MUST LOVE GHOSTS: COFFEE AND GHOSTS 1

THE COMPLETE FIRST SEASON

CHARITY TAHMASEB

COLLINS MARK BOOKS

COPYRIGHT

CONTENTS

AUTHOR'S NOTE

COFFEE & GHOSTS is a cozy paranormal mystery/romance serial told in episodes and seasons, much like a television series. Think *Doctor Who* or *Sherlock*.

I've consolidated the episodes into three season bundles. This makes the episodes easier to find and—I hope—more enjoyable to read.

If coffee hasn't yet topped your list as the most versatile substance on Earth, consider
"The Ghost in the Coffee Machine" by Charity Tahmaseb.
~ **Lori Parker, Word of the Nerd**

COFFEE AND GHOSTS, THE SEASON LISTS

Season 1:
    Episode 1: *Ghost in the Coffee Machine*
    Episode 2: *Giving Up the Ghosts*
    Episode 3: *The Ghost Whisperer*
    Episode 4: *Gone Ghost*
    Episode 5: *Must Love Ghosts*

Season 2:
    Episode 1: *Ghosts of Christmas Past*
    Episode 2: *The Ghost That Got Away*
    Episode 3: *The Wedding Ghost*

Season 3:
    Episode 1: *Ghosts and Consequences*
    Episode 2: *A Few Good Ghosts*
    Episode 3: *Nothing but the Ghosts*

COFFEE AND GHOSTS

THE COMPLETE FIRST SEASON

GHOST IN THE COFFEE MACHINE

COFFEE AND GHOSTS: EPISODE 1

WHEN IT COMES TO GHOSTS, my grandmother has one solution: brew a pot of coffee. Like today, in Sadie Lancaster's kitchen.

Sadie clutches her hands beneath her chin and stares at our percolator, her eyes huge. The thing gurgles and hisses as if it resents being pressed into service. My own reflection in its side is distorted. When I was younger, I thought this was how ghosts see our world.

In places with bad infestations, they swirl around the percolator. I can reach out, touch hot moist air with one hand and the icy patch of dry with the other. One time, a ghost slipped inside. It rattled around until the percolator sprang from the table and hit the floor, splashing scalding water everywhere.

I still wear the scars of that across my shins.

But Sadie's ghosts are barely ghosts at all. I'd call them sprites. They might annoy you on the way to the bathroom at three a.m., but little more. They also, as my grandmother points out, help pay the bills. So I remain silent while she pours the coffee: three cups black, three cups with sugar, three cups with cream, and three cups extra light and extra sweet. Twelve cups. Always. If anyone complains, my grandmother snorts and says, "As if no one has a preference once they've died."

Don't get her started on instant coffee, either. Since I was five, my job involves carrying the cups throughout the house, up and down stairs, into bedrooms, dining alcoves, walk-in closets. We never skip the bathroom, no matter what.

"The last place you'd want a ghost," my grandmother says to Sadie. "Lecherous little beasts."

I walk past the two women, my steps slow and steady. I still burn myself, make no mistake. My hands wear the scars of multiple scaldings. We keep a burn kit in the truck. But as I place the last cup on the edge of the sink, I smile. At least I won't need that today. I rush back to the kitchen for the Tupperware.

Some ghost catchers use glass jars, but ghosts confined to small spaces can manifest images—grotesque or obscene or both. Ghosts, generally speaking, are pissed off and rude, which is why you don't want one in your toilet. We buy the containers with the opaque sides, since what you can't see won't offend you. I use several at Sadie's that afternoon, although truthfully, I only snag three little sprites in the den.

"She's imagining things," I whisper to my grandmother.

"Yes." Her hand steadies my shoulder. "But how many repeat customers do we get?"

She has a point. We're good. When we're really in the zone— the right type of coffee beans, perfect brewing temperature, clean catches—a house might stay ghost-free for decades. If we're not careful, there won't be any ghosts left to catch.

With the sprites in the back of our pickup, we rumble down the county road that leads out of town and into endless fields of corn and soybean. Ten miles out, there's a windbreak with a little creek. This is where we'll set the sprites free. They'll be, if not happy, content at least, and in no hurry to find other humans to haunt.

I'm setting the sprites free—legs braced, container at arm's length —when my grandmother speaks.

"When I'm gone, Katy-girl, I'll come back and show you how to rid them once and for all."

I sigh. I've heard this before. "But then I'd be getting rid of you."

"You wouldn't like me as a ghost. Besides, they don't belong on this plane. This has been my life's work." She touches three fingers to her heart. "I don't see why it shouldn't be my afterlife's work as well."

She always says this. I always tell her she'll live a good long time. Then we drive home, empty containers rattling against the flatbed, percolator perched between us, belted in, our third—and quite possibly most important—passenger.

THAT WAS THREE MONTHS AGO. If my grandmother raged against the dying of the light, it didn't show in her expression the following morning when I found her. She left me her house, the family business, and of course, the dented, silver percolator. I have yet to see a hint of my grandmother's ghost. I'm not sure I want to.

The house is quiet without her in it. Even the ghosts have stayed away. I shake the canister of roasted beans, give it a sniff, certain I'll need to dump it and buy fresh within a matter of days.

Sadie Lancaster calls as the first cascade of beans hits the garbage sack. I decide on those fresh beans now, and instead of running next door, I jump into my truck and head for the Coffee Depot.

Ten minutes later, I pull up in front of Sadie's house, but I don't find her cowering on the porch (her usual position pre-eradication). Percolator under one arm, I ring the bell.

"Oh, Katy," she says, urging me inside. She beams like she has a secret. "There's someone I want you to meet."

This is it. My grandmother has chosen Sadie's house as the spot for her grand reappearance and that's why Sadie isn't scared. My steps quicken, heart fluttering something crazy. Do I want to see my grandmother like this? I've never been afraid of ghosts, but this is different.

The aroma hits me first—rich, aromatic, turmeric, saffron, and a hint of rose petal. Sun glints off the sides of a samovar squatting in the center of the kitchen table, in the very place I always set the percolator. I clutch the thing to my chest as if that can protect us from its flashy usurper on the table. The samovar is gold-plated brass—I squint at it—in the Persian style instead of Russian.

"Katy," Sadie says, throwing her arms wide, "I want you to meet Malcolm Armand. He catches ghosts with tea the way you do with coffee." Her fingers twitch as if she's urging us closer together. I stand my ground. "You two have so much in common," she adds.

Malcolm runs a hand over smooth, dark hair. His white dress shirt gleams in the sunlight streaming through the kitchen windows. I'm in torn jeans and a T-shirt. Why anyone would attempt ghost catching in something so fancy is beyond me. Even so? I can't help but feel grubby in comparison.

"It's nice to meet you," he says, extending that same hand, one without a single blemish or scar.

I fight the urge to whip my own hands behind my back, out of sight. I gulp a breath and shake his hand, breaking contact the second it's polite (okay, maybe a couple of seconds before it's polite). I try not to stare too hard at Malcolm, so I let my gaze travel the kitchen, the dining alcove. No ghosts here. I'd be surprised to find even the weakest sprite. And certainly, my grandmother isn't in residence.

That leaves me alone with Malcolm—and the tea-scented suspicion about where all my business is going.

WHEN I WALK INTO SPRINGSIDE LONG-TERM CARE, the first thing I see is Malcolm standing in the center of the common area, enchanting all the residents, the gold-plated samovar glowing on a side table next to him. I freeze, so every time the automatic doors try to close, they bounce back open again. This draws attention. I sigh, give up my plan to sneak out, and step forward to meet the facility manager.

"Oh, Katy," she says, a flush rising up her neck, "I meant to call, so you wouldn't make the trip out here." She waves a hand at Malcolm. "He offered a "try before you buy" and well ... the residents just love him."

Or at least most of the female ones do. They gather around Malcolm and his shiny, shiny samovar, their *oohs* and *ahhs* mixing with the scented steam.

I don't point out that Springside is—and always has been—a gratis account. Older people, my grandmother always said, are haunted by many things. It's only right that we chase some of their ghosts away.

I'm backing toward the door, willing myself not to inhale a hint of rose petal and saffron, when a bony hand grips my wrist. The percolator crashes to the floor, adding one more dent to its history.

"Katy-girl, are you going to let him get away with that?" Mr. Carlotta nearly growls the words. He may hold the world's record for longest unrequited crush, in his case, on my grandmother. Even now, sorrow lines his eyes. His fingers tremble against my wrist.

"What can I do?" I wave my free hand toward Malcolm. "He's so flashy."

"More like a flash in the pan. Mark my words."

A part of me grabs onto what Mr. Carlotta says. Be patient. Business will pick up the second it's clear you can't catch ghosts with tea. Because honestly, who ever heard of that? My practical side—the side that pays the property taxes and utility bills—wonders if the local coffee shop is hiring.

I TRACE THE SCARS on the backs of my hands while waiting for the Coffee Depot's assistant manager. My qualifications are thin. I know ghost hunting and how to brew a damn good cup of coffee. But customer service? Well, when you ghost hunt, people don't mind if you shove them out of the way, not if you trap the otherworldly thing shaking their house to the foundation.

At the Coffee Depot? They probably frown on customer shoving. Still, the converted train station is quaint and life as a barista can't be that bad, can it?

The assistant manager plops down across from me. He wipes fake sweat from his brow and gives me a grin.

"So," he says. "Tell me a bit about yourself."

"I make the best damn coffee you've ever tasted." I declare this because I've read online that you should be confident in your interview.

He chuckles but doesn't sound amused. "I'm sure you do. But tell me," and now, the amusement is back, "what about frothing milk?"

I like cappuccino, even if frothing milk is something I've never done. Likewise, I'm sure there are many fine answers to his question. I do not choose any of them.

Instead, I say, "Why would you want to do that?" It's like I'm possessed by the spirit of my grandmother, since in that moment, I sound just like her.

"Right," he says. He clears his throat, then gives me a long look. "I'll take that challenge. Go make me the best damn cup of coffee I've ever tasted."

So I do. I stand, and with his nod, round the counter so I'm on the other side. My fingers barely brush the silver, industrial sized coffee machine when it starts to tremble. The thing wheezes. The tile beneath my feet shudders, sending a shockwave that resonates from toes to jaw. Next to me, the barista's teeth clack together, and she pitches toward the cash register, clinging to it. Then, the machine erupts, spewing water and coffee grounds with so much force, they coat the ceiling, the walls, and all of the tables.

I OFFER TO CLEAN UP. I offer to rid their machine of its ghost— for free. Everyone is damp, but since the water was only lukewarm, no one was scalded. This is why the assistant manager pushes me out of the store instead of calling the police.

As the door closes, his voice echoes behind me. "Yes, do you have the number for Malcolm Armand ...?"

Something won't let me leave the sidewalk in front of the shop. My feet remain rooted there, next to the planters with the sugar maples. I stand there so long it's a wonder I don't sprout leaves. But since I do stand there so long, I'm treated to the view of Malcolm Armand double parking and springing from his two-seater. In the passenger seat, belted in like a trophy girlfriend, sits the samovar.

"That's not very practical," I say.

He halts in his trek up the walk, samovar held away from me. "What?"

"Where do you put the ghosts? I mean, once you capture them." I point at the convertible. "There's no room."

He eyes me, my coffee-soaked shirt, stained slacks, and all. He sniffs, nose wrinkling, and tromps into the shop without another look in my direction. I turn, uproot my feet, and inch toward the front window.

Inside is the mess I made, but I ignore that. What I want to see is how Malcolm works, what he does, how he entices the ghosts. I stare so long, the sun dries the back of my shirt. I study the inside of the shop, the placement of the samovar, and track Malcolm's every move until the assistant manager jerks a cord and Venetian blinds block my view.

Whatever grips me about the shop—the ghost or Malcolm—loosens its hold. Dismissed, I trudge home, leaving a set of coffee-colored footprints in my wake.

~

"K-K-ATY? ARE YOU THERE?"

The call comes at nine in the morning, on a day so sunny and bright, only the most dedicated pessimist could remain that way. Since I have all my overdue bills spread out on the dining room table, I'm well on my way to joining their ranks.

"Sadie?" It sounds like her, but I've never heard her voice so shaky.

"Please hurry."

"What's going on? Where are you?"

"My porch. They won't let me inside."

"Who won't?"

"The ghosts."

"Why don't you call Malcolm?" The question comes out sharp, laced with acid and jealousy.

"He's t-trapped inside."

"Trapped?"

"Dead?" Sadie's voice hitches.

"Ghosts don't ..." *Kill.* No, normally ghosts don't. But they can. "I'll be right over."

The second I pull the half and half from the fridge and give it a good whiff, I realize *right over* isn't happening. I toss the reeking carton into the garbage and head to the canister with the beans. A few lone ones rattle in the bottom. I haven't been back to the Coffee Depot since my disastrous interview, but it looks like I'll be stopping there today.

With the percolator strapped in its seat, a four-pound bag of sugar snug against it, and several containers of half and half on the truck's floor, I run two red lights on my way to the Coffee Depot. By the time the little bell above the door stops jingling, the assistant manager is rounding the counter. He stalks forward, arms loaded down with bags of coffee beans. He skids to a halt and shoves the beans at me.

"But—" I begin.

He holds up a cell phone. On the screen, a message reads:

Malcolm: Give her anything she wants.

Still uncertain, I blink at the words. In my arms, I hold everything I want, or at least need. For now. I head for the door.

"Call or text if you need a resupply," the assistant manager shouts after me. "I'll have someone run it over."

The door whooshes closed before I can say thanks.

I TEST OUT THE FRONT DOOR, the garage, even the window to the bathroom. Every surface I touch ices my fingertips. Sadie Lancaster's house is in full-on ghost infestation. Usually something like this takes years to build up, or a sudden invasion of strong ghosts—a group of them. True, I haven't cleared the sprites in a month or so, but that can't be the cause of this.

My gaze travels the structure, from chimney to foundation. All the windows are black, the cheery blue paint molting into a dead gray. I need to get inside. I need to do that now. So I do the most logical thing. I march up the porch steps, press my palm against the doorbell, and let it ring for an entire minute. Then I cross my arms over my chest and tap my foot.

"Nobody's getting any coffee if someone doesn't open up this door." I sound bossy, just like my grandmother. I kind of like it.

A moment later, the door creaks on its hinges. I scoop up the percolator and my bag of supplies and race for the kitchen.

"Malcolm?" I call out. "Are you okay?"

Is he even here? Maybe he went out the back once the ghosts released their hold on the doors. I plug in the percolator and take a few deep breaths so I don't rush the preparations. Ghosts this strong will need the best coffee I can brew.

I survey the beans the assistant manager shoved at me. One hundred percent Kona? Really? Shame to waste that on ghosts. But the air prickles the skin on my arms. It must be fifty degrees in here and getting colder. One hundred percent Kona might not do the trick if I don't hurry.

"Katy?" A voice rasps.

For a second, I mistake it for a ghost.

"Katy?"

No. Too deep, too human for that.

"Malcolm?"

"In the dining room."

I set the percolator to brew and run. On the threshold, I trip over something bulky and sail through the air. I land hard, but manage to tuck and roll. When I stop, the blown out end of a gold-plated samovar fills my view, the brass twisted into vicious curlicues.

A groan comes from the threshold. Malcolm props himself up on one elbow, his cell phone clutched in one hand, his shirt, torn and tea-stained.

"What happened?" I say.

"It just ... blew. I was adding in a sprite when—"

"Wait. You've been storing all the ghosts." I heft the samovar, careful of the edges. "In here?"

He nods.

"You don't release them?"

"Never have." He shakes his head, eyes downcast. "Honestly? I don't know how."

This sad, honest confession tugs at me. We don't have time, however, to go over the finer points of ghost hunting.

"Can you stand?" I ask. "Walk?"

"I think so."

"Then you can help."

In the kitchen, I pour the twelve cups. Malcolm adds the half and half and sugar. His hands are steady, and he stirs each cup without spilling a single drop. My grandmother would approve.

From there, we divide and conquer, carrying the cups to various spots in the house.

"Be sure to put one in the master bath," I call from the living room. "There's bound to be one in there."

"It won't let me in," he says a moment later.

Oh, really? Nasty little bugger. Ghosts and their toilet humor.

At the door to the bathroom, I ease the cup of coffee from Malcolm's hands then kick on the door. It flies open with all the strength of the supernatural behind it.

Malcolm places a hand on my arm. "I don't think—"

"It'll be okay." I hear it for the lie it is, and so must Malcolm, but he lets me go.

I close the door and place the coffee on the vanity. That icy patch of air flutters past, swirls into the steam, and revels in it. Oh, it is having the best time—at everyone's expense, too. Before I can trap it beneath some Tupperware, that same feeling from the coffee shop washes over me. This is the ghost in the coffee machine. This is ... my grandmother.

The realization makes me drop the container. Malcolm pounds on the door, but I ignore him.

"Grandma?"

Now, the ghost swoops around me, a frigid caress against my cheek.

"What are you doing? I thought—"

Something that sounds like *hush* fills the air. Whatever her mission, it's not for me to question.

"I love you," I say. "And I miss you."

I pick up the container and my grandmother flows inside, compliantly. I secure the lid and hug the Tupperware to my chest. During her life, my grandmother was right about most everything. But here's where she was wrong:

I do like her as a ghost.

~

WE DRIVE OUT TO THE NATURE PRESERVE, a good thirty miles from town. In a deserted campsite, I demonstrate how to open containers and set ghosts free. I even let Malcolm release a few. (Only the sprites, but you have to start somewhere.)

"Will they come back?" he asks.

"The strong ones can, but most choose to stay here, or find an old barn to haunt. Something's got to scare all those Scouts on camping trips, right?"

Malcolm studies the backs of his hands. The beautiful olive skin is pink from scalding.

"You should put something on that," I say. "Before it scars."

"A little scarring never hurt anyone. I'm sorry for a lot of things." He raises his hands. "But not for this."

I nod and he gives me a piercing look that I swear could scar—if I let it.

"You know something," he says, "I think this will work."

"What will?"

"You and me. I'm all sizzle, and you're the steak."

"I'm a vegetarian."

He throws his head back and laughs. And while I have no clue what he means, I can't help but like the sound of his laughter.

~

I LET MY FINGERS TRACE the gold lettering on the window—

14

for the tenth time in as many minutes. I can't help it, can hardly believe the words are real.

K&M Ghost Eradication Specialists

In the store window, the gold-plated brass samovar sits, backside hidden in midnight velvet. Somehow, Malcolm talked the bank manager into a small business loan. Somehow, we're on retainer with the only law office and investment firm in town. Somehow, my worry about bills and property taxes has evaporated.

Malcolm still wears the scars from what we call the day of the ghosts. He boasts a few fresh ones as well. So do I. We take a new, electric samovar with us when we go out on a call. Because even I must admit: some ghosts prefer tea. Sometimes I feel that particular presence and an icy caress along my cheek. Sometimes I say things that make Malcolm throw his head back and laugh.

What I don't tell Malcolm: I do it on purpose.

What I don't tell my grandmother: I know what her afterlife's mission really is.

And I love her for it.

GIVING UP THE GHOSTS

COFFEE AND GHOSTS, EPISODE 2

CONTRARY TO POPULAR BELIEF, it's hard to find a ghost in a cemetery. But a mausoleum? Like the sterile one Malcolm and I are now walking through? That's going to be even harder. We trek along the endless halls. Wall after wall. Drawer after drawer. The interior is all windows, steel, and marble. Sunlight pours through the glass and makes me wince. Even so, Lasting Rest Mausoleum is—quite possibly—the coldest place on earth, or at least in this county.

"I don't sense a thing," I say to Malcolm. Actually, I whisper it, which is ridiculous, since we are the only two people on the third floor.

"Let's keep going," he says, voice equally hushed. "Maybe there's something. Plus, I promised."

We seldom turn down a ghost eradication job, it's true. Often it's no more than a mischievous little sprite. They love to play jokes. If anything might haunt a cemetery, it would be a sprite. Whatever else you think you sense, see, or experience is a product of your imagination, fears, and repressed feelings. You don't need an exorcist. You need a psychiatrist.

I know how to deal with ghosts. But this place? The space feels hollow in the wrong sort of way. At least in a cemetery, grass cushions your feet. The grave markers hint at stories, lives, and loves. Birds chirp. Dragonflies buzz.

"They should pipe in some music." I glance toward the ceiling as if in search of hidden speakers. Nothing disturbs the smooth marble surfaces.

"I read an article once, about the cleanup at Chernobyl," he says. "They had to pipe in music for the workers since there were no other sounds."

I wonder if he realizes he's compared the Lasting Rest Mausoleum with the world's largest nuclear disaster.

He coughs, glances around—maybe so I won't see the blush in his cheeks. "But it's a clean, well-lighted place."

Yes. He realizes. "I don't think this is what Hemingway had in mind," I say.

Malcolm chuckles. I love his laugh, but it's the wrong sort of sound for this place. "Let's replay the video," he says. "We're getting close to the spot."

I think it's an excuse to hear something other than our footfalls and breathing. He pulls out his phone and brings up the recording. In it, our client, Doug, is touring the mausoleum much as we are, only with a video camera in his hand. Occasionally he speaks directly into the lens, but mostly it's a rocky, virtual trip through these halls. I sway, motion sickness overtaking me.

"You okay?" Malcolm steps closer, places a hand at the small of my back. A hint of saffron from the tea he carries reaches me.

He is very much warm and alive in a place that is not. He smells of nutmeg and Ivory soap. I like being close to him, but I don't want to give him the wrong idea. I don't want to give *myself* the wrong idea.

I keep my distance.

On the screen, Doug's trek continues.

"Doug didn't even notice the ghost while he was filming," Malcolm says. "It was only after he reviewed the video that he noticed something odd."

This does not lend credence to Doug's claim, but I remain silently skeptical.

"There!" Malcolm says. The cold marble walls bounce the word back at us and seem to gobble it up all at once. The space is greedy for all things alive.

What looks like a white bed sheet flutters on the screen. It's a child's idea of a ghost. I've said as much to Malcolm, but feel compelled to mention it again.

"Ghosts don't look like that. It's probably something he edited into the video."

"I don't think so. He's not that tech savvy."

"You don't have to be that tech savvy these days. You could hire someone to do it."

Malcolm turns to me now, arms crossed over his chest, phone still clutched in his hand. "Why would someone do that? He's paying us money, good money that we need, to investigate—"

"And eradicate."

"And eradicate, if necessary. Why go to all that trouble and expense?"

Oh, there are so many reasons. When I worked with my grandmother, we encountered them all. Some people crave the attention, or are so lonely, they desperately need it. Having a ghost select them—or their house—to haunt? Well, that must mean they're something special. Or so the reasoning goes.

But Malcolm is new to the business. He is what my grandmother would have called feral—not in a bad way. Ghost hunting is both an inborn trait and a skill that is passed down through generations. Long ago, his ancestors no doubt made a living doing what we're doing now. But when I met him, he didn't even know how to perform a proper catch and release.

We match our steps to those on the video to where that white fluttering vanished into the wall. A fan is stationed at this corner. In fact, several fans are positioned throughout the building. Clean. Well-lighted. Not ventilated. But then, the dead don't need to breathe, do they?

"The fan would account for the fluttering," I say. "Some fishing line, a bed sheet or an old bridal veil? Instant ghost."

"And they rigged it up how, exactly?" His gaze searches the walls and ceiling.

Oh, yes, he has a point. No place for a pulley and ropes. No place for a co-conspirator to hide. It's a mystery, but I doubt it's an otherworldly one.

"Malcolm, I just don't think—"

"I'll be honest, Katy." His words are rushed, anxious. "I've already spent the deposit."

I know ghost hunting, but Malcolm knows business. His words send a chill through me that rivals the temperature in this place.

"Rent, on the office space," he says. "Bargain eradications aren't going to keep us in business. Some people are starting to embrace their sprites and live with them." He shrugs. "It's sort of a thing now."

My grandmother and I always made ends meet—more or less. It took Malcolm to untangle the mess of property taxes on the house I inherited from her. I don't have any savings and only just started a retirement account—and only because Malcolm insisted. When it comes to money, I trust him.

I ease the pack from my shoulders. "I guess it wouldn't hurt to set up the coffee, at least. If there's a ghost, it will come out for that."

The long marble bench makes an excellent station. Malcolm unloads the cups and thermoses. I pour. Twelve cups, like always: three black, three with sugar, three with cream, and three extra light and sweet. Everyone has a favorite, even ghosts.

"We could get out the tea, too," I say to him.

The smile melts some of the worry from his face. "Let's see how picky they are."

Usually, I brew the coffee on the premises, but we decided for this first run to use the field kit. If it works well enough in abandoned barns and warehouses, then it should work here. Steam rises from the cups, warming the air, infusing it with a tangible thickness.

"Ow." Malcolm sticks a finger into his mouth, although that's no way to treat a burn. "Careful, it's still scalding hot."

"Good. Have you ever seen what a ghost does with a lukewarm cup of coffee?" I ask.

He shakes his head.

"It's messy." I have a dozen coffee-stained shirts to prove it.

He holds his hands over the rising steam. "It feels better in here."

It does. Even so, the air is devoid of everything but the coffee's aroma. No glimmer. No swirling in the steam above a cup. I have the Tupperware ready for the catch, but at the moment, there's nothing to catch.

I'm about to suggest tea, since perhaps this is a particular sort of ghost, a choosy sort who is only lured by the exotic. Malcolm's tea recipe, an old Persian one, is all kinds of exotic. Before I can say a word, a screech echoes down the long hallway, the sort of sound that raises the hairs on the back of your neck.

Something swoops. Something flutters. Bed sheets. Bridal veils. It might be either or both of those things. The force of the swoop upends the coffee cups—all of them. The liquid splatters everywhere. On the tombs, the silk flowers that adorn them, the floor.

Me.

Black coffee strikes my thighs, the scald instant. I yelp, then pluck at my jeans, the material too hot, too tight, too slippery for me to grip. I can't move fast enough, pluck hard enough. My skin flashes with pain. At last, I unbutton the fly and yank.

By the time the material is past my knees, it no longer has the power to burn. I slump on the damp, coffee-covered floor and push my palms against my eyes. *I will not cry. I will not cry.*

"Katy!" Malcolm slides to the floor next to me. "Jesus, let me look."

He eases me back. His intake of breath is not reassuring.

"How bad?" I ask, palms locked on my eyes.

"Hospital bad, as in I'm dialing 911 bad."

I peer through my fingers at him. "We don't have money for an ambulance." We are two townships from home. An ambulance will cost what? More than I think we should spend, perhaps more than we have to spend.

"We'll make the money, somehow."

"My truck. It'll be just as fast, and there's a burn kit in the glove compartment."

"The EMTs—"

"Can't do anything more than I can on my own." Honestly, he can't lecture me about finances then expect me to be fiscally irresponsible.

"Compromise." He holds up a finger. "You're not walking anywhere." He tugs off his fine white dress shirt, which is now speckled with coffee and less than fine. He helps me stand, helps me ease the jeans off my legs, then creates a makeshift skirt from that shirt.

Then, in knight-in-shining-armor mode, he sweeps me into his arms and carries me down the hall.

"I can walk," I protest.

"But you're not going to." He heads down the stairs.

"There's an elevator," I point out.

"And with our luck, we'd end up trapped. No thanks."

He has a point. Whatever that thing was, it has a vendetta. Messing with the electrical system is something a strong ghost might do, on occasion, although I'm still uncertain that's what we encountered.

"Maybe we should've served it tea," I say.

He grunts a laugh and crushes me closer to his chest. Nutmeg. Ivory soap. If there's an upside to being a damsel in distress, it might be this.

Malcolm secures me in the truck, seatbelt and all, as if he's afraid I'll bolt back inside to fight more ghosts. His instincts are spot-on, for I point and say, "Our stuff. We just can't leave it."

Those are precision-made German thermoses and matching cups, not to mention everything else in our field kit.

"But I'm not sure you should go in alone," I add.

His gaze darts from the mausoleum to me. Fine grooves form around his mouth and eyes. "You're right," he says. "But someone has to. Stay."

Like I'm going anywhere half-dressed. I give him a mock salute. Malcolm rushes off, and I stare after him, tracking his progress inside through the window as he dashes up the stairs. Then, he vanishes.

I wait. And I wait. My thighs sting with enough force it steals my breath. I should pull out the burn kit, start in on first aid, but my eyes are locked on the mausoleum. My shoulders tense, and I inch ever closer to the windshield. That's when I see it. That's *why* I see it. Something white. Something that flutters. Bed sheets. Bridal veils. Whatever it is, it circles the mausoleum in what can only be described as a victory lap. The thing is ... gloating.

Malcolm bursts through the glass doors of the mausoleum, field kit clutched to his chest. I nearly tumble from the truck with my efforts to point toward the sky. But the thing is gone, and when Malcolm turns to look, all that greets him is blue sky.

He throws the field kit at my feet and clambers into the driver's side. "Katy?"

"I saw it," I say.

"It?"

"The thing. The thing from Doug's video."

"Do you know what it is?"

The truck rumbles to life and he throws it into gear. The way is smooth, but the suspension bad, so we bounce down to the main road.

In all my years of ghost hunting, in all the stories my grandmother told me, I've never seen or heard anything like this.

"I have no idea."

MY ARM ACHES from the tetanus shot. This small annoyance bothers me more than the swath of bandages across each thigh, and the fact I can't tug any of my jeans up and over the bandages. I'm reduced to wearing a short, flirty skater skirt. This skirt, which is really too short for most activities, might be the only thing I can wear for the next week.

This does not bode well for ghost hunting.

I sit on the couch in our office, tray propped up and over my thighs—a bridge over my bandages. In a wise move, Malcolm brings in a cold lunch—sandwiches and icy lemonade from the deli next door. I am not in the mood for coffee.

"You okay?" he says. Actually, he has said this about once every fifteen minutes. Until now, I haven't felt like answering.

"I've never blistered like this before," I tell him.

"The doctor said it wouldn't scar—"

"That's not what bugs me."

Oh, I have scars, many of which are on view, thanks to the skater skirt. I look at them more as badges of honor, a legacy of working with my grandmother. "I was totally unprepared for what happened."

"We both were."

"But I shouldn't have been."

This still eats at me, hours later, has led to endless Internet searches, and has left me so frustrated, I'm afraid most of my words will emerge with more than a growl—I will bite, too.

"It's different for me," I add. The words hang in the air, and I realize just how arrogant they sound, and how it's too late to take them back.

He studies his sandwich, a Black Forest ham with baby Swiss, on rye, his favorite. Instead of eating, he sets it on his paper plate.

"You know what I think?" he says.

"What?"

"You're right, sort of. It *is* different for you, but not because you think you went in unprepared. No one is more prepared than you are."

"Then what was it?"

"I think it was ... a trap, an ambush. Whatever that thing was, it targeted you."

"You think that?"

Malcolm tips his head; it's a slow, thoughtful sort of movement. He rubs his jaw. "I don't have proof, but I sense it. There was nothing when I ran back inside. I couldn't even smell the spilt coffee."

"You were in a hurry—"

"And I had to pick up all the cups and the thermoses. You know the smell of cold coffee."

Do I ever. An involuntary shudder runs through me and has Malcolm securing a fleece throw and wrapping it around my shoulders. I don't refuse.

"The place should've reeked." He sits on the coffee table so his gaze strikes me dead on. "I'm telling you, there was nothing, no odor, and it's not like that place smells of anything except stale air."

"The fans?" I suggest. "They were going full blast."

Instead of responding, he pulls the field kit out from under the table. Inside, the contents rattle. He lifts a silver thermos from the pack, the one we use for the extra sweet, extra light concoction. The sides should be damp and sticky. No matter how carefully we pour, this is our messiest thermos. The silver gleams. Malcolm unscrews the cap. He waves it under his nose, then mine.

Nothing.

"That's weird," I say, "but it doesn't prove this thing is after me."

He directs a pointed look at my thighs. Okay, maybe it does.

"Vendetta," he says.

"What?"

"The word is stuck in my mind. Vendetta. Only I can't figure out why. Who, or what, would have a vendetta against you? You've never done more than catch and release, have you?"

I shake my head. No, that was always our strict policy. Ghosts can be nasty, it's true, especially those who resent their afterlife. For the stronger, meaner ones, the solution is nothing more than driving them farther out, and around in circles, until they lose all sense of direction. Sure, once released, they might make their way back. More likely, they'll find a new spot to haunt.

"What about your grandmother?"

"Not that I know of, and I learned everything from her."

He props his elbows on his knees and plants his chin on his fists. His dark eyes are fringed with black lashes. This close, the effect is breathtaking. No wonder the women who work the deli counter toss in dessert for free.

"Maybe we need to expand our search," he says. "Maybe this thing isn't a ghost. I told you about the old Victorian I lived in back in college."

It's where he picked up his ghost catching ability—or maybe it picked him.

"People thought it was funny I could catch ghosts and put them in my samovar, but I always thought it was kind of sad."

By *people*, he means his fraternity brothers, and he had amassed quite a collection by the time I met him. I had to teach him how to release ghosts, although he still doesn't have the knack. Half the time, they double back and smack him in the head.

"But there was other stuff going on. Not ghosts, but ..." He pauses, presses a finger against his lip. "Definitely supernatural. I never knew what they were, only that I couldn't catch them."

I don't like the idea of things that can't be caught. I think of that white fluttering—of bed sheets and bridal veils. Merely a ruse, then? Something to grab our attention—or the attention of a potential client? If so, it worked.

"Maybe you should talk to Doug," I say. "Give him an update."

Malcolm groans. "If I do that, he's going to blather it all over the internet."

"One, there's already so much ghost crap all over the internet, what's a little more? Two?" I catch Malcolm's eye. "Maybe that's not such a bad thing."

I DON'T KNOW what it is about the internet and ghosts, but it has a way of bringing out the frauds. Or maybe that's the internet in general. Long ago, I stopped trying to explain properties of light to potential clients. It simply doesn't matter. If someone wants to see a ghost in a spot in a photograph, they will see one.

I've never once captured an actual ghost on film, although I've taken hundreds of lousy pictures trying to do so. Even when they swirl in the steam of a hot cup of coffee, ghosts simply don't show up on film or the digital version of it.

Less than twenty-four hours after Malcolm updates Doug, the phone calls and emails flood in. I am still couch-bound and still in my skater skirt. I scroll through the photos attached to those emails, and scan the paranormal chat boards, looking for a connection.

When my cell phone rings, I answer automatically. "K&M Ghost Eradication Specialists."

"You're on the wrong track." The voice warbles, like it's streaming through an electronic filter. I place the call on speaker and wave Malcolm over.

"What did you say?" I ask the caller, then press a finger against my lips.

Malcolm nods, once, and crouches next to the coffee table, ear aimed at my phone.

"You're on the wrong track, and your client's an idiot."

"How so?"

"Do you really believe he can see ghosts? Capture them on film?"

"Well, whatever he saw, I did too."

The caller snorts. The resulting burst of static has me clamping my hands over my ears.

"But you're not dim enough to call it a ghost."

"You don't like Doug," I say.

The silence stretches for so long I think the call has dropped.

"This has nothing to do with Doug. You should know that ... Malcolm. Yes, I know you're listening in."

Malcolm slams a hand on the coffee table. I jump back, my heart thudding.

"Who is this?" he says. "I demand to know who this is."

He's always so cool, so calm, so Malcolm. But this? This is a side I've never seen of him. My ears strain for the caller's response, but it's Malcolm who holds all my attention.

"Can't you figure it out? Oh, Malcolm, really? I never thought *you* were that dim." A static-laden sigh travels through the speakers. "And your business partner is so pretty. Be a shame if those burns ended up on her face, wouldn't it?"

"Who is this?" Malcolm's voice cracks.

Mine doesn't. "Don't be stupid," I say to the caller. "An empty threat is just that, empty and stupid."

"Who says it's empty?"

"I do. The victim has to care, and I don't. Burn my face. I don't care. I don't care at all. But I do care about my friends—"

"Are you sure you know who your friends are?"

The speakers let out one last burst of static before going silent. My gaze meets Malcolm's.

"What the hell was that?" I say.

"Katy." He shakes his head. "Katy, I—"

"Please tell me this is not where you make some horrible confession that changes everything."

I consider my demand—and the call. I've only known Malcolm for four months, and for one of those he was my rival in the ghost hunting business. How well can I claim to know him? Would I swear he is good and honorable and all those things a person should be, especially your business partner? Would I? What's the alternative?

"Oh," I say, the realization sinking in, my lungs pulling a full breath at last. "Of course. Seeds of doubt. Who hates you—or me —enough to do that?"

"Then—" he begins.

"I think we're being played. What do you think?"

He props his elbows on the coffee table and rests his head in his hands.

I ignore this. "This is personal, not paranormal." Bed sheets and bridal veils. The thought strikes me hard. "You didn't break an engagement or something before you moved here, did you?"

I'm praying he'll say no, or shake his head, or something. He remains statue-like still, as if in mourning.

"Malcolm." I lean forward, smooth his hair, and then place a gentle hand on his shoulder. "What's going on?"

"Once upon a time, I had a brother," he says. "Nigel."

Once upon a time? Despite the fairy tale start, something tells me this is going to be a dark story. "*Had* a brother." I say the words slowly.

"Technically, I still do. Around the time I discovered I could catch ghosts, my brother did too. Only instead of putting them into something, he swallowed them."

"Swallowed them? Is that even possible?"

Malcolm gives me one anguished nod.

"He's filled with ghosts?"

Malcolm nods again.

"And resents you because?"

His eyes meet mine. They are dark and damp and filled with so much sorrow, my heart constricts.

"Because of you."

I SINK into the couch cushion as if Malcolm's confession has knocked the wind from me. Perhaps it has, figuratively, at least. An eater of ghosts. I've never encountered such a thing; my grandmother never mentioned it.

"How do I figure into all of this?" I ask.

"You ... saved me. I was using the samovar as a holding place, so I wouldn't swallow the ghosts, wouldn't be tempted to." He heaves a sigh. "Now that I know there's an option, that I don't have to carry them with me or inside me, I can live a normal life. You know why I was fired from the brokerage, don't you?"

"I thought it was the recession."

He shakes his head. "That's the excuse. A layoff. After I graduated, my brother followed me there. My first job after college. I thought I was all set. Then Nigel shows up one day. He ..."

Malcolm breaks off and searches the ceiling as if the words he needs are there. "He would stand in the public lobby, like some sort of crazed prophet, talking about ghosts—and of course, me. He harassed people, the women brokers in particular. It was..." He shudders. "Awful."

"Why didn't you tell me?"

"I thought it was all over. I took one suitcase and left everything else behind, except the samovar, and drove until I was nearly out of gas. I stopped here. I liked the town. I heard about you and your grandmother. I thought maybe you had the same problem I did." Here, he shrugs. "It made sense to stay."

I guess it would. "I kind of hated you when you first showed up."

Malcolm tips his head back and laughs—the first light sound I've heard from him since yesterday. "I know," he says once he's caught his breath.

"Do you want to swallow ghosts now? Is it like being an alcoholic?"

He shakes his head, his smile still there, although his eyes grow somber. "No, fortunately. I don't think I could function when we go out on calls if I did."

I wonder how true this is, but don't contradict him. "What happens to the ghosts once your brother swallows them? Do you know?"

"He says they give him strength, but I don't know if they're there inside, if they disappear or dissolve." He shrugs, palms skyward. "Maybe they become part of him."

At his words, one horrible thought strikes me. "My grandmother!"

"What?"

"She's ..." I choke back the words.

I've never told Malcolm my secret, that my grandmother's ghost haunts me. Or rather, she has a series of haunts, and when our bank balance dips to a certain level, she kicks up a ruckus—and we get a call and some much-needed cash.

"My grandmother is a ghost," I admit, at last. There. Now we've both confessed. I want to sink into the cushions, but the expression on Malcolm's face won't let me.

"How can you know? You've said yourself that most ghosts lose their human personality."

"Most do, or they cling to one aspect of it. In life, the thing my grandmother wanted most was to take care of me. So in her afterlife?"

"She's still taking care of you—or us." This time, his laugh is soft. "Last month's ghost in the bank vault?"

I nod.

"I suppose she's the one who shows up in the law offices as well."

"That too."

"What about Sadie?"

Sadie Lancaster is my next-door neighbor, one who believes herself continually plagued by ghosts. "No, Sadie just has a low tolerance for sprites. But that isn't my point."

Malcolm raises an eyebrow.

"What if your brother finds my grandmother and swallows her?"

WE'VE RETURNED to Lasting Rest Mausoleum. Autumn chills the air. Although I've pulled on a pair of over-the-knee stockings, the strip of flesh between the wool and the bandages breaks out in goose bumps. But my feet are toasty in leather hiking boots, the rest of me in a leather jacket.

I've spent the entire drive here ignoring glances from Malcolm, but now in the parking lot, I spit out an annoyed, "What?"

"You look—" he begins.

"Like you've walked out of his dreams, my dear."

It's the voice from the phone, but where it comes from, and how it seems to echo both in my head and all around us, I can't tell. It is yet another thing that defies logic and physics, like the floating bed sheet of the ghost from earlier.

"Is this what you meant by harassment?" I whisper. "He made it ... personal?"

Malcolm's face contorts. He gives me one quick nod.

"I'm sorry." I mean it, too. I suspect this first volley is merely a hint of what his brother can deliver.

The world around us has gone quiet. A breeze flutters my skirt, but I don't hear the wind. No birds sing. It is nearly as quiet as I'm sure the inside of the mausoleum is. But this is where we need to be, if only because there are no ghosts here. My grandmother isn't here. At least, I don't sense her. Would she face off against this ghost eater if she thought he might hurt me?

I know the answer and decide not to think about it, not now.

"Why are we here again?" Malcolm asks.

"Because this is where it started, because when you have so many different people inside you, you probably need a quiet place. Isn't that right, Nigel?"

Silence answers me. Malcolm eyes me. I want to protest that no, I have not suddenly lost my mind. Instead, I say:

"Let's set up the camp stove."

We are outside, in the parking lot. If someone protests, we can point out that there isn't a sign that states: No brewing coffee. Or tea, for that matter. Malcolm sets up the stove on the tailgate of my truck. I unpack the percolator and the Kona blend. A job like this, with an untold number of ghosts? Well, we need the good stuff.

But his hands move slowly. His gaze darts to the bandages on my thighs. At last, he drops any pretext of starting the stove.

"I can't do this," he says. "I can't see you hurt again."

"I won't be hurt."

He turns and cocks his head at me.

"How about, I probably won't be hurt. I'll jump out of the way. We know what to expect."

"That's just it, Katy. You don't know him. I do. And he'll go to any lengths—"

"Ah, poor baby brother." The strange voice is back. "Always

trying to play knight in shining armor. It's too bad your damsel in distress doesn't want to be rescued."

It's clearly the wrong thing to say, since the metallic words send Malcolm into a frenzy of activity, and soon the camp stove is pumping propane and heat into the air. I set the percolator on it, and the aroma of coffee joins the heat. Then I pull three more percolators from the front seat of the truck.

Malcolm scowls at the sight. "Katy, what the—?"

"How many years has your brother been swallowing ghosts?"

His mouth draws into a thin, hard line. "I'm not certain. At least three, maybe more."

I expect that strange, metallic voice to cackle, but all is still. "That's a lot of ghosts, and they're going to want some coffee."

Malcolm blinks. "Or possibly some tea."

"Or possibly some tea," I echo. I want to hug him, but I'm not certain I should. That might only give Nigel more ammunition, and Malcolm is already skittish.

Wouldn't I be? I scan the parking lot. If we can hear him, his brother must be close. "All those ghosts," I say. "Do you think that helps him throw his voice?"

"Yes, actually, it does."

I jump and whirl around, but no one is behind me. Malcolm stands next to the tailgate, clutching a samovar, one he'll use to brew tea.

"Oh, you're clever," I say. "Isn't he clever, Malcolm?"

Malcolm stares as if I've lost my mind. Perhaps I have. "But there's a difference between clever and smart, and you're not being very smart."

A howl of protest goes up, but it's all air and golden leaves and little more.

"Because it isn't very smart to swallow ghosts." When there's no response, I continue. "How do you keep them all in check? Each one wants something, right? How do you manage? How do you keep them from leaving?" I return to the tailgate and the camp stove.

There, Malcolm sets out the cups. I pour. He adds sugar. I add cream. We work like my grandmother and I used to, our movements like a perfectly choreographed dance routine. I smile at him. Worry crinkles the lines around his eyes, but he gives me a small smile in return.

Scented steam fills the air. The parking lot is thick with the aroma, and combined with the cool autumn day, this could almost be paradise, or at least, a version of it. Barring Lasting Rest Mausoleum looming over everything, of course.

A cry rends the quiet, followed by a choking sound.

"They want out, don't they?" I say. I get no response.

"Katy, look!" Malcolm points, then reaches for one of our Tupperware containers.

Above one of the cups of coffee, something swirls. It's a puny thing, hardly more than a sprite, but its presence tinges the air, makes it glimmer in a way steam alone can't. Malcolm traps it easily in the container. The thing doesn't even put up a fight, but merely sinks to the bottom as if it needs a good rest.

He peers at the container and then at me. "It's exhausted."

I nod.

"Ghosts get tired?"

I shrug. "Maybe from being inside someone else, with so many others?"

Maybe. And maybe it simply doesn't matter, not when a second, third, and fourth swirl above two cups of coffee and one of tea. We trap them, one by one, and place the containers in the back of my truck.

The stillness catches us off guard. We've been so busy catching ghosts that only now do I notice that the air is stale. The steam sinks into the cups as if it has acquired weight. The world is silent and devoid of everything—smells, sounds. I inch closer to Malcolm, but even his Ivory soap and nutmeg scent eludes me.

"It's like the calm before the storm," I say.

He nods toward my truck, not so much at it as the space beneath it. He taps his fingers against his thigh, a countdown.

Three ... two ... one.

We both dive beneath the tailgate. The asphalt tears at my stockings, scrapes my bare skin. Malcolm tugs me close while around the truck, coffee and tea rain down. It's a storm and it's unrelenting. The laugh that follows rings hollow and makes my heart squeeze tight.

"Bravo, bravo. But did you really think *coffee* would work?" That metallic voice is triumphant.

Malcolm eyes me. I'm afraid my expression must convey it all: yes, I really did think coffee would work.

"The ghosts are exhausted," I whisper. "They really want to leave. They need a reason to break free."

That's when I feel the familiar and icy caress against my cheek. She must swoop in and nudge Malcolm as well, for his eyes go wide.

"Katy, that's not—"

"It is," I say. "That's my grandmother."

She continues to swoop and nudge, as if she could push me from beneath the truck. I flip over and low crawl my way from its shelter. I roll and miss most of the larger coffee puddles. They've lost all their scent, and the air above them is cold and stale, but as my grandmother whirls around the truck, a glimmer returns to the day.

Somewhere in the far-off tree line, a howl reverberates.

"More coffee," I say. "And tea."

Malcolm fires up the camp stove. I measure out the grounds. In the back of the truck, my grandmother swoops around the Tupperware containers, the ones with occupants. The ghosts rattle, then sink, rattle, sink. She darts back and forth before streaming across the parking lot. I catch the barest glimmer of her near the tree line.

I grip Malcolm's wrist. "She's using herself as bait."

His face is stricken. He shakes me off, then, before I can say or do anything, he bolts across the parking lot, toward the tree line, his brother, and the ghost of my grandmother.

FROM THE MOMENT Malcolm vanishes into the trees, my world goes quiet. Make the coffee, I order myself. Make the coffee, pour the cups, add the cream and sugar. Move your hands and everything will be okay. Move your hands.

My legs twitch. It's all I can do not to tear across the parking lot after them. But if the coffee isn't brewed, if the containers aren't out and ready to capture ghosts, then whatever happens to my grandmother and Malcolm will be for nothing.

I count the cups. I pull out extra containers and count those too. What I don't count on is seeing the fluttering bed sheet, that pretend ghost, in my peripheral vision. I cast my gaze toward the tree line, then back toward the fluttering. My heart sinks.

"Bed sheets and bridal veils," I say out loud.

That strange, metallic voice laughs.

"Vendetta?" I venture.

This time, there is no response.

"There are two of you," I say. Has it been this ... thing all along? I think I know the answer and dread washes over me.

"Ah, close enough, my dear. You are far cleverer than ... who is he, again? Your business partner?"

I clutch one of the percolators to me. It's not much of a weapon, but the metal heats my frigid fingers, and the handle is sure and steady in my grip.

"You are not Nigel," I say.

"Again, brava."

"Who are you, then?"

That laugh fills the air. With it comes the absence of everything

—the aroma of coffee, the saffron from the tea. It's as if this thing —whatever it is—sucks up everything with a hint of life.

"It gives me substance," he says, as if reading my thoughts. "Not much, but I do appreciate your effort. You do make a damn fine cup of coffee." A sigh kicks up some dried leaves. "I miss drinking coffee, almost as much as I miss walking. It's strange, really, how much I miss the simple act of moving myself from one place to another. Of course, there are other ... *pleasures* I miss as well."

I scan the parking lot, but every time I catch sight of that fluttering bed sheet, it somehow whisks away.

"People imagine that to be ethereal is to be divine. It isn't, of course. In fact, you might say it's rather hellish, especially when all you want to do is stroke the cheek of a pretty girl."

That bed sheet appears before my eyes. It flaps as if draped from a clothesline. An edge touches my cheek. Before I can leap back, it entwines itself around my neck. Pressure against my windpipe makes me drop the percolator. Coffee splashes my shins, but I barely feel the heat. All my attention is on getting air into my lungs. I clutch at my neck, but all I do is rake fingernails across my skin.

Then, in a flash, the bed sheet flies away, once again teasing my peripheral vision.

"See? It's just not the same. Now, if I had a body ..."

I cough, unable—at first—to respond with words. I hold a protective hand over my neck; the other clutches the side of the truck. "Nigel," I say at last. "You want Nigel. You lured him here."

"With some help. You. His brother. That imbecile Doug. You see, my dear, for a ghost eater, I'm the ultimate prize. Of course, I'll have to do a little housekeeping once I'm inside. Kick everyone else out, for starters—"

"How does a ghost get so powerful?" I turn in a slow circle. His voice comes from everywhere. There must be some sort of trick.

The stale silence of the parking lot greets my question. "How does a ghost become so self-aware?"

Most, I believe, run on instinct, my grandmother a possible exception. But this thing?

"I am older than your grandmother. I am older than her grand-mother. I am older than you can possibly begin to imagine." The voice fills the parking lot, seems to fill me. "I was here when mankind first crawled from the slime, and I'll be here when you bomb yourselves back into it."

"Then why would you want to be a puny human being?"

"I believe I already gave you my reasons. Indeed, I may have just added you to my list of those reasons."

"Seriously?" My neck aches, but my words come out strong. "Is that supposed to scare me?" I pick up a percolator, although this is only a ruse.

"It should."

I walk around the truck and open the driver's side door. I lean in, as if reaching for one of the bags of sugar. The bed sheet strikes the windshield. I pull my legs inside the cab and slam the door before it can follow me in. I start the engine. I'm about to peel out of the parking lot, in search of Malcolm, when in the rearview mirror I see that bed sheet flutter and dive.

The tailpipe.

I shift into first anyway. I press the accelerator. The engine sputters and dies. I reach for the key, determined to try again.

"I wouldn't, my dear. Carbon monoxide poisoning is a nasty way to go."

I concede that this obnoxious entity is correct. So I blast the horn instead.

Now, in the side mirror, I see two figures. Both run. Both glimmer. My grandmother must be keeping pace with them, blurring their images. No matter what Nigel has done, I need to warn him. He can't swallow this creature. This ... thing will kill him, erase any trace of the brother Malcolm knows and—I suspect—still loves.

But I can't leave the cab without the stupid thing choking me again.

"No, I'm afraid you can't."

"Stop that," I order.

"I'm not reading your mind, not really. It's just that all your thoughts play so clearly across your face. It's like watching a stage actress."

"Watch this." I hold up my middle finger.

The entity merely laughs that grating, metallic cackle. The sound freezes both Malcolm and Nigel in place. Then they both race forward again. This time, though, it's as if Nigel is bolstered by supernatural strength. He's thinner than Malcolm, but his legs stretch farther with each step, and he outpaces his brother easily.

He is nearly to the tailgate when I fling open the cab door.

"Nigel, no!" I shout. My throat aches and my words emerge with a croak. "It's a trap."

I'm right. It is. But not in the way I think. That bed sheet bursts from beneath the hood of my truck and drops down on top of me. Someone screams, but I don't think it's me. My mouth is too full of what feels like mist. I cough and choke. I push, but there's nothing to push against.

Nigel crashes into me. For a moment, we're both trapped beneath a fluttering white bed sheet that is there, and at the same time, not there. But he's done this before and knows what to do. He opens his mouth as if for a big yawn, and then I am free.

Nigel falls to the ground. His legs and arms twitch. I am only two feet away, but the chill that rolls off him is a force pushing me back. I can't get close. I can't help him. Malcolm catches me from behind, wraps his arms around my waist.

"The ultimate prize." Malcolm's voice is ragged in my ear. "That's what he kept saying. The ultimate prize for a ghost eater."

"A trap. That thing will ... use your brother, maybe already has been using him. I'm sorry."

Malcolm's arms tighten around my waist. He buries his head against my neck. "I'm sorry, too, Katy, for bringing this to you."

I don't want to watch, but know I should. If I must fight this sort of being, then I need to know all its tricks. Nigel rolls on the asphalt, through puddles of coffee and damp leaves. He clamps his hands over his mouth.

"He's not giving up the ghosts," I say.

"Is that good?"

"I don't know, but it isn't part of that thing's plan."

When I notice the darting glimmer, I can't say. Perhaps at first, I only think it a trick of the September afternoon light. But this light has purpose. It moves and swoops—just like my grandmother.

"Oh, my God, she wants in," I say a second before Nigel uncovers his mouth.

My grandmother dives inside.

This time, the scream is mine.

NIGEL STOPS TWITCHING. He rolls onto his back, closes his eyes, his face almost serene. An infant asleep. Or a man near death. In my mind, I hear an echo of a voice, a command from long ago.

Katy-Girl, the coffee, now!

"Coffee!" This comes out as more air than word, but understanding lights Malcolm's eyes.

We race for the camp stove. Except for the pot I removed earlier, the rest remains, brewing and steaming and filling the air with an aroma to rival the best coffee shop. Malcolm pours cups of tea from the samovar. When that heady mixture of saffron and spice strikes the air, I think I hear a cheer, the sound both joyful and otherworldly.

"Katy, look!" Malcolm points and we round the truck together. "Do you see them?"

"I do!"

One by one, glimmers emerge from Nigel's mouth. Tiny ones, no more than sprites. They streak toward the brewing coffee. They dip and dive in the steam before compliantly sinking into one of the Tupperware containers by the truck's left rear wheel.

"They're happy to be free," I say.

And they are. Happy. Grateful. A few swoop by me, giving me a ghostly kiss on their way to a container. Granted, one smacks Malcolm on the back of the head, but it's more of a ghostly version of a buddy shove than any sort of retribution.

Sprites are one thing. Nigel has just swallowed something very nasty. We will have to face that.

During my years of ghost catching, I've only witnessed a full-on ghost infestation three times, two in homes, once in an old barn. Never have I seen one inside a person, but that can only explain Nigel's current state. He appears glazed over, as if a thin sheet of ice covers him. His lips turn blue; his eyelashes are frosted.

"More heat," I call to Malcolm. "More steam." I refill the percolator. Malcolm turns the knob of the camp stove to high.

"Let's bring the cups to him," I say a moment later. "Tempt them out."

When the coffee is ready, I pour. Malcolm adds the cream and sugar, the spoon clinking against the sides of the cups.

"Three black," he says, "three with cream."

"Three with sugar," I say, picking up the chant. "And three extra light and extra sweet."

"Because even ghosts have a preference."

Twelve cups. Always. The way my grandmother taught me. We rush the cups of scalding coffee across the parking lot. Hot liquid sloshes over the sides. My hands throb with the scalding, their skin bright pink. I keep up the run until a circle of coffee surrounds Nigel, the ceramic mugs gleaming in the sunshine, bright blues to rival the sky, the green deeper than the chemically enhanced lawn of the mausoleum behind us.

With all twelve cups in place, it's like Nigel is some strange offering to the god of caffeine. Steam rises into the autumn air, the vapor clouding my view of him. He is hazy, as if we've tucked him in for the night in a blanket of fog.

His entire body trembles. He cries out, once. Then, the world glimmers.

From his mouth, ghosts stream. The more powerful ones jostle the mugs, send coffee splashing across the asphalt, my hiking boots, Malcolm's loafers. They whirl, kick up leaves and pebbles with the force of their escape. We grab containers and catch the slower ones. Some bypass the coffee, intent on freedom—and that is anywhere but our Tupperware.

I don't sense my grandmother. I detect no hint of that ... thing, the one who flutters bed sheets and makes me think of bridal veils. Nigel bolts upright. He coughs. He strikes himself in the solar plexus as if giving himself the Heimlich maneuver.

What emerges from his mouth is an inky swirl of dark purple, tinged with green, like storm clouds during a tornado warning. It does not glimmer. It oozes. I take a few steps back and bump against Malcolm. He grips my shoulders, and it's his heat that keeps me steady.

The thing floats inches from my face. The air around it is stale, devoid of scent. Its presence fills my head. Cold metal. Gray sleet. And thoughts I force myself not to think. Bed sheets. Bridal veils.

"Know this, Katy," the thing says in its strange, metallic voice, words clicking against my eardrums. "You can't run."

Malcolm pushes himself in front of me, but the thing drifts skyward as if filled with just enough helium to give it lift. The breeze takes it and carries the inky mass away until the blot against the sky at last vanishes.

Malcolm swears softly in my ear, giving voice to my thoughts. Then I whirl.

"My grandmother!"

We rush to Nigel's side. He is still, his face pale, eyes shut. Malcolm sinks to one side, I land on the other. I close my own eyes to hold back the tears. True, I've lost my grandmother to death. That she follows me now during her afterlife has been more of a comfort than I'm willing to admit. Now I fear the goodbye is for real.

"Katy." Malcolm's voice is soft. "Look."

So I do. There, emerging from Nigel's mouth, is a soft, shimmering glimmer, robust and able to withstand the breeze. Thirsty, perhaps, for a cup of coffee—two sugars, extra cream.

"It's the yellow cup," I tell her.

Before she swoops in for her reward, my grandmother's ghost swirls against my cheeks and dries my tears.

Malcolm holds his brother's hand. "He's breathing, his pulse is fast, but I think that's to be expected."

"Should we—?" Before I can suggest calling 911, Nigel bolts upright.

He coughs, a shudder convulsing his body. His eyes clear. "Malcolm?"

Malcolm nods.

"I ... I ..." Nigel surveys the parking lot, the coffee cups. His gaze follows the tree line. I see the instant the memories come flooding back. The chagrin on his face is painful to witness.

"Oh, God," he murmurs and buries his face in his hands. "I am so ashamed."

Malcolm hugs his brother, but Nigel won't stop his litany of regret and shame.

"I don't know what I've done, and yet, I remember it all. I can't explain it."

"You weren't in control," Malcolm says. "It was the ghosts."

"Oh, but I swallowed them."

Malcolm casts me a desperate look. I inch closer. My red and

44

white striped stockings are ruined, so what's a little more asphalt? I kneel and peer up at Nigel. Then I offer him my hand.

"Hi, I'm Katy. You saved my life."

Now I have the attention of both brothers. And yes, the resemblance is there, although where Malcolm's hair is a gleaming ebony, Nigel has a shock of pure white. Their eyes are dark, but Nigel's have the look of a man who has seen far too many things.

"I ... saved your life?" he says, each word its own question.

"That thing." I touch my neck. It's tender, and I suspect a bruise is already forming. "It tried to kill me. It would have, or taken me over, or something. You crashed into me on purpose, didn't you?"

Nigel is silent.

"You had second thoughts about it, didn't you?"

"I don't know." The words are rough and honest.

"I think you did, and you didn't have to save my life, but you did anyway." I'm still extending my hand. I nod to it.

He takes my hand, his skin nearly as warm as his brother's. A second later, he exclaims, "You're freezing." He turns to his brother. "Malcolm, she's freezing."

"I think there's some tea left," Malcolm says.

We huddle around the tailgate and sip the last of Malcolm's tea, my grandmother turning lazy circles in the steam from the samovar.

WE RETURN one last time to Lasting Rest Mausoleum. After Nigel gave up all the ghosts, a few mischievous sprites found their way inside. Apparently, they've been nipping at visitors and knocking over the fans. Personally, I think they liven up the place. But a client is a client, as Malcolm points out, especially with our cash flow the way it is.

On our final circuit through the building, we find a discarded bed sheet, some fishing line, and what looks like a pulley from a child's toy. The innocuous items feel menacing, but the air in the space smells merely recycled, not devoid of everything, not like before.

Still, when Malcolm gathers the things, worry carves a frown in his brow.

"Why bed sheets and bridal veils?" I ask both brothers later in the week. We've settled now into a new routine, one that includes Nigel. He lives with Malcolm, and knows his way around a computer. He plans to build us a ghost hunting database.

To my surprise, it's Nigel who speaks up first.

"Sex and love," he says. "That's what most of them want, some form of it. Attention, love, acknowledgement, to be desired." He shakes his head. "Even now, I can hear their chatter. It fills you up, but it leaves you empty."

And then he is silent. We've grown used to this, having him quiet, his gaze somewhere in the middle distance. I don't ask him what he sees. I know he will tell us when he's ready.

In the meantime, Malcolm and I have an incident at the local law firm.

"Your grandmother can't keep doing this," he says. "Someone will figure it out."

"You didn't." I have graduated back into jeans, my thighs healed, or mostly so. I've added a plaid blazer, but still feel under-dressed for the gauntlet of lawyers we will need to pass.

"How about this," he counters. "She needs to be careful." He stops our trek down the sidewalk. "You need to be careful, Katy. That thing—"

"Is gone."

He stands firm in the center of the sidewalk so a mother with a stroller must scoot past us.

"I can't get that word out of my head," he says once she passes. "Vendetta. It wasn't about Nigel, and I don't think it was about me. That leaves you."

"That thing is gone," I say again.

"For now."

"Yes, exactly. And in the meantime, we have a job to do."

"But—"

I press my finger against his lips, a quick touch, there and gone. This close, he is all Ivory soap and nutmeg. "Let's go catch a ghost."

To my surprise, Malcolm doesn't protest. He merely takes my hand and starts walking.

To my surprise, I don't mind. Not at all.

THE GHOST WHISPERER

COFFEE AND GHOSTS: EPISODE 3

AS FAR AS GHOST ERADICATIONS GO, clearing sprites
from Sadie Lancaster's house almost never varies. I suspect
they are the same two sprites, although with sprites, it's hard to
tell. I suspect they hold a certain amount of affection for Sadie
since they always return. They don't mind my efforts to catch
them. At least, they don't mind the coffee I use to do so. All in all,
clearing Sadie's house of sprites guarantees a certain amount of
cash flow each month.

K&M Ghost Eradication Specialists appreciates and counts on
that certain amount of cash flow.

"You know, Katy," Sadie says to me, hands fluttering. "I've been
talking to someone who says I should embrace my sprites."

"You could," I say, mentally weighing cash flow against honesty.
In my hands, I cradle a cup of coffee, one I plan to place in the
master bath. Ghosts of all varieties love toilet humor. You really
don't want one in your bathroom. The mug stings my fingertips
and steam rises from the coffee's surface. In that steam, something
glimmers. I may have my first catch already.

"She says they won't hurt me," Sadie adds.

"They won't," I say. "But they will play pranks."

Sadie gives her head an emphatic shake. "They're only trying to communicate. You should know that, Katy."

Well, no, they're not. And no, I don't know any such thing. True, ghosts have desires, but not in the way most people think they do. None of them want to sit down for a chat. They don't want to unburden themselves, no matter what you see on television. Like most things supernatural, information on ghosts is very misleading.

"Anyway," Sadie is saying. "Mistress Armand—"

"Wait. Mistress *Armand*?" My partner—the M in K&M—is Malcolm Armand.

"Well, yes. I just assumed she's a sister, or an aunt. Same beautiful black hair and all." Sadie waves a hand, dismissing my question.

Aunt. Sister. Imposter? My hands tremble at the thought. Coffee sloshes over the rim. My skin smarts. I swallow back the pain. When I reach the bathroom, I'll run some cold water over the burn. Now? Now I want to know more about this Mistress Armand.

Sadie clutches her hands beneath her chin. "She did a reading, right here in the living room." Her eyes glow. "She knows everything, about Harold, how even though he cheated, he still loved me ..."

What else would you say to a widow, especially one both grieving and wronged? I sigh, my breath chasing steam from the top of the cup. The sprite is there, waiting to be caught. This one is a tease.

"Cold reading," I murmur to myself.

"Pardon, dear?"

"I said, the coffee is getting cold. I need to take it to the bathroom."

What I need to do is think, and possibly call Malcolm, and catch a ghost. I can do all three in the bathroom.

I set the cup on the vanity, then return with a Tupperware container. I hold it open next to the rising steam. The coffee is cooling, and the sprite has had its fill.

"In you go."

I don't even need to scoop up the tiny thing. It floats compliantly into the container, settles at the bottom, and makes no protest when I snap on the lid. I hold the container at eye level and stare through the opaque plastic.

"We've met before."

In response, the sprite thumps the Tupperware's side.

Sprite secured, I text Malcolm. Nothing. I call Malcolm. Still nothing. As a last resort, I try the main number of the Springside Long-term Care Facility.

"Oh, hello, Katy," the manager says, her voice clear and light and full of humor. "Yes, Malcolm is here."

The fact I'm speaking with the manager—and she sounds so happy—can mean only one thing: Malcolm is holding court. The Springside staff and residents love him. Or rather, most of the *female* staff and residents love him. For a man so obsessed with our cash flow, he certainly doesn't mind spending hours at one of our few gratis accounts.

In the background, a cry goes up, a gasp as if a magician has pulled a bouquet of flowers from a hat and presented them to someone in the audience. Since Malcolm knows a handful of magic tricks, this is entirely possible.

The manager laughs. "Oh, his visits brighten everyone's day ... yours do too, Katy, I didn't mean—"

Whenever I visit, I only manage to mess up everyone's bridge game. So no, I doubt I'm a day-brightener.

"It's kind of important," I say. "Could you put him on the line?"

The manager sets the phone down. Sounds filter through the receiver, chatter and laughter. Someone squeals. When Malcolm picks up the phone, his voice is tinged with warmth.

"Malcolm Armand."

"It's Katy."

There's a pause in which I hear him mentally berating me. Yes, I know. I'm interrupting the Malcolm Armand variety hour and all his fun.

"Do you have a sister?" I ask.

This is a fair question—and not out of the blue as you might suspect. Up until a few weeks ago, I never knew Malcolm had a brother, one who swallows ghosts. It's entirely possible his family tree includes a medium.

"No."

"An aunt, then? Or a female cousin?"

"Maybe a second cousin. Or is that first cousin, once removed? I can never remember."

"How about a mistress? Do you have one of those?"

"Katy, what the hell is this about?"

"Someone is in town. She claims to be—" I pause and glance at Sadie, eyebrow raised in question.

"A medium between this world and the next," Sadie rattles off. She sounds like she's parroting an infomercial.

"A medium. She's been advising Sadie." Possibly for a great deal of cash, but I'll investigate that later. "And she calls herself Mistress Armand."

"Seriously, Katy," Malcolm says. "Assuming I had a mistress, which I don't, would she really go around calling herself Mistress Armand?"

"No .... I was just trying to get your attention."

The line goes silent, and then his laugh fills my ear. It's a rich sort of laughter that—if you could brew it and pour it into a cup— would taste like a sweet, dark roast.

"You've got it," he says, humor returning to his voice. "You always do."

My throat tightens. I'm not entirely certain what he means by this. However, I am certain I won't ask. Or at least, I can't ask. My throat won't let me. Through the receiver I hear the volume of the chatter in the facility drop, a collective hush that sounds like the rushing of air. Malcolm sucks in his breath.

"Uh, Katy, do you know what Mistress Armand looks like?"

I repeat the question. It's barely out of my mouth when Sadie hands me a trifold brochure.

"Long, dark hair," I say.

"Check."

"Could be anywhere between twenty-nine and forty-nine."

"Check."

"Long, flowing robe-like thing?" I add.

"I think they're called kaftans."

Yes. Leave it to Malcolm to know the correct term.

"Whatever," I say. "She's wearing a pink and yellow one in her photo. It's fancy."

"Blue and green. But yes, and it looks expensive, like it's made out of silk."

"It is made out of silk."

I jerk around because the lilting female voice seems to come from both the phone and the air around me.

"Speaker," Malcolm murmurs.

I mute my own phone and then press it close to my ear, unwilling to miss a single word of this exchange.

"I hear we share an interest in the supernatural and a surname," that same lilting voice says. "I am Mistress Armand."

"Malcolm Armand."

He sounds impressed, or like he's trying to impress. From the brochure, her image stares up at me. I assumed Photoshop. Perhaps I assumed wrong. My throat clogs again, the taste of it thick and salty. *Don't be stupid. Malcolm is your business partner. He's free to impress anyone he likes.*

If only I weren't so impressed.

"We need to embrace our otherworldly friends," Mistress Armand is saying. Her voice wavers in and out, like she's turning as she talks.

"Physically speaking," he says, "that's not possible."

Her laugh tinkles as if he's uttered the funniest thing ever.

"But you do catch them, don't you?" she says. "They must have some substance."

Well, yes, but not enough for a hug.

"And then you just set them free?" she asks.

"Of course." Malcolm's voice is sturdy and sure. "We are strictly a catch and release operation."

"But, in some ways, isn't that just as cruel?"

Cruel? My ears strain to hear what Malcolm says, what she will say.

"I don't see how," he says. "We set them free."

"Unmoored, unprotected, lost, in all that air? It's like releasing a laboratory animal or a house pet into the wild. Without their familiar surroundings, they're unable to survive."

Worry pings inside me. I'd never thought of what we do as deliberately cruel. It's a service, really, for both humans and ghosts. Most ghosts are more than willing to be caught. Many, like Sadie's sprites, find their way back to haunt yet again. My grandmother—who taught me everything I know about ghosts and ghost hunting—always said we were doing everyone involved a favor.

"I don't think that's true," Malcolm says, but the conviction in his voice bears cracks. At least, I can hear them even if no one else can.

"Here." Something rattles, something that sounds like paper, quite possibly a replica of the brochure Sadie handed me earlier. "I'm holding a séance tonight. Bring your little partner."

Little partner?

"Cups of coffee and Tupperware?" She snorts a laugh, one that does not tinkle, thank goodness. "Come tonight and watch how a real ghost whisperer does it."

~

MALCOLM IS NOT at our office by the time I arrive there, but his brother Nigel is. Nigel, who is also an Armand. Nigel, who knows a thing or two about ghosts, even if those things came from swallowing them. He's recently recovered from his addiction to that. Although sometimes his eyes glimmer, like he's contemplating a tasty sprite. He is also our resident computer expert. I hand him Mistress Armand's brochure.

"Whoa." Nigel runs a hand through his pure white hair. "She's ... intense."

"A relation?"

"Not that I know of, but—" He shrugs. "The Armand family tree is kind of scattered."

He studies the brochure for a moment, then glances up, dazzling me with a rare smile. "She has a domain name. Where there's a domain, there's a trail. Let's follow it."

His hands fly over the keyboard while I pull up a chair to watch.

"Here we go," he says. "Looks like she maintains a static webpage. Not much here."

I lean forward for a glimpse of Mistress Armand's website.

Let Mistress Armand whisper the ghosts from your life. Guaranteed. Effective. Heal yourself and watch the ghosts flee.

I roll my eyes.

"Not impressed?" Nigel asks.

"Not really. She knew all about Sadie's marriage, and how Harold cheated on her, and probably how he died, too."

"How did he die?"

"In bed, with another woman."

Nigel cringes. "Really? Poor Sadie."

"Do you think she researches a town," I say, "then uses that as a starting point for cold readings?"

Really, it wouldn't be that hard to scan the newspapers for tidbits and then ask a few questions around town. Harold

Lancaster's obituary was coy, but if you knew what to look for, you could read between the lines.

And although I haven't met her, Mistress Armand strikes me as the sort of person who knows how to read between the lines.

"Probably," Nigel says. "You can find out almost anything on the Internet these days."

"But why use your last name?"

"To get our attention?" A new voice joins the conversation.

Malcolm stands in the doorway to the conference room, which also doubles as Nigel's work area.

"What's your take on all this?" Nigel asks.

Malcolm gives a half laugh and shakes his head.

"Is she ...?" Nigel points to Mistress Armand's portrait. "In person?"

"Oh, yeah, and then some."

"What?" I demand. "She's what?" I glance from one brother to the other, but neither one will meet my gaze.

Nigel clears his throat. "Anyway, here's the thing about having a domain name. Even though her registration is private, we can take a trip in the Internet Wayback Machine to see if she's always been Mistress Armand."

He clacks the keyboard some more. Then, in triumph, he pushes back from his desk, fists raised in the air. "Lady and gentleman, meet Mistress Ramone."

Malcolm leans over one shoulder. I take the other. The website is unchanged except for the last name in the center of the screen.

Nigel peers up at his brother. "We should get on the ghost forums, see if anyone is chatting about her."

I almost never bother with the ghost forums since anything there is either completely wrong, or so filled with hyperbole it might as well be. But in this case, maybe it's just what we need.

Nigel pulls his chair closer to the desk and leans forward like he's about to run a race. "I'm on it."

WHAT DOES one wear to a séance? Certainly not a skater skirt paired with over-the-knee, plaid socks. Unless you're me. Because that's exactly what I'm wearing. The only other dressy item in my closet is the suit I wore to my grandmother's funeral. I can't bring myself to pull it on; I doubt I ever will. I can't bring myself to donate it, either, so there it hangs, haunting my closet.

Outside the Springside Community Center, a crowd is gathering. Residents from the long-term care facility make their unsteady way down the steps of the shuttle bus while others wait for the wheelchair ramp. I wave at Mr. Carlotta, who has just landed on the sidewalk.

"Katy-Girl, do you believe this bunk?" He takes my hand, like he always does. We proceed inside as if I'm his date for the evening, one of the attendants pushing his wheelchair.

"Bunk, I tell you," he says again. "You don't believe it, do you?"

"Of course not."

"Then what are you going to do about it?"

People swarm the lobby. A sticky, sweet smell rises in the air. Some enterprising soul from the school board has set up a cotton candy machine. Someone else—just as clever—is selling bottled water. Sweat trickles down my spine, and despite the two-dollar markup, I buy a bottle.

"I don't know what we're going to do," I say to Mr. Carlotta. "I'm meeting Malcolm here and—"

He snorts, a response that encompasses his entire opinion of Malcolm. Then a cloud passes over Mr. Carlotta's eyes. I see it, feel it, and kneel next to his chair.

"God, Katy-Girl, but I miss her." He clutches my hand harder, as if that could bring my grandmother back.

"I miss her too."

He was so in love with her. That he mourns—still—makes me

just a little bit angry with her. She never encouraged him; it was true.

"It wouldn't be right," is what she always told me. "And it's not something I can do."

Before she died, I agreed. Mr. Carlotta's gnarled fingers pass across the top of my head, tangling in a few wayward strands of hair. Now I wonder if it really would have hurt that much. I disengage, slowly, standing first, then giving his hand a squeeze.

"I've been meaning to ask," I say. "How's Jack?"

At the sound of his grandson's name, Mr. Carlotta's spine straightens. The clouds clear from his eyes.

"Just passed the bar exam and got a job offer from one of those fancy law firms in downtown Minneapolis."

"Very impressive," I say.

"He's a good catch for a girl, steady job and all. Hard to make ends meet as a ghost hunter."

I swallow back the sigh. "Last I heard, Jack was engaged."

"Flighty thing. I knew it wouldn't work out."

I went to school with Jack Carlotta. We were in the same graduating class, and he once set my hair on fire with the Bunsen burner in science class, although not on purpose. I adore Mr. Carlotta too much to tell him that it's actually his grandson who's the flighty one.

"I need to find Malcolm," I say instead.

Predictably, I'm treated to another snort. "You tell him, for me, that I've got my eye on him. He mistreats you, Katy-Girl? Well, I'll have something to say about it."

"We're business partners."

"Yes. Of course." He gives me a sly look. "How silly of me."

Only after I turn toward the gymnasium do I roll my eyes.

At the far end of the gym, a platform sits beneath the basketball hoop. Except for an overstuffed chair in midnight blue, the platform is empty. From where I stand, the material looks like velvet and it matches the ruffle that surrounds the platform itself. The fabric—on the chair, around the platform—is so conveniently draped, it makes me wish I were five so I could lift it up, crawl beneath, and discover all the secrets that are no doubt hidden there.

But I'm not five, so instead I walk up the center aisle, gaze searching for Malcolm. I catch sight of his ebony hair first. He's in the front row, chatting with a reporter from the weekly newspaper. I don't want to sit in the front row. Indeed, nothing about the front row entices me, as a person or as a ghost eradication specialist. The back is the better option, the place where you might see the sleight of hand of the technical crew.

In the back, you can slip out and no one notices. In the back, you can see who is truly engaged from their posture. But Malcolm is in the front, so I continue my trek and take the chair two seats away from his.

When the reporter leaves, Malcolm eyes the space I've left between us, then skewers me with a look.

"What?" He raises an eyebrow. "Do I smell?"

Normally, yes, like Ivory soap and nutmeg. It's one of the best things about working closely with him. But when he scoots over, I end up with a nose full of musk. I scrunch up my face.

"Yeah, you do smell. Are you wearing cologne?"

He pushes a strand of hair from his forehead. "A little."

A lot. His white dress shirt bristles with starch. His loafers gleam. So does his hair. Extra product, I think.

"Are you going on a date later?" I ask at last.

He casts a glance at my stockings. "Are you?"

I look away.

Several banks of lights shut off, leaving the rows of chairs in the dark. A collective intake of breath echoes through the gymnasium. A hazy glow illuminates the chair in the center of the platform, the midnight blue like the night sky, sparkling with hundreds of tiny stars. It's low budget stagecraft, to be sure, but it's effective. I can feel people in the rows behind us leaning forward. The soft plinking of some new age tune fills the air. I turn toward Malcolm. He gives me a shrug.

Mistress Armand ascends the platform from the back, using stairs none of us can see. Her caftan flutters and glimmers a ghostly white. The image reminds me of a child's idea of a ghost. It also reminds me of something I saw very recently, something I can't explain, and something that tried to kill me. I lurch backward. My chair tips. The legs wobble, then Malcolm's arm steadies me. As an encore, the chair legs thud against the wood floor. The jolt travels from the base of my spine to my jaw.

"You okay?" he whispers.

I place a hand against my neck. That thing—the entity that attacked me—is not here. Nothing is choking me. I can still breathe. I nod.

Perhaps it's the light, but Mistress Armand is somehow lovelier than her own retouched image. Another murmur cascades through the crowd. Certainly Malcolm sits up straighter, as if she's captured his full attention. His arm slips from the back of my chair.

I pretend not to notice.

"Welcome!" Mistress Armand calls out. "Welcome friends of all kinds, human and otherworldly. We are here today to dispel myths about our friends on the other side. We are here today to communicate with them, to learn from their knowledge. We are here to heal past hurts."

I can't tell if she means all of us or is speaking in the royal third person. I'm not sure it matters, since most everyone is here to speak to ghosts.

If only the ghosts could talk back.

I listen, trying not to judge or roll my eyes. I fail on both accounts. I squirm in my seat, the metal folding chair making my hips ache. A chill rolls through me despite the body heat warming the air. Up on stage, Mistress Armand wants us to confront our ghosts, which is something I do every day.

"They are merely a manifestation of our inner turmoil," she says. "Rid yourself of that, and you rid yourself of ghosts completely. You will heal your body, soul, and spirit."

I raise my hand.

For a second, Mistress Armand's face contorts. "Let's save questions for the end, shall we?"

"But I have one now," I counter, and before she can cut me off, continue with, "Didn't you say earlier, in fact, earlier today, that ghosts are real and that our policy of catch and release was cruel? How can they be both things? Real and merely a manifestation of our inner turmoil?"

"You simply don't understand, my child. They are both. Don't you see? Catch and release is like denial. You're not facing your problems, simply pushing them aside. They return, stronger than ever."

"But—"

"Who would like to be healed of their ghosts?" Mistress Armand's caftan flutters with her movements. It billows as if to embrace us all.

Around me, hands shoot into the air until I'm surrounded by a forest of arms.

"You there, in the gray sweater and blue skirt. Yes, you."

I crane my neck to see who she's selected. To my horror, Sadie Lancaster makes her way down the aisle, hands clutched under her chin in excitement and pride at being picked.

"Ah, there you go, my dear." Mistress Armand extends a hand and helps Sadie climb the stairs to the platform. "You are plagued by ghosts, then?"

Sadie nods. "Normally I call Katy or Malcolm, but the ghosts always come back."

"Perhaps theirs is not the most effective business model."

Muted laughter ripples through the audience. I'm leaning forward, ready to raise my hand or possibly storm the stage, when Malcolm grips my wrist.

"Not worth it, Katy," he says under his breath.

"But—"

"Not. Worth. It."

I sit back, defeated—for now. Mistress Armand leads Sadie to the chair and rests fingers with long red nails against Sadie's temples.

"Ah, yes. I see your ghosts, my dear. The philandering husband. Am I right?"

"We have to stop this," I say to Malcolm.

"It's common knowledge. Everyone in town knows." He's still gripping my wrist as if he's worried I'll charge up on stage. He should worry, because I'm *this close* to doing so.

On stage, Sadie gulps a plaintive, "Yes."

"I count one, two … oh, my, *five* affairs."

I spear Malcolm with a look. So Mistress Armand wants to talk cruel? *This* is cruel. Sadie's lower lip quivers. She shuts her eyes only to have Mistress Armand snap her fingers in front of her face.

"No, my dear, you must face your inner demons, stare at them straight on. For this business, we keep our eyes open. *Always.*"

Mistress Armand goes on, although the details hardly matter. Malcolm is right. Everyone in town already knows. Everyone in town, except perhaps my grandmother, was party to the deception. When Mistress Armand is done, Sadie is in tatters, her mascara carving two dark rivers down her cheeks. Bits of tissue dot her skirt.

Mistress Armand clutches hands to her chest and turns her gaze toward the ceiling. "Wasn't that cathartic?"

"Actually it was horrid," I say, not caring who hears me.

Mistress Armand's jaw twitches.

"Now, my dear," Mistress Armand continues, "you will see the benefits and a distinct lack of ghosts. Mark my words on that."

Sadie makes her shaky way down the stairs. The assistant manager from the Coffee Depot helps her down the final steps and she gives him a wan smile. When she passes my chair, however, Sadie refuses to even glance at me.

"Who's next?" Mistress Armand calls out. "Who else wants the benefit of ridding their lives of ghosts?"

This time around, the forest of arms is not quite as thick. Still, plenty volunteer. To my surprise, Malcolm releases my wrist.

Then he raises his hand.

"How about a gentleman this time. You there, sir, are you haunted?" She points a red-lacquered nail at Malcolm.

"Constantly," he says.

She gestures toward the stairs. "Then Mistress Armand awaits you."

Oh, I bet she does. I cross my arms over my chest, then cross one leg over the other. Without Malcolm at my side—on my side—things feel wrong in a way I can't pinpoint. Mistress Armand doesn't lead him to the chair. Instead, she has him stand center stage, then circles him as if he's something she might like to buy.

"Oh, dear," she says. "Such a sad tale, such a heavy heart. Do you want to tell Mistress Armand all about the girl you left behind?"

"Yes." And Malcolm breathes this word more than says it. It's as if someone has hit him in the stomach. "The girl I left behind."

The *what*? I come undone, or at least, unfolded. My mouth? Hanging open. Yes, Malcolm's past is murky. I've only just learned of—and met—his brother. Still. Have I been too focused on my own mourning and the business of ghost catching to notice he was suffering from a broken heart?

I don't think so. But ever since Mistress Armand first uttered her breezy proclamations—just this afternoon, no less—I've started to doubt a great many things.

"Oh, you poor boy," she murmurs, her voice like velvet. She cups his face, fingers caressing his jaw. Malcolm stares at her, mouth agape, expression rapt.

I push from my chair and head, not toward the stage, but down the aisle. I can't take anymore. In fact, I may have taken too much already. I doubt I can scrub the image of her hand caressing Malcolm from my mind. At least, not any time soon.

I push through the gymnasium doors. Before they shut completely, Mistress Armand's lilting voice follows me.

"There are always unbelievers."

Police Chief Ramsey is standing in the lobby outside the gymnasium, arms folded over his chest, his serious-police-business scowl firmly in place. For a moment, my mood lifts. Yes! Mistress Armand is a fraud and Chief Ramsey is here to arrest her—or at least to shut down the séance.

The hope must show on my face, since an almost-grin appears on his.

"Sorry, Katy, you'll have to deal with the competition on your own. I'm just here for traffic control when the séance lets out."

Mistress Armand was right about one thing: there are always unbelievers. Chief Ramsey? He's one of the biggest in town. When my grandmother was alive, every few months, she'd offer to help clear some of the unsolved cases clogging the files of the Springside Township Police Department. Half the vandalism in town is really the result of energetic sprites.

Chief always refused. Some people can't detect ghost activity. They chalk up odd occurrences to Mercury in retrograde or bad luck or superstition.

I glance back at the closed gymnasium doors. "Does she have—?"

"A permit? Why, yes, she does. You'll also notice she isn't charging anyone anything."

"Yet," I add. "She isn't charging them yet. The first hit is always free."

"Isn't that how you operate? Funny how the ghosts"—he draws little air quotes around the word *ghosts*—"always come back."

Yes. Like mice. Or insects. I don't say this. Instead, I say, "K&M Ghost Eradication Specialists is registered with City Hall. We're a limited liability company, and our business license is up to date."

Most of that is thanks to Malcolm. At the thought of him, my gaze once again goes to the closed gymnasium doors.

"Lose something?" Chief asks.

I choose to ignore this. "Let me know when you want me to capture the ghost in your garden shed."

Without waiting for a reply, I walk from the lobby area and head into the night.

The air cools my heated cheeks. Part of me insists I charge back into the gymnasium and put a stop to the séance. Part of me wants to argue with Chief Ramsey, but I can't force someone to believe in ghosts. I can't force anyone to believe anything at all.

I take a final look at the community center doors and wonder if that applies to me.

There are always unbelievers.

Maybe I'm one of them.

∼

ON THE SIDEWALK, I find Mr. Carlotta. He glowers at the entrance of the community center. For a moment, I fear that glower is for me.

"Bunk!" he shouts. "Pure bunk! If only your grandmother were here, Katy-Girl."

Yes. If only.

"She'd know what to do. Oh, she'd take that charlatan down a notch." He wags a finger at me. "That young man of yours—"

"He's not my young man, Mr. Carlotta. He's my business partner."

"He's a disgrace, picking her over you."

"I don't think he's picked anyone." Although why, at the moment, I'm defending Malcolm, I can't say. Maybe I simply can't believe it. So instead, I say, "Can I wheel you home?"

"I know you *can*, Katy-Girl."

I sigh. "May I wheel you home, Mr. Carlotta?"

"No, but you may wheel me back to the care facility."

I sigh again.

The facility is lightly staffed. The few employees on shift seem resentful and disgruntled, as if we've kept them from all the fun at the séance. From what I saw, it was less of a séance and more of an exercise in public humiliation. They should probably thank us.

"Bunk!" Mr. Carlotta tells them, not that it helps. But he's right. It was that, too.

The wheels on Mr. Carlotta's chair whisper against the carpet. His room is near the end of the wing, and I wave at the residents still here and still awake. When we reach his room, a glimmer and flash of cold greet us.

"Oh, Mr. Carlotta, why didn't you tell Malcolm your ghost was back?"

He makes a noise, something that sounds like *harrumph*.

"He can catch ghosts just as well as I can."

"No, Katy-Girl, that's where you're wrong. Besides, I don't want just anyone catching this particular ghost."

It's a strong one, that's for certain, its vibe more sad than malevolent. For something ethereal, it weights the air as if it carries many burdens. It feels, if not ancient, then very old.

"Had it since Guadalcanal," Mr. Carlotta told me once.

I don't know if that's true, or if one ghost has been swapped for another. In the past few years, I've sensed it's the same one. Why it chooses to haunt Mr. Carlotta, I can't say, although I'm certain Mistress Armand would be willing to take a guess.

But that's all it would be. My theory? Ghosts latch onto emotions, either an overabundance of them or a complete lack, depending. It's why you so often find sprites annoying a humorless person. They think it's funny.

Sometimes it is.

But in Mr. Carlotta's case, I suspect this spirit merely wants to commiserate. Maybe it was a soldier, like he was during World War Two. Maybe it suffered a great loss and feels that same loss in him. But it makes the air hard to breathe in here, dims the overhead lights. A well of sadness forms in my chest.

"Let me see if they have any coffee in the staff break room."

Mr. Carlotta waves away my suggestion. "You won't catch this one with that swill."

He's right about that.

"Go home, Katy-Girl. I've lived with this ghost for many a year. One more night won't matter."

"I'll be here first thing in the morning," I tell him. "With the Kona blend."

"Extra cream and sugar?"

"Of course." I lean down and let him kiss my cheek.

"Close the door and shut the light off on the way out?" His voice is quiet, just shy of plaintive. I don't want to leave him here, alone, in the dark. But I do.

On my way toward the lobby, a quavery voice calls out.

"Katy, dear, is that you?"

I pause in front of another resident's door. "Shouldn't you be asleep, Mrs. Greeley?"

"I wanted to tell you how much I've been enjoying your grand-mother's visits."

I push open the door. The room is shrouded, the space lit by single nightlight. Not that Mrs. Greeley needs it. She's blind. I'm conscious—maybe self-conscious—about how I step, as if Mrs. Greeley can detect worry and stress in my footfalls. When I reach her bed, I take her hand.

She folds my hand between hers. "Are you all right, my dear?"

Nope, I'm not fooling her. "Tired," I say. "I went to the séance, then pushed Mr. Carlotta all the way here."

"Old fool. He should've called for the shuttle."

"I wanted to walk," I say.

Her skin feels papery thin against my own. She is so frail, her fingers like twigs. And yet, despite her blindness, I suspect she perceives more than the rest of us combined.

"I haven't seen your grandmother for a few days," she says.

"It's a busy time of year. Close to Halloween. Sprites like to make mischief then."

Mrs. Greeley chuckles. "Indeed they do. If you see her before I do, tell her I'd love to continue our chat."

"I will," I promise.

The night manager meets me in the hall, a few doors away from Mrs. Greeley's room.

"Oh, Katy, I'm so sorry." He's the sort of man who wears his anxiety all over his face, and now lines crease his forehead. "We've had her in for testing. Her memory is fine. Why she insists that she can talk to your grandmother, no one can figure out."

"It's okay."

"But it's not. You already do so much for the residents here. That you're reminded of ...."

He can't bring himself to say *your grandmother's death*, so he lets the sentence trail.

"Every single time," he adds, with more conviction.

"It's really okay," I insist. "In some ways, it's like my grandmother lives on through Mrs. Greeley."

The night manager looks unconvinced. He crinkles his forehead, multiplying the lines there, then gives me a shrug. "How was the séance?" he asks.

"A waste of time."

With that, I leave, before I can confess more, before I can tell the night manager that Mrs. Greeley does talk to my grandmother. For my grandmother still makes rounds here at the care facility—as a ghost. Perhaps Mrs. Greeley has always been sensitive. Perhaps it's her blindness. Whatever the cause, she can communicate with my grandmother's ghost. The only other person who can is me. Not that we've actually chatted. Sometimes words or images float into my head, unbidden. Most of the time, I don't know what they mean. It's like putting together a puzzle, and so far most of the pieces are missing.

Outside, the wind ruffles my skater skirt, the night air colder, the sky black with a few pinpricks of stars. Goose bumps pucker on my bare skin above the stockings. I consider asking the night manager for a ride in the shuttle. But my feet have their own ideas. I'm two blocks away before I truly regret my decision to walk.

I ignore the car at first. Because it's cherry red and a convertible, this is hard. The driver revs the engine. He doesn't tap the horn because it's late, this town tucks in early, and he's far too polite for such things. Then he says my name.

"Katy, come on, I'll give you a ride home."

I stop my trek, turn to face the car, my arms clutched close for warmth. It really is too cold for the top down, but then, that lets Malcolm wear the scarf. It's dark gray wool, and he has it flung jauntily around his neck.

"You were brilliant tonight, by the way," he says.

"Brilliant?"

Did I miss something about the séance? I remember storming out, a lot like a jealous girlfriend might. I remember being rude and disgusted. Brilliant? I doubt that.

"She made a couple cracks about you," he adds.

Oh, how lovely. Of course she did.

"It was perfect. It's almost like you're here." He taps his temple. "Right inside my head. We couldn't have planned it any better if we tried."

I clutch my arms tighter. "I have no idea what you're talking about."

"The whole jealous routine. She totally bought it."

I still have no idea what he's talking about. Instead of responding, I shiver, icy air sneaking up my skirt, the cold making me feel both sleepy and wide-awake at the same time.

Malcolm frowns. "You weren't really ... jealous, were you?"

I'm not the sort of girl who might flip her hair and pretend the image of red lacquered nails running along the jaw of her partner-not-boyfriend doesn't bother her. So I tell Malcolm the truth.

"I was ... am." I shrug as if there's nothing more to say after confessing that.

"But why?"

"Because you're my partner, and—"

"I'm still your partner."

"Then—?"

"If you tried to fool her, pretended to be interested, tried to get close to her," he says, "do you think she would've believed you?"

"Probably not."

"Add your reputation to that, not to mention your grandmother's. Mistress Armand seems to know a lot about everyone in this town."

Yes. She does. Disturbingly so.

"But me?" Malcolm touches his chest. "When I'm, you know—"

"Soft-headed and easily swayed by a pretty face?"

My words ring cold in the night air. Perhaps I've shattered our partnership, which after declaring it so important is a rather stupid thing to do. Then Malcolm throws his head back and laughs.

"Get in the car, partner?"

"It's freezing out and you have the top down."

"And the heat cranked. Trust me, there's no better way to ride."

I don't bother with the handle. Instead, I plant my hand on the side of the car and vault over. I'm halfway into the front seat when I remember the skater skirt. The material flares, and I flash him a generous portion of my thighs and a glimpse of my underwear—pink with black polka dots. A fierce blush chases the chill from my face. Before I can read his expression, Malcolm glances away.

Then he puts the car into gear and we fly down the road. Whenever we go out on a call, we take my truck. The old, battered thing grumbles, but it runs. Plus, once we catch the ghosts, we can store them in the back until the release. There's no room in the convertible for ghosts. There's barely room for two. Despite the gearshift that separates us, I feel close to him, but not trapped or confined. No. Close. I feel close to Malcolm.

And yet? Not.

I exhale, sending my frustration streaming into the air that buzzes past us.

"Cold?" Malcolm asks.

"Tired. I pushed Mr. Carlotta all the way to the care facility."

"Oh, damn, that reminds me. I think his ghost is back."

"It is. But I didn't have any decent coffee with me. I'll stop in tomorrow."

"It's just as well." And here, I think the wind also steals Malcolm's sigh. "He doesn't much like it when I catch his ghost. Actually, he doesn't much like me."

I want to contradict this, but can't. Why this bothers Malcolm, especially when most everyone else in town adores him, I don't know.

The convertible rolls to a stop in front of my house. Next door, light blazes from all the windows. A muted glow comes from the bedroom. I suspect this night will be long for Sadie.

"I feel like I should sneak over and scoop up her sprites," I say. They're back already; I can tell. That accounts for the lights, and the enormous electric bill she'll need to pay at the end of the month.

"If you did, it would only prove Mistress Armand's point. I don't think we want to do that."

I turn toward him. "What happened at the séance?"

Malcolm sinks into the car seat. "What didn't? I know there

aren't many secrets in a town this small. Still." He swipes a hand over his face. "I'm not sure we needed so much bloodletting. I don't know what else to call it. She left everyone bruised and bloodied up on that platform."

"Even you?"

He shifts in his seat and raises an eyebrow as if to ask, *Whatever do you mean?*

"You know," I say. "The girl you left behind."

"Oh. That." His laugh is soft. "I'll give Mistress Armand that. She's good at a cold read. We can't underestimate her. I must have twitched my jaw. She picked up on something, but she got it all wrong. There is no girl I left behind."

"Oh." Questions burn in the back of my mind. If there's no girl, then what is there? What is it I'm missing about him? After all, he's my business partner, and maybe my friend. Yes, he's my friend. So what does Mistress Armand see that I can't?

"Anyway," Malcolm continues, "she convinced everyone to embrace their ghosts and promised they would vanish. Business could be ... thin for a while."

Like it wasn't already. My gaze is drawn back to Sadie's windows, which continue to pour light into the dark.

"Do you think it's on purpose?" I ask him.

"Well, yes, she's being very intentional with all this, most likely to fill her bank account, even if she hasn't charged anyone yet."

"No, not that. I mean, why. She claims to be getting rid of ghosts. So they must vanish, at least temporarily. If that's the case, where do they all go?"

We stare at each other, and I detect the moment horror fills Malcolm's eyes.

"Oh, no. No," he murmurs. He shifts into gear and makes a tight U-turn, nearly hitting a car parked opposite my house. It's a good thing I never undid my seatbelt. I'm tossed from one side to the other as we race down the road toward the center of town. Before I can ask, Malcolm speaks.

"Nigel," he says.

With that one word, I understand his fear.

MALCOLM RENTS an apartment at the center of town. The old, restored building has lots of brick and wood. We jog through the lobby. Malcolm punches the button for the elevator, but he's so jittery, I think he might rush up the stairs. The doors open with a soft ding before he's able to.

The fourth floor hallway is quiet. Either the walls are thick or his neighbors are polite. No drone of a television set. No loud music. At the end of the corridor, he pulls out his keys to unlock the door, and we step inside.

And I realize this is the first time I've seen where Malcolm lives.

He holds up a hand, stopping me from venturing farther than the living room. "Let me check," he says, voice low.

I nod.

While he's gone, I scan the space. A flat screen TV takes up most of one wall. A blanket and pillow sit neatly at one end of a worn futon. Is this where Malcolm's been sleeping? It strikes me as both uncomfortable and a little sad.

On the coffee table rests a laptop computer that I know belongs to Malcolm. On all sides, I'm surrounded by stacks of books, magazines, and newspapers. One pile teeters, then cascades over my feet the moment Malcolm emerges from the apartment's lone hall.

"Sorry, sorry," he says, scooping papers into his arms and a soiled coffee cup from the table. "The place is a mess." He dumps the papers into a bin and the cup into the sink. "Hey, do you want something to drink?"

"I'm okay," I say, even though my throat is dry.

Malcolm returns with two bottles of water despite my protest.

"It's a long walk from the community center to the care facility," is all he says.

I nod toward the hall. "Is Nigel—?"

"Sound asleep. If there are any ghosts inside him, I can't tell, but I doubt it. Insomnia is one of the signs, or at least it was before." Here he shrugs. "Still."

"Are you worried?"

"I'm worried how addictive it is, this ghost eating thing."

I wonder if some of that worry extends to Malcolm himself. He's new to ghost catching. It would be easy to slip, I think, to try something, to end up liking that something.

"Other than the name, I'm not certain there's a connection between Mistress Armand and either of you," I venture. "And I don't think Nigel—"

"It just ... it just hit me all at once. Things got bad between us before I left Minneapolis. Addicts lie, all the time. Nigel has only been clean for a few weeks. And I thought—"

"Me, too."

My legs ache. Malcolm was right. It *was* a long walk from the community center to the care facility. I cast a quick glance around. I don't want to sit on his bed. I decide on the coffee table.

"Before I left for the séance, I scanned the ghost forums." Malcolm kneels next to the coffee table and flips open his laptop.

"See?" He points to a message thread. "Someone called Mistress Ramone was in Waunakee, Wisconsin a few months back. And six months ago, a Mistress Williams was in Kendallville, Indiana. Oddly enough, there's a Williams in Kendallville who's a ghost hunter, and a Ramone who was retired school teacher in Waunakee."

"So she borrows names? To get people to trust her?" I ask.

"Apparently."

"To do what? Séances?"

"People, it seems, were reluctant to talk about it. Lots of 'don't trust her' or 'stay away' messages, but nothing concrete, and nothing, really, to prove that either one is Mistress Armand."

"So what's her angle? What does she really want? I mean, other than to humiliate an entire town. Is that why people won't talk about it? I don't see the purpose in that."

"I don't either, except that some people are intentionally cruel."

Malcolm stands and shakes out his trousers. Despite the evening, he still looks clean and pressed and ready for a date. I'm fairly certain I look rumpled, disheveled, and ready for a shower.

"Come on," he says. "Let me drive you home."

"YOU DON'T HAVE to walk me to the door."

I've said this before. Actually, I've said it a hundred times, at least, since Malcolm and I started working together. Even though my street is quiet and half my neighbors leave their doors unlocked (the others keep a key beneath one of those fake rocks), if the sun is flirting with the horizon, Malcolm makes the trip up the front porch steps and makes sure I reach my door.

He says nothing in response. I never push the issue and in return, he isn't pushy. He's just there, solid and sure. This one small thing defines who he is.

"In the morning," I begin. My hand lands on the doorknob. A second later, I jerk it away. What happens first, I can't say. Do I yelp? Or do I clutch my hand to my chest, the sharp sting of freezer burn making its way through my skin?

"Katy! What is it?"

I'm doubled over, but straighten just enough to test the door again. Frozen solid. My house? Malcolm probes the door, but yanks his hand back.

"Damn." His gaze meets mine. "It can't be."

But it is. My house is in a full-on ghost infestation.

He scans the porch, the roof, the yard. "Back door, maybe?" He takes my hand. His fingers are so warm, I don't want to let go. We race around the house, clatter up the back porch steps, and confront a door hoary with frost. Instead of letting go, Malcolm grips my fingers tighter.

"Now what?" I say.

"What did you do last time?" He nods toward Sadie's house.

Oh, yes! Of course. The full-on ghost infestation at Sadie's might count as our very first job together—even if we didn't realize it at the time. I clear my throat.

"All of you are aware that coffee doesn't brew itself, right?"

At first, nothing but icy silence greets my proclamation. Then, slowly, the back door creaks open. We're allowed only as far as the kitchen. When we try to push through to other areas of the house, a force pushes us backward, toward the percolator. Something much stronger than a sprite rattles the bin where I keep the Kona blend.

"Looks like we have our marching orders," Malcolm says.

Over the past few months, we've brewed so many pots of coffee together it's like a dance routine. He knows what pitcher to use for the half and half, which spoon for the sugar. It is, perhaps, not strictly necessary to use the same items in the same manner, but routine soothes both humans and ghosts. The air vibrates around us, a whole pack of ghosts anticipating the first hints of rich brew from the percolator.

I pour the coffee into the twelve cups lined up on the kitchen table. Malcolm adds the half and half and sugar. It's always the same: three black, three with half and half, three with sugar, and three extra light and extra sweet.

Aromatic steam fills the kitchen. It wavers, not just with air currents, but with the ghosts that fill the space, soaking in the warmth and flavor. The temperature in the house also rises, the thermostat nearly back to normal. I sag against the sink.

"What's going on?" I ask.

As if in answer, cold swirls around my ankles. Ghosts urge me forward. I glance at Malcolm, and he takes my hand again. Together we creep into the living room, the dining area, explore the entire house.

It's filled with ghosts, from attic to basement. I lose count sometime after ninety. Some I recognize, or at least they feel familiar when they brush against my skin. Others are strange, wild things, the sort that haunt deep woods or old, abandoned houses. The only ghost I don't sense is my grandmother's.

"Why are they here?" I ask Malcolm.

It isn't logical, not on the surface, anyway. I've been catching and releasing ghosts since I was five years old. I'm not scared of them, although I've encountered my share of stubborn ones. Still, ours is a relationship where I—more often than not—spoil their fun.

Malcolm holds out a hand, turning it in the air. The ghosts are so thick, I can see them swoop between his fingers. "I think they're scared," he says.

"Of what?"

"Mistress Armand?"

"Is she really a danger?" I ask.

Sure, she's a fraud and is planning to bilk people out of money —at least, I'm pretty sure she is. But dangerous? I don't see it.

"What if it's a distraction?" He points between the two of us. "For us." Now he waves that same hand in the air. "And for them. We're all in one spot. Who would want us all in one spot?"

"If I have all the ghosts, then it looks like Mistress Armand's methods work, right?" I say.

"What if it's more than that? What if she's the distraction?"

"You mean that thing …?" I begin, but my words dry up. Dread fills my stomach; it feels as cold as the ghosts around me.

"Yeah, that thing that attacked you at the mausoleum."

"That was weeks ago."

"That's just it," he says. "I don't think it was the sort of thing that cares about time."

He's right. The thing—for I have no other name for it—is not a ghost. I don't know what it is other than some sort of entity. But maybe a few of my current houseguests might.

"Okay, you guys." I cup my hands around my mouth, letting my voice carry throughout the space. "Who wants more coffee?"

The air shimmers with excitement. A few sprites whirl around my head. Malcolm raises an eyebrow, a quizzical look on his face. It's really kind of adorable when he does that. But when I hold out my hand, he doesn't hesitate.

"You may have to make a bean run to the Coffee Depot when it opens," I tell him on the way back to the kitchen.

"What did you have in mind?"

"We're going to get these guys drunk."

"It's like pulling an all-nighter in college," Malcolm says. His eyes are both bright and half-lidded.

Because yes, we have indulged in several cups ourselves. There's no sense in letting the very fine and very expensive Kona blend go to waste, even if ghosts have been dancing in it all night. And dance they have. Several float in the air, languid and spent. Sprites still zip around, tripping me up whenever I try to go somewhere that isn't the kitchen. But then, sprites are like puppies—almost always active and nearly always causing trouble.

"You had a reason for doing this, right?" he adds.

"They might be able to tell us something," I say.

"I thought you said ghost whispering was a fraud."

"Oh, it is. I'm not talking about personal demons or healing, or messages from beyond the grave. I'm talking about what they see and hear. Each one might have a little piece of ... something that won't make sense. But together? We might figure out what's going on."

"And you know this how?"

"Lately my grandmother's been talking to Mrs. Greeley," I say, and then add with some reluctance, "and lately, I think I can hear her too."

"And you're telling me this now?" His eyes are wide, their expression tinged with fatigue and anger.

"I just found out about Mrs. Greeley." I shrug. "And it's not like I've been having actual conversations. I never thought you could talk to ghosts. I still think that. But I get words, usually ones that don't make sense. What if everyone here—" I wave a hand. "Has a word for us?"

A tired smile replaces some of the anger. "Especially if we ply them with a fresh batch of coffee?"

"Especially then."

"What if you lie down on the floor and I place the cups of coffee around you?" he suggests.

I eye him, uncertain if he's joking or not. "No. That's just creepy."

He laughs, the sound tired, but still, a laugh. "Kidding."

"But lying down sounds nice," I say.

He stifles a yawn. "It does."

We shouldn't, I know. Despite the coffee, I feel the night press against my eyelids. And lying down with Malcolm, even if it is on the living room floor, even if a good two feet of space separates us, is also a bad idea. But we do, gazes fixed on the ceiling. The ghosts there are so thick, their outlines swirl before our eyes, and the ceiling shimmers as if covered with tinsel. Although our fingertips don't touch, he's close enough that the warmth of his skin reaches mine.

"You," he says in no more than a whisper.

"Me?"

"The ghosts. They're talking about you. That's what I hear, or it's the word in my head. Katy. Katy. Katy." He falls silent. "They like you."

"I don't know why. I'm always spoiling their fun."

"I don't think they mind that."

I don't respond. Above us the ghosts continue their dance. A sprite nudges my foot.

"Do you hear anything?" Malcolm asks.

"I don't know. It's too silly to be anything real."

"What is it?" he says.

"Boo."

"What?"

"Just that. Boo. You know, when you want to scare someone. You pop out and say, 'Boo!' It's a little kid thing."

"A child's idea of a ghost."

With his words, we both turn our heads to face each other.

"No." And I hate the way the word emerges from my mouth, pathetic and small.

"He's not here, Katy." Malcolm pushes up on his elbows. "He ... it ... whatever it is. We're safe, you're safe, in this house."

"And you know this how?"

He glances around, waves his fingers through a ghost. "Probably because they're here. They're scared, too, remember?"

"I'm not sure this makes us safe," I say.

"Then what does it make us?"

"Trapped."

The walls around us shudder as if that single word has triggered such a trap. I scamper to my feet, Malcolm reaching a hand to help me up. We stand there, clutching hands, the walls trembling around us.

"Whatever it is," Malcolm says, "it's outside the house. We're safe."

I'm not so sure.

The greatest trembling comes from the front. That's where the threat is. That's where we must go, if only to see what we're up against.

"Come on." I nod toward what used to be the formal dining room of the house. The windows look out onto the front lawn.

We leave the dining room light off. Malcolm splits two of the venetian blinds with his fingers. He swears and lets the blinds fall back into place. Then he doesn't move.

So I repeat the exercise. There on the sidewalk is not the creature that haunts my dreams, not the thing that tried to kill me mere weeks before, but Malcolm's brother.

Nigel looks nearly ghostly himself, that shock of white hair, his thin, drawn face. He hasn't fully recovered, at least not physically, from ghost eating. He stares up at the house as if it's a banquet.

No wonder the ghosts are shaking my walls.

"It's okay," I call out to them. "He won't swallow you."

The trembling continues. Malcolm heaves a sigh. No one in this house, human or otherwise, believes me.

"I won't let him," I add, slipping through the pocket door that leads to the front entrance. I touch the handle, flinch and jerk my hand back so hard, I smack Malcolm in the chest.

"Sorry." I clutch my freezer-burnt hand with the other. "Come on, guys. Let us out."

Nothing. The doorknob is pale with frost. I know if we brew another pot of coffee, I'll be sick.

"He won't come in, but you need to let us out," I say, using my most reasonable voice. "You want to go back to haunting someone other than me, right? I'll just catch you all right now and drive you out to the nature preserve."

The doorknob thaws, warm brass breaking through the frost. I don't even have to turn it. A bevy of ghosts obligingly push open the door for us. We spill onto the front porch. The door slams behind us.

It will take another round of bribery to get them to open it again.

"Nigel?" Malcolm grabs the porch railing, the knuckles of his hands turning white. "What's going on?"

"Katy's grandmother," he begins.

I cut him off. "My grandmother!" I start for the steps, but Malcolm stops me with a gentle hand on my shoulder.

"She ... your grandmother sent me," Nigel says. He stares up at the house, his eyes wide with both horror and hunger. "Mistress Armand. She's chased all the ghosts away from the care facility. She's there now ... feasting."

"Feasting?" I can barely force the word through all the bile in my throat.

"Not like you think," Nigel adds. "She consumes shame, humiliation. In some ways, she's like me. I'm—" His gaze goes once again to the house. "Addicted to ghosts. She's addicted to shame—as long as it's someone else's. That's why she gets everyone to confess their deepest regrets, their most shameful experiences."

The notion hits me hard. "And she's at the care facility because people with long lives often have a long list of regrets."

"It's the ultimate in schadenfreude," Malcolm observes.

Joy in the misfortune of others. Joy and money. And how terrible is it to steal everything from someone?

"We should go," I say, casting Malcolm a wary glance. "They'll need our help."

Malcolm rests his head on my shoulder. "I can't leave him here," he says in a voice meant only for my ears. "I can't. You know that. And you can't go alone."

"I can go alone," I insist.

"No, you can't!"

The voice isn't Malcolm's. Nor is it Nigel who speaks these words. From next door, Sadie charges down her porch steps, her pink fleece robe flapping in her wake. Matching pink slippers encase her feet, and their soles slap the concrete with each fierce stride. She holds a broom like a sword. She is so ferocious that I take a step back, into Malcolm's embrace.

"I will guard the ghosts!" she declares. "I won't let this young man hurt himself further, and I won't let them"—she brandishes the broom at my house—"get into any trouble, either."

"Sadie, are you sure?" I say. This? From the woman terrified of sprites?

"You know who left me, right?" she says. "Harold. The whole town knows that, thanks to Mistress Armand. You know who didn't leave me?"

I can only shake my head.

"My sprites. Even though they were scared—yes, I could tell—they stayed with me all night. After reliving the humiliation of Harold at the séance, after everything I've tried to do to get rid of them, they stayed. Well? I'm here to return the favor." She shakes the broom at Nigel. "Don't get any ideas, young man."

Nigel steps off the sidewalk and lands in the gutter.

Sadie turns to us, broom at the ready. "Well? Don't just stand there. Go!"

"We can take my car," Malcolm says. "It will be fastest." He pats his pockets. "Damn, my keys are—"

My front door flies open. A second later, a key fob sails through the air and lands at Malcolm's feet.

"Well?" Sadie prompts again.

Malcolm grabs the keys while I launch myself into the convertible's passenger seat. We leave behind a motley crew in the exhaust. A reformed ghost eater, a woman petrified of ghosts, and a house filled with every spirit in town, except for one.

THE SUN RISES with a burst of orange and pink that makes the sandstone buildings along Main Street glow. Malcolm's red convertible streaks along the road, its reflection in the storefront windows like something from a movie.

"Do you think it's that ... thing?" I ask Malcolm over the roar of air. "He ... it was looking for a body." Not to mention, the thing had captured Nigel's for a short time.

Malcolm shakes his head. "No. She touched me, remember? On stage?"

Oh. *Yes.* I remember.

"I don't know who she really is, but she had too much substance and warmth to be anything but human."

I'm not certain that's proof. Then again, I can't shake away the image of her red nails clutching Malcolm's jaw, so my view is definitely skewed.

Malcolm parks in the roundabout driveway. From the moment he shuts off the engine, I can hear the cries. Sobs, heartfelt and deep—the sort that shake your entire body. I cast a glance at Malcolm. His worried frown must mirror my own. The crying continues, each wail squeezing my heart so hard it hurts.

My legs wobble when I hop out. Unsteady, I clutch the side of the car, not quite ready to burst through the double doors and into the care facility itself. Sweat bathes my forehead. A wave of dizziness pushes me back against the car door.

"Katy?" Malcolm is at my side. He appears to sway before my eyes.

"The all-nighter? I feel ..."

"Weak," he finishes. "Me too."

The cries continue unabated.

"I felt fine when we left," I say. "Tired, but fine."

He nods and rubs his temples.

Near the entrance, someone has left a walker. I stumble across the outdoor carpeting and make a grab for it. I miss. I tumble onto the ground and trigger the automatic doors. They whoosh open. From inside, the sound of crying increases, louder, more heart wrenching.

I pull myself up and onto the walker, triggering the doors each time they try to close. By the time Malcolm reaches me, his skin has gone a horrid shade of gray.

"You look awful," he says.

"That makes two of us."

We hobble toward the facility entrance, the doors wide open now. With each step, the cries grow until I'm certain the sound is thickening the air around us.

"I have the strangest urge to tell you about the time I lost my shorts during a soccer game," he says, his breath labored.

"During the game? You mean on the field, in front of everyone?"

"Yes, it was ... humiliating, to say the least, and I wasn't wearing any—"

I place a finger over his lips. "Not now."

"But—"

"Someday, when this is all over, if you still want to tell me, you can. But not now. She only wants to feed on your shame."

Understanding dawns in his weary eyes. "Of course. That explains why I want to also tell you about all my bad dates."

"I can't believe you ever had a bad date," I say. He's too smooth and charming.

"I'm refraining." Somehow, he manages a wink. "Later, and you can tell me about yours."

"There isn't anything to tell."

I start up our trek again. We're almost to the lobby and the carpeted floor there. I'm not certain how much longer I can walk, and falling there, rather than the hard tile of the entrance, feels like the better option.

"So all your dates have been amazingly good?" he asks.

"There haven't been any dates," I say, palms sweating against the walker's handgrips. "Good or bad."

Malcolm halts, so I plunk the walker forward a foot or two without him. I'm on the carpet now, and the surface steadies my footsteps. When Malcolm doesn't catch up, I crane my neck to peer at him.

"You've never been on a date?" His gaze surveys me, from wobbly feet to the top of my head, his look incredulous.

"No." Only now that I've confessed do I realize how odd it is for a woman my age to have never dated. How ... humiliating.

Something crackles in the air, raises the hairs on my arms and the back of my neck, like a surge of electricity. A second later, a force knocks me across the room, into the reception desk and onto the floor. I fight to regain my breath, my bearings. My vision tunnels to a single point before expanding.

"Thank you, ghost hunter," a voice says, melodious and feminine, and just this side of seductive. "That was a most delicious bite of shame you served up. I do hope there's more where that came from."

Mistress Armand is still lithe and tall, her glossy black hair streaming down her back, her white caftan fluttering around her. And yet, something about her is massive. I'd call it her aura, but I don't believe in such things; my grandmother never did, anyway. Something surrounds Mistress Armand like a force field. It glows and crackles and gives off the occasional spark.

Any words I might say would be lost in the electricity that fills the air. Silence may be golden; in this case, I suspect it may be the only thing that saves us. *Don't speak. Don't utter a word. Don't feed her.* I frown, hoping to convey this idea to Malcolm with thought power alone. All I get for my efforts is Mistress Armand whirling to follow my gaze.

"Oh, and there he is, the man with so many secrets, and some of them are oh, so shameful, you bad boy. Do tell, Malcolm. I'm certain Katy will want to hear all of them. You know I do."

He is a man frozen, is what he is, whether from shame or for other reasons, I don't know. Then I see his fingers twitch. They twitch again, toward the hall that leads to the wing with the resident rooms, the wing from which all the crying still echoes. In that slight twitch, I discern a single message:

Go!

I crawl, knees scraping against the rough carpet. Before I vanish down the hallway, I hear Malcolm's voice, so strong and steady, I wonder how he manages it.

"I'll tell you my secrets, Mistress Armand, but you have to tell me some of yours."

~

THE SOBS and wails from the residents' rooms weaken me further. I continue forward on hands and knees. Every time I try to push to stand, another cry assaults my ears. At last I reach Mrs. Greeley's door and slump against it.

"Mrs. Greeley? Are you in there? Are you okay?"

"Katy, dear, is that you?" Her voice is anxious, but free of tears.

"It's me."

"I'm trapped. That witch jammed something in the door handle."

"Give me a moment," I say. Oh, the handle is up so, so high. Can I stand up to reach it? How can I not try? I let my head thump against Mrs. Greeley's door, the sound that of defeat.

"Close your eyes, dear," Mrs. Greeley says.

"What?"

"Close your eyes. They're blinding you to the falseness of her voice. With them closed, you will hear her for what she is."

Certainly I've blinked since entering the facility, but I haven't left my eyes closed, not for more than a moment, if that. I don't want to fight ... blind. But that's exactly what Mrs. Greeley is doing, and so far she's the only one not caught in this web of sorrow and shame. I think about the séance and how Mistress Armand insisted Sadie keep her eyes open. To confront her personal demons? Or to let Mistress Armand feast on some shame?

I shut my eyes. At first, nothing changes. The crying rings louder in my ears. But strength returns to my limbs. I reach up and open Mrs. Greeley's door. It creaks, and Mrs. Greeley claps her hands together.

"Well done!" The tap of a cane accompanies her voice. "Now, we must get down the hall and tell the others to shut their eyes."

A shriek echoes through the hallway, wretched and other-worldly. In it, I detect the barest hint of Mistress Armand. There is no seduction left, but an occasional musical tone breaks through, tempts me to open my eyes.

"Don't," Mrs. Greeley says. "Yes, I feel the urge too," she adds, "but I simply can't comply. I'm certain Mistress Armand didn't count on me."

Indeed she didn't. I push to stand, then hold my hands out in front of me, fingertips straining against the air. I will crash into something on my trek down the hall, without a doubt.

"Stop!" The command is robust, so much so that I do falter in my steps. That low, musical tone is stronger. My eyelids flutter before I squeeze my eyes shut again.

"Go," Mrs. Greeley urges.

Yes, but where? I don't dare open my eyes. Before I can move in any direction, something crashes into the backs of my legs.

"Oh! Katy-Girl, is that you?"

"Mr. Carlotta?"

"Keep going," he says. "You're covered. Annabelle and I will guard your back."

"Old fool," Mrs. Greeley mutters, but her voice is nothing but tender.

I still don't know which way to walk, not with my eyes closed. Then something cold and familiar brushes my cheek. The words *Katy-Girl* float into my mind. My grandmother. She's here, and she's showing me which way to go.

Gingerly, I take a step, then another. My grandmother nudges my face, first the right cheek, then the left, helping me navigate around obstacles. Every few feet, I call out.

"Shut your eyes. Don't open them."

Bit by bit the sobs subside. Bit by bit, the care facility quiets. Despite the fact that Mistress Armand's words now cajole and mock, they hold no power. Not over me, and not over anyone in the facility who has their eyes closed.

Even so, or perhaps because of this, she comes for me. Where Malcolm is, I don't know, and I don't open my eyes to find out. Mrs. Greeley cries out. Mr. Carlotta calls, "Hang on! She's broken through."

I hold still. I've reached the lounge area. From the television comes the muted hum of a morning news program. The crying has all but ceased. Perhaps it's my imagination, but I think I detect snoring. My grandmother swirls around me like this alone will protect me. I feel her against my eyes, as if she's trying to remind me not to open them. Then the other presence enters the room.

"You think you know him," Mistress Armand croaks. Without everyone's shame, she is a weak thing. "That will be your undoing."

It's nearly enough to tempt me, nearly enough that I open my eyes. But I don't. I clench my fists against the urge. My grandmother whips around me like a cyclone. I think we might stand like this forever—Mistress Armand too weak to attack with anything but taunts, me not daring to open my eyes.

Then a thump echoes in the lounge area and her presence vanishes.

"You can open your eyes, Katy." Malcolm's voice is calm and welcoming, and with my eyes closed, its rhythm is startling. I think I could listen to him like this for a long while. But instead, I open my eyes. When I do, his are the first thing I see. He glances downward.

There, on the floor, his foot secures a Tupperware bowl. Inside the bowl, the misty and shrunken image of Mistress Armand floats.

"Nice work," I say.

"You too."

We don't lift the container. Instead, the night manager brings us a thin cookie sheet from the facility's kitchen. We slide it beneath the bowl, and now our trap is mobile.

Malcolm drives. I clutch the two pieces—bowl and cookie sheet—until my hands ache. We drive past our usual release point, the windbreak with a little creek. We drive past the nature preserve and state park where we release the meaner ghosts.

We drive for another full hour after that. The wind chases my hair around my head, into my eyes and mouth. I still clutch the bowl and cookie sheet. Malcolm leaves the freeway, navigates back roads until he finds a deserted gravel road that's barely more than a path. Next to a plowed-under cornfield, he stops the convertible.

He holds up a hand. "Hang on," he says and rounds the car to open my door.

I step out, Malcolm's hands joining mine. Together, we stumble through the ruts and rows of the cornfield. We stand in the center of what must be the most desolate spot on earth—or would be if Malcolm weren't next to me. Then we set the container on the ground. We don't bother to remove the cookie sheet. The wind or an animal will knock it off soon enough. In the meantime, Mistress Armand can stew in her own mist.

We return to the convertible without looking back. Halfway across the field, Malcolm takes my hand.

~

"THINGS ARE CHANGING," I say to Malcolm right before we enter Springside Township. It's the first words we've spoken since leaving the cornfield. "I used to know what to do, how to capture ghosts. But ghost eating? Mistress Armand? None of this makes sense. I can't believe my grandmother wouldn't tell me about such things."

Malcolm is silent, jaw tense. In front of us, the stop light for Main and Fifth turns red.

"What do you think she was?" I ask. "You said before you thought she was human."

"I did," he says. "I think at one time, she must have been. I think the addiction ate away at her. I mean, look at Nigel compared to me. He's only two years older."

But looks at least twenty.

"I wonder if my grandmother ever knew of such things?" I think she must have. Maybe she died too soon to tell me.

"About what Mistress Armand said—" Malcolm begins.

I cut him off. "I doubt you have any shameful secrets. And if you do? So what? That's in the past."

I want to reach over, pat his knee or something. I don't. Instead, I clutch my hands together and hope I've said the right thing.

He sighs. The light turns green. With a single nod, he puts the car in gear.

Malcolm slows the convertible when we reach my street. We crawl up the road, well under the speed limit. In fact, I could walk home faster. All appears quiet. Still, my heart thumps with worry.

Inside my house, warm air greets us. The frost has melted from all the brass doorknobs. I do a quick circuit, but not even a sprite is in residence. The only proof I have of last night's ghost infestation is the mess—cold cups of coffee scattered all over the place, brown stains on the carpet, a splatter pattern on one wall that would be creepy if it were blood rather than Kona blend.

Malcolm casts a wary look around. "Where's Nigel?" He bolts and is out on the street before I can suggest an answer.

We find Nigel next door, in Sadie's kitchen, drinking coffee. Sadie chats happily over the drone of a talk show host. Nigel stares into the middle distance. Whether he hears Sadie or not doesn't seem to matter. Odd contentment lights his face, and the man who stared mere hours before with horror and hunger is banished. Malcolm places a hand on his brother's shoulder and squeezes.

To my surprise, Sadie's sprites are basking in the steam of an extra-large cup. But other than that, her house is also ghost-free.

I point to the sprites. "Do you want me to take them with me?" I ask her. For certainly they are up to no good, no matter how complacent they appear to be.

Sadie considers, hand on her chin. "Maybe tonight, if they start acting up. But for now?" She throws them a stern look. "They can stay."

Malcolm's pocket buzzes. Or rather, his cell phone does. He pulls it out, raises an eyebrow, then meets my gaze.

"Looks like we're back in business," he says. "Want to go catch a ghost?"

"My grandmother?" I whisper on the way out.

"Possibly."

"Law firm again?"

"Bank. The manager is locked in the vault. "

"That's probably my grandmother."

"The tellers want us to bring extra coffee." He checks his phone again. "And one wants tea."

"We're going to have to charge extra if we're supplying drinks for ghosts *and* humans," I say.

Back in Malcolm's convertible, I realize I'm still in last night's clothes, the skater skirt limp, my stockings sagging well below my knees. I haven't brushed my teeth. My hair? After that ride in the country? I'm afraid to look. But when he puts the car in gear and gives me a grin, none of that matters.

"Ready, partner?" he asks.

"I am," I say into the wind. "I am."

GONE GHOST

COFFEE AND GHOSTS: EPISODE 4

I STAND OUTSIDE THE DOOR to the Springside Long-term Care Facility, my hands clutching an insulated carafe of the best Kona blend. I have a ghost to catch, one who is picky and prickly. Even with the most expensive beans, I might not be able to tempt it from its haunting.

The melancholy ghosts are the hardest to catch.

My business partner, Malcolm Armand, stands next to me. In the canvas bag we use as a field kit, he carries a collection of thermoses. They jangle as he halts, a hand on my shoulder to keep me in place. His brow wears a worried frown, and his lips are pursed.

"Malcolm?" I say. "What—?"

"Where is everyone?"

Through the glass double doors, I can see the woman who works the reception desk, but no one else. Above us, the sun is doing its best to pretend that summer hasn't faded. It's one in the afternoon, activity time. Most residents should be doing something. But the building feels quiet, as if everyone is tucked in for the night.

Malcolm's cell phone buzzes. He pulls it out and holds it so we both can read the text message from the facility manager.

Please stay where you are. I'll be out in a moment.

Malcolm and I lock gazes.

"Did we do something wrong?" I ask.

As if in answer, a breeze catches strands of my hair and chases them into my mouth. Since I'm holding the carafe, I blow and spit, and it's entirely unladylike. I ponder our last visit here: we rid the place of a rather obnoxious (if preternaturally beautiful) being, a woman who claimed to be a ghost whisperer, but instead feasted on everyone's shame. And when you've lived a very long life, you have plenty of shame in reserve.

The double doors whoosh open. The facility manager strides out, her heels clicking on the sidewalk, pant legs fluttering in the breeze and from her gait.

"I'm sorry you had to come all the way out here." She holds out her arms as if to herd us back toward my truck. "There's been a change in plans."

"Do you want us to come at a different time?" I ask.

I've been coming here for years, first with my grandmother, then on my own. Now, Malcolm and I visit. Springside Long-term Care is one of our gratis accounts. We don't charge for catching ghosts. My grandmother always said the people here already had enough ghosts to contend with—why not make things a little easier on them.

"Actually, we're changing our routine, and we won't be..." The manager trails off, bites her lip. "Needing your services from now on."

"But we're not charging you anything." It's a stupid protest. We all know this.

Malcolm's grip on my shoulder tightens. With the slightest bit of pressure, he eases me back, steps between me and the manager, and turns on the charm.

"Vanessa, what is this about? Have there been any complaints? I've been promising a taste test between Katy's coffee and my tea." He gives the canvas bag a shake, jostles the thermoses, and the aluminum sings out. "Today's the day. I'd hate to disappoint the residents."

By *residents*, he means the female residents, or at least most of them. While the Malcolm Armand variety hour goes on in the common area, I'm always down the hallway, in residents' rooms, catching picky and prickly ghosts.

Vanessa wavers, swaying back and forth in the breeze and under Malcolm's gaze. Then she shakes herself and shakes a good dose of resolve into her features.

"This is hard for us," she says, "but we took a vote on it. And by we, I mean all the residents and the staff. We no longer want you visiting Springside Long-term Care. I'm sorry."

She turns and bolts toward the glass double doors, high heels striking the concrete like icepicks. With each step, I feel a sharp stab in my stomach. I loosen my grip on the carafe and press a hand against my belly, my pulse beating frantic beneath it.

I survey the building, the drawn curtains, and the now-empty reception desk. "They took a ... vote? What does that mean?"

He shakes his head. "I don't know."

"But I promised Mr. Carlotta that I'd take care of his ghost. No one else can catch it."

"I know."

Not even Malcolm. And for a while, I doubted my own ability to do so. Mr. Carlotta's ghost is very old and very sad. It weights the air, makes it hard to breathe in Mr. Carlotta's room. He claims the ghost has been with him since Guadalcanal, but I don't know how true that is. What I do know is that something about this is wrong.

I step forward, determined to find out what—exactly—that something is.

"Katy, no." Malcolm jogs to catch up. "If they don't want us here, and we barge in, that's trespassing."

"What are they going to do? Call the police?"

He points. "Maybe."

Through the glass double doors, I see Vanessa, cell phone pressed against her ear. But it doesn't matter. When I reach the entrance, nothing happens. The sensor that opens the doors automatically is switched off. I stand there, peering into the space, my fingers leaving smudges on the glass.

Malcolm takes that hand, the one glued to the glass, and folds it in both of his. He tugs me away. The movement is gentle, like a mother reluctantly pulling her child from a swing, a father urging his son away from a toy that's far too expensive. I think he might wrap his arm around my shoulder on the way back to the truck, but all he does is clutch my hand.

I can't explain how much this hurts. I can't explain why it plants an ache in my heart. It's just business, isn't it? But when Malcolm holds out his palm for the keys to my truck, I know he understands. I pass him the keys, not because I can't drive. I certainly can. But I want to take a long, hard look at the care facility. I want to study each resident's room. And when the curtains flutter in Mr. Carlotta's window, I want to make sure it's something I've really seen.

IT'S THE LATE AFTERNOONS, when the buildings across from our office fracture the setting sun, that are the hardest to endure. That tender light signals another day without a client, another day without income, and one day closer to giving up this space if we can't make the rent.

I love our office, all of it. I love the gold lettering on the front window, proclaiming us *K&M Ghost Eradication Specialists*. I love that we have Malcolm's old samovar in the window, along with a vintage percolator that belonged to my grandmother, one I've recently retired from service. I love how unlocking the door every morning makes all of this feel real.

But when lunch rolls around without a call or email, when I peer through the large bay window and see the bank closing down for the day, it feels as though the ventilation system isn't pumping in enough air. It's been two weeks since Vanessa at Springside Long-term Care told us not to return. I've gone out on a few jobs, nuisance calls involving sprites that I handled on my own. But after that? Silence.

I've been here before.

"Maybe it's the change in the weather," Malcolm says.

We haven't been talking about the lack of work, but clearly it's on both of our minds.

"In college," he continues, "nothing supernatural happened until at least October."

"You were probably too busy to notice," I say.

Ghosts love autumn, and Halloween in particular, especially the sprites. They love to play pranks, and Halloween is perfect for that.

"Then maybe that's it," he counters. "People are too busy going back to school and with sports and all of it to care about a few ghosts."

"Maybe." I rub my neck. Across the street, the bank manager pulls the shades on the entry doors. I'm too far away to hear the click of the lock, but that doesn't stop me from imagining that I do.

"Staring out the window isn't going to get us any clients," Malcolm adds.

"It was just like this, you know."

"What was?"

"When you came to town and stole all my clients."

He bursts out laughing. "Oh, come on. I didn't steal all your clients."

I pivot from my contemplation of Main Street and confront him instead, hands on hips. "Didn't you? What would you call it, then?"

"Free enterprise?" He crosses the distance between us. "Besides, we both know how it turned out."

For a month, Malcolm was my rival, and he did steal all my clients, no matter what he says. For a month, I loathed the sight of him. And now?

He puts his hands on my shoulders. "Didn't it turn out?" His voice is lower, a near whisper, as if he doesn't want anyone to overhear what he might say next.

My heart thuds hard against my ribcage. I don't want to feel this way about my business partner. I'm not even certain what *this way* means, except that at times like this, his nearness clouds my head. He smells of Ivory soap and nutmeg and that does nothing to clear my thoughts.

"Katy," he says, "I've been thinking—"

The door to our office swings open, the chime promising a customer. Malcolm drops his hands as if my shoulders burn him. In the entrance, Officer Deborah Millard stands. She's been a police officer for as long as I can remember. Her partner is new, practically a boy. He gnaws on his bottom lip while the creases around Officer Millard's eyes deepen.

"Katrina Lindstrom?" she says, although why, I don't know. We've known each other forever.

"Yes?" I answer, although again, it seems silly, both my answer and the sound of my full name.

"I have a warrant for your arrest."

Or not so silly.

She pulls out a pair of handcuffs. "You have the right to remain silent..."

"No, really." Malcolm inserts himself between Deborah and me.

"This is ridiculous. What are the charges? You just can't come in here and—"

"Sir, step to the side and let me do my job." Deborah's words lack any inflection. "There are penalties if you don't."

I shake my head at Malcolm. "You can't get arrested too." I let Deborah take my hands and secure them behind my back. The metal is cold against my wrists, and I'm shackled. There's no way I'm jerking free of this. At least she doesn't pat me down. Then again, it's not like I can conceal and carry a carafe of coffee.

"... Anything you say can be used against you in a court of law..."

"What are the charges?" He is fierce, but hovering, one eye on Deborah and one on the boy, who has pulled out his own set of cuffs. "At least tell us that."

"Grand larceny," Deborah says. "Seven counts."

I know I must be gaping. My jaw feels loose; air rushes into my mouth. I can't imagine it. What is it they think I've stolen?

"Katy?" Malcolm's eyes are wide and uncertain.

Well, yes, I've had money troubles. But I've never stolen anything, not even clients.

"You have the right to an attorney," Deborah is saying.

A lawyer! My gaze meets Malcolm's and his eyes brighten.

"I'll run down to the law offices," he says. "Don't say anything until I get there with a lawyer, okay?"

I nod. But really, what is there to say? I don't know what Deborah is talking about. Then again, maybe that makes this even more dangerous.

When I'm cuffed and Deborah has finished speaking, she leads me from the office. A town the size of Springside doesn't have much of a rush hour. But today, I'm on display for the one it does have. Malcolm locks the door and charges down the sidewalk.

"I'll be there as soon as I can," he calls over his shoulder.

Then he sprints, loafers clacking the concrete, his destination the law firm at the corner of Main and Fifth, where we're on retainer. Ghosts with a grudge like to pester attorneys, divorce lawyers in particular.

I glance around as if the people gathered can rescue me from this fate. Someone will step forward and confess or provide evidence of my innocence. But the only thing that happens is that people glance away. No one meets my eyes. Except for my neighbor, Sadie Lancaster, who drops her shopping bag on the ground, her mouth round with shock.

My cheeks flame and I duck my head. But a whisper, my name on the breeze, has me jerking it back up again. In the doorway of the deli, Malcolm's brother is hiding. Nigel steps toward me, but I shake my head. He can't help me, not now. Then my attention goes to Sadie. He follows my gaze and nods to show he understands. When Deborah places a hand on my head and eases me into a patrol car, Nigel slips from the shadows.

As we drive away, I crane my neck to peer from the back window, the hard, unforgiving seat digging into my hips. There, on the sidewalk, Nigel has his hands on Sadie's shoulders. The gesture is so like Malcolm only a few minutes earlier, my heart lurches. Then she's in his arms and he's holding her close. He picks up her shopping bag and seems to be talking to both the items inside and to her, comforting words, judging by the expression on Sadie's face.

And then we turn a corner and there's nothing left to see.

"Oh, goodness, Katy, I'm so sorry. Can we do this again?"

The metal bench I'm sitting on is secured to the wall. My spine is flush against that same wall. I stare at the blue dot next to the camera's lens. I don't smile.

"Of course," I say.

"Sometimes this thing goes haywire. You haven't moved, so I don't know why each picture is so blurry." Penny Wilson blows air through her bangs. She is the booking officer, the police chief's administrative assistant, and quite unaware of the two sprites darting around the camera.

They dip and dive. While you can't capture ghosts on film, they can certainly do plenty to mess up your glamour shot. Or, in my case, a mug shot.

"Cut it out," I whisper.

"What, dear?" Penny raises her head so her eyes peek above the camera.

"I said, maybe the power cut out?"

"Maybe that's it!" She ducks beneath the desk.

"You and you." I mouth the words and point at each of them. "Let her do this." Not that they'll listen to me. I don't recognize these two sprites in particular. But then, sprites have such a slight presence that that doesn't mean much. It's a sure thing, however, that I've caught them before—sometime in the past—and have spoiled their fun.

I don't suppose I can really offer my services now. Not that Penny would accept. She has an unusually high tolerance for sprites. The fact she hasn't noticed these two is proof of that. Also, Police Chief Ramsey has never been a fan of ghost eradication.

"It's not science!" he always told my grandmother.

He's right. It's not. Really, that's the point.

Besides, the charred swill wafting from the break area wouldn't tempt these two in the least. I'm surprised it hasn't repelled them, not to mention all the humans in this place. The scent alone makes the back of my throat ache. Then again, maybe that's something else, something like waiting for my mug shot to be taken.

Penny pops back up, her curls swinging in triumph. She slaps a hand on the camera, catching the sprites off guard. "There!" she cries out. "Perfect."

Oh, but there's still the fingerprinting to endure. This, too, is digital.

"Springside PD has gone high tech," I say.

And because this is Penny, and she's known me all my life, she brightens at my conversation starter, despite the circumstances. "We have! They even sent me to training."

Unfortunately, this training didn't include how to take a print when two sprites are covering your subject's skin. I blow at them— discreetly. Or rather I try, but I don't think there's a discreet way to blow.

"Although sometimes," Penny concedes, "the old-fashioned way is better."

By the time she's through, my hands are covered in black ink. There's a smear across Penny's cheek and several in her hair. The sprites zip around us, far too pleased with themselves.

"Wait," I whisper on the way to the holding cell. "Just you two wait."

Then Penny locks me in, and it's official. I'm a criminal.

A figure is huddled on the plank bed connected to the wall. I grip one of the metal bars, smearing it with black residue, and sigh.

"Katy?"

A voice creaks behind me. I whirl, heart thumping. A woman emerges from that huddled mass, her hair a blonde tangle that still catches the light despite its current state. Her blue eyes water, but I remember what they look like when they shine. Last time I saw Belinda Barnes, she was in rehab. The center called me since dealing with an alcohol addiction and a particularly nasty ghost is more than anyone can handle.

"Oh, Belinda." It's all I can think to say. The alcohol is stealing everything from her—her beauty, which is phenomenal, her brain, which is equally so, and her life. She could be anything, go anywhere. But she drinks and the ghosts find her. So she drinks some more. It's been that way since high school.

This must show on my face, for she gives me a rueful smile. "I know. I know. I already got the lecture from your grandmother."

I suck in a breath. True, my grandmother's ghost haunts me.

Malcolm recognizes her presence, and Mrs. Greeley at the long-term care facility senses her as well. But this? This is new. I move to the bench and sit next to Belinda. This is not a conversation that needs to be overheard.

"Sorry." Belinda tucks the flaps of her overcoat beneath her thighs and then plucks at her shirt. "I refused the shower. I like to make them suffer."

An earthy smell rolls off of her, one laced with dead leaves and whisky. In some ways, it's a relief from the charred coffee stench in the booking area.

"You can talk to my grandmother?"

"She caught me drinking." She raises her palms skyward as if to say *obviously*. "She read me the riot act. At least that's the feeling I got. I know she cares. She's not like some of the ... others." She pulls her coat closer.

"Have they been bothering you?"

She shakes her head. "Clearly, I'm dry at the moment, right?"

"If they do, come find me. I mean that. No charge."

"Katy, you don't—"

"I do, and I don't mind. It would make me feel better. Okay?"

She nods, and it almost looks sincere. Nasty ghosts have a tendency to attract even nastier ones. Sprites are annoying and sometimes take their pranks too far. But the nasty ones linger. They clutch and cling, and those who carry that burden really are haunted.

"So, you know, I hate to ask," Belinda says. "But what on earth are you doing here?"

"Grand larceny, seven counts, only I can't tell you what I've stolen."

She snorts. "Idiots. They spend all their time rounding up drunks and arresting the wrong people."

"Are there right people to arrest?"

"Of course. Whoever's been stealing everybody's stuff. You haven't heard about the break-ins?"

Not at all. This worries me, as does the fact I haven't heard from my grandmother for a few days. Usually she's a ghostly presence, an icy kiss against my cheek when I go out on a call. But we haven't been out on any calls. Sometimes, when things get slow, she'll kick up a ruckus somewhere so we'll get a little business.

That hasn't happened either. This worries me even more. I shift on the hard bench, pulling my knees to my chest, wrapping my arms around my shins.

"Oh, no," Belinda says.

I turn my head so my cheek rests against my knees.

"You don't suppose that they"—she points through the bars, toward the front of the station—"think you're the one stealing, do you?"

"Grand larceny," I say. "Seven counts."

For a moment, we stare at each other. Belinda's eyes are clear now, like the September sky. Then she huddles into her overcoat, drawing the collar up around her jaw as if she's chilled. I turn to face the bars and the long night ahead of me.

～

"KATRINA LINDSTROM, YOU HAVE A VISITOR."

Really, I don't think my full name is necessary. The holding cell is hardly teeming with violent offenders. Belinda stirs and shifts. I hope whoever called my name hasn't woken her. Sleep without alcohol or ghosts would do her good.

"Katy?"

This voice is different—low, masculine, familiar. But not Malcolm. I can't place it, not until its owner comes into view. Jack Carlotta bursts through the door. By the time he reaches the cell, I'm gripping the bars with both hands and peering out at him.

"Jack? How—?"

"My grandfather called me. He said you were in jail and that I needed to rescue you. His words, not mine. So I called down, and yes, you are in jail. So here I am." He holds out his arms. "Here to rescue you."

"But ... how did he know?"

Jack shakes his head, gives a little shrug. He's all suited up, very much the lawyer. Crisp pleats in each leg of his trousers, a tie with a red stripe. This is good. I need a lawyer, especially since Malcolm hasn't returned with one.

"You drove all the way down here?" I ask. "From Minneapolis?"

"It's not that far, and I've been meaning to visit anyway. Look, I've already made some preliminary calls—"

"On your drive down?"

"I multi-task. Anyway, they can't hold you. The evidence is way too thin. If it went to a hearing, the judge would throw it out."

"Then why arrest me in the first place?"

"Well, there was some pressure to do something about this rash of robberies, or so I'm told. There's the fact Chief Ramsey and your grandmother often had ... words."

"Neither of which have anything to do with me."

"The pattern of thefts does. Three to five days after you stopped in on a call, something goes missing."

All those nuisance calls. The thought of them makes me vaguely uncomfortable, like I should've noticed something about them. "And they told you all this?"

"They have to." He gives me that winning grin I remember from high school. "I'm your lawyer."

"Can you get me out of here, too?"

"Working on it."

"More multi-tasking?"

"Of course. I'm a pro at it."

The door bursts open again. This time, Malcolm rushes in. He lurches forward as if there's nothing more he wants to do than plant his hands on his thighs and suck in lungfuls of air. The sight of Jack in front of the jail cell halts him, but only for a moment. He starts at a run again and grips one of the bars next to my hand.

"Katy, I'm sorry. They closed the law offices for the day, and I wasted an hour calling around, trying to get someone at home. In the morning—"

"Katy has a lawyer," Jack says.

When Malcolm simply stares, Jack adds, "Me. Jack Carlotta."

He takes Malcolm's hand and it's all handshaking and elbow gripping. I think they must be passing secret messages to each other, since Malcolm's eyes narrow and Jack's lips curl into a grimace. Malcolm looks rumpled next to Jack, as if he's been tearing up and down Main Street, which, I concede, he probably has been.

I cough, hoping to get their attention. I am the one in jail, after all. "Jack," I say, "this is my business partner, Malcolm Armand. Malcolm, this is Jack Carlotta, Mr. Carlotta's grandson. We went to high school together."

"I even asked Katy to prom, but she turned me down." Jack winks.

I'm not sure if this is aimed at Malcolm or me. But, yes, it's true. In the week Jack was in off-again status with his on-again/off-again girlfriend, he did ask me. And I did turn him down. He ended up at prom with his girlfriend, as I'd known he would. I don't mention this detail.

Instead, I say, "Jack just passed the bar exam. Mr. Carlotta called him. He'll be my lawyer."

Malcolm's eyes light with the same question turning in my mind. "How did he...?" He trails off, casting a look at Jack.

I give my head the slightest of shakes and mouth, "I don't know." Later. We'll sort all this out later.

"Listen," Jack says, "no friend of mine is spending the night in jail. I'm getting you out. In the morning, I'll get all the charges dropped. This won't even go to a hearing. It's ridiculous. Give me ten minutes and you'll be on your way home."

He strides from the holding area very much like he entered it— a full swagger, suit coat swinging. Malcolm tracks him as he leaves, his eyes still narrowed, an odd expression on his face, one I can't read.

"Go with him," I say.

"I don't want to leave you alone." His gaze flickers to the lump that is Belinda.

"I'm fine. Nothing can hurt me in here, and the only two ghosts are the sprites in the booking area. Besides," I add, and lower my voice, "Jack can get ... distracted. He'll end up having drinks with Chief Ramsey and forget all about me."

"Are you sure?"

"Positive."

When Malcolm leaves, I sag against the bars. I don't know what to make of Jack's sudden appearance. I'm not ungrateful. I can get more done if I'm not in jail. Still, I must find a way to speak to Mr. Carlotta. I take a deep breath, and then slowly, I turn toward Belinda.

"Hey." I keep my voice low, in case she really is asleep.

"Katy, don't..."

"Okay, I won't, but I was just thinking—"

"You just promised you wouldn't. You said it yourself. He's easily distracted. I take more concentration these days. A lot more. And promise me this as well. You won't say anything once you're out, either."

"What makes you think I'm not spending the night?"

"The two guys out there who're about ready to fight over you."

"Don't be stupid," I say. "No one's fighting over me."

The lump that is Belinda stirs. "Don't think so?"

"No, I don't. I'm not that kind of girl."

"Well, take it from someone who used to be that kind of girl. Watch yourself, Katy. And choose carefully."

I don't know what to say to that, and she burrows further into her overcoat, cutting off our conversation. When the officer comes to release me from the cell, Belinda doesn't move, almost seems content in her pile of ragged clothes.

So I step from the cell and let the officer lock the door on the woman who went to prom with Jack Carlotta.

∾

I AM RIGHT ABOUT one thing. By the time I meet both Malcolm and Jack in the main office area, Jack is slapping Chief Ramsey on the back. I sense more than hear the suggestion of Finnegan's Pub.

"Katy, come with us," Jack says. Deftly, he goes from slapping to urging, his fingers finding the small of my back and pushing me forward.

"Isn't that a conflict of interest?" I whisper. Isn't it? My lawyer with the police chief? It must be.

"I was thinking more of mending a few fences." Jack's mouth is close to my ear, his lips brushing the sensitive skin. It's almost like a kiss or a caress, these words in my ear. "Like the ones your grandmother burned down."

"I think you're mixing metaphors," I say, and I am trapped between his lips and his fingers.

"I was always lousy at English." Jack steps back, pulls his hand away as if he senses my discomfort. "It's why I'm a lawyer."

"I can't go." I scour my mind, searching for an excuse, any excuse. I never drink. Ghosts are not kind to drunken ghost hunters.

"We need to get back to the office," Malcolm says. And now his hand is at the small of my back, but this I don't mind nearly as much. "Ghosts don't wait, after all," he adds.

Of course, in our case they do, given our lack of clients. I decide not to contradict him.

"Next time." Jack leans closer, and it's almost like the three of us are conspiring, our heads are so close together. "Really, it would be good for your business to have the police chief in your corner."

Jack leaves me with that bit of advice and a kiss on my cheek.

OUR WALK back to the office is silent. Main Street has rolled up for the night, with only the pub casting a beacon into the dark. Even the deli next to our office is closed, and I despair that I must cook dinner for myself.

The samovar that sits in our front window throws a golden glow onto the sidewalk. This feels like home, but Malcolm is quiet, oddly so. I want to say something to him but don't know where to start. When I cast him a sidelong glance, he turns toward the door, wrinkles his nose. I step back, pluck my shirt, and bring the fabric close to my face. I sniff. The holding cell comes flooding back—all stale, burnt coffee, that earthy aroma, and a hint of whisky.

"I stink, don't I?" I say.

"Maybe a little."

"Maybe a lot?"

His laugh is soft. He nods toward the door. "Let's go inside."

Once we're inside, it strikes me. I can't smell him. Normally, he smells so warm, but when I inhale, all I get is stale air. The smallest bit of dreads worms its way into my stomach. This is so like before, when we confronted that entity, the thing that seemed to suck up all the life—and scents—around itself. I shake my head and try to shake away that idea. I can't smell Malcolm simply because I reek. Nothing more.

"So," he says to me now. "You and Jack Carlotta."

"Me and Jack Carlotta what?"

"You went to high school together?"

"Same graduating class."

"Who did you end up at prom with, if not him?"

"No one," I say. "You ... I mean, I told you that I've never dated anyone."

Before we managed to put an end to Mistress Armand, she had coaxed that bit of shame from me. Even now, it stings. Even now, I know how odd it sounds, how odd I sound, how odd I am.

"No one wants to date the local ghost catcher, okay?" I shrug. "Maybe it's different in the city, at college, but here? They just don't."

"It's just that he—" Malcolm begins, his voice thick with something I can't name.

So instead, I don't. I refuse to name it, and I don't let him finish either. "Why are we even talking about this?"

Malcolm rubs his jaw. "I realized tonight that I don't know a whole lot about you or your life in Springside."

"I don't know a lot about you, either."

He takes up a perch on the desk, making certain to adjust the leg of his trousers first. "Maybe we should do something about that sometime."

His meaning is lost on me. I'm not certain what he wants. We're already business partners. I'd like to think we're friends. I'm not sure what comes after that.

"Maybe we could play truth or dare," I say.

He throws his head back and laughs. The sound of it is so rich, so real, and that earlier dread loosens its grip. Tension melts from my shoulders.

"What do you think?" he says, once his laughter has subsided. "Should we call it a day?"

"I need a bath," I say.

"You kind of do." He softens this with a grin. "I can give you a ride home."

"I'm fine," I say. "Really. But you can walk me to my truck."

He does, and even helps me inside it. Malcolm's brand of chivalry is solid and sturdy. It never feels like a trap.

I'm a block away, ready to make the turn off of Main, when I check the rearview mirror. In it, I see Malcolm, standing on the sidewalk, hands in his pockets, gaze on my truck.

Then I turn the wheel, the signal clicking, and he vanishes from my sight.

THE RINGTONE on my cell phone jolts me awake at three in the morning. This isn't too unusual. Even the gentlest sprite can morph into something fearsome after midnight—at least in the imagination. Some people simply can't—or won't—wait until morning. Of course, when we inform them that all eradications between the hours of midnight and six a.m. are at double our normal rate, most find a way to embrace the supernatural—at least until the sun comes up.

But the number on the screen is for Springside Long-term Care. My heart thuds, the beat strange and worried, as if no matter how fast it goes, it can't push enough blood through my veins.

I answer, more dread filling my stomach.

"Katy-Girl," the caller says, voice low and hushed. "Is that you?"

Only one person, other than my grandmother, has ever called me that. "Mr. Carlotta?"

"Sorry to call you so late. I've been waiting for the night manager to take his long weekend. The substitute they get always falls asleep. I had to wait until no one was around."

"Why not shut the door and call from your room?" Every resident has a phone, after all. This seems like the most logical solution.

"They monitor outgoing calls," he says.

This I doubt, but I suppose it's possible. "Won't they know you called out tonight?"

"Just that someone did from the front desk. They won't know it's me."

Honestly? I think Mr. Carlotta is just having a bit of fun, maybe at my expense. Of course, if not for the fact that Springside Long-term Care is no longer a client, I might say this was a joke.

"Katy-Girl," he's saying now, "I'm sorry for what everyone did to you. There was nothing Annabelle and I could say to change their minds. It was our two votes against everyone else."

"But what did I do?" There's something awful about knowing that a large number of people simply don't want you around, that you're that repulsive or unpleasant or whatever it is Mr. Carlotta is about to tell me.

"It's not what you did, it's what you heard, when Mistress Armand was here."

"What I heard?"

The echoes of that day rattle around in my head—confessions and shame, sorrow and regrets. The things that tear at your heart decades later, big and small, the things you can't shrug off, pretend never happened, the things you keep locked away.

"You're like a granddaughter to us, Katy-Girl. For some of the residents here, the ones without actual grandchildren, you are the closest thing to it."

"Then—"

"No one wants their granddaughter learning those sorts of secrets, the indiscretions, the infidelity..." Mr. Carlotta breaks off, his voice rough as if it's coated with its own layer of shame.

Springside Township is small enough that no one can grow up here and remain ... ignorant to all the goings-on. Still, gossip is different than confession, and truth trumps rumor.

"So they didn't want us to come back?"

"They were too ashamed. Don't hate them, Katy-Girl."

"I don't. And maybe you could tell them I can't even sort out what I heard. It's all a jumble, and I don't know who did what to whom."

Mr. Carlotta snorts. "You're better off not knowing. Trust me."

In this case, he's right. I would very much like to remain the ignorant granddaughter. I would also like our account back as well, even if it's a gratis one. If I am the surrogate granddaughter, then these people are my grandparents.

"But here's the thing," he says. "We have worse trouble now."

"Is it the ghosts?"

"Someone new came around, claiming they could exorcise the ghosts from haunted objects."

"That's convenient," I say. I scoot up in bed and plump the pillow. I have the feeling I won't be falling back asleep after this conversation.

Mr. Carlotta snorts again. "It did work."

My heart sinks. This is just how it was when Malcolm first came to town and stole all my clients with his flashy golden samovar and tea. (Ghosts prefer coffee. At least, most ghosts do. A few odd ones go for the tea.) Someone new. Someone doing something different. It's the shiny factor.

"But there's a problem," he adds.

"And that is?"

"Not all of our items came back."

For a moment, I can't speak. I feel as if the breath has been knocked from me. Grand larceny. Seven counts. I kick off the covers, my feet bicycling furiously.

I think I've been framed.

I don't voice my suspicion to Mr. Carlotta—not yet, anyway. I want to hear the whole story, or at least, his version of it.

"There were three of them," he says. "But I think only one of them, the woman, could sense ghosts. The other two looked like hired muscle."

"But she didn't try to catch them?"

"No."

Sensing ghosts—where they are, their size, what they're up to —is an inborn trait. Actually catching them takes skill, finesse, hours of practice, and in my case, plenty of scalding with cups of coffee.

"Could you tell if all the items they took were haunted?"

"I'm sure they weren't. They took Annabelle's jewelry box. According to her, it's never been haunted."

Annabelle Greeley is another resident at the care facility.

Whether it's because she's blind or extraordinarily sensitive, she has a feel for ghosts—my grandmother's in particular. She'd know if she owned a haunted jewelry box.

"Here's the thing, Katy-Girl. They brought that back."

"As a ruse?" I suggest. The jewelry box is something her grandchildren bought her, probably at a dollar store. I doubt you could pawn it or fence it or do whatever it is thieves do. Its only value is sentimental.

"My thoughts exactly!" His voice is charged with excitement.

"And I was in Mrs. Greeley's room not too long ago," I add. "But I wasn't there for the jewelry box." My grandmother likes to visit Mrs. Greeley and often swirls inside a cobalt blue vase on the nightstand—or the Kona blend I might happen to have in a thermos.

"And you were in my room," Mr. Carlotta says.

"Are you missing something?"

"My Purple Heart."

"They took that?" It's good I live alone. My outrage would wake the entire house.

"And my ghost as well."

Oh, well, this is different. I hadn't pegged his ghost as one that would haunt an item. Its connection to Mr. Carlotta feels far more personal than that.

"Have you told Jack this?" I ask.

"Yes, but don't you dare say anything to him. He's convinced I just misplaced it and forgot."

Mr. Carlotta still advises the Springside High School chess team. Of all the residents, I'd say his memory is the sharpest.

"But you called him ... Why did you call him? How did you know I was in jail?"

"Your grandmother, of course. She told Annabelle, Annabelle told me."

And then Mr. Carlotta embarked on his secret, after-hours

mission. I sigh. "But Jack got me out of jail. He can make Chief Ramsey take this seriously."

"He'll just say I shouldn't bother you."

His voice tears at me, so glum, so forlorn. Mr. Carlotta is eighty-nine years old. I did the math once, figured out that he must have lied about his age to enlist during World War Two. Maybe this, too, is one of the reasons he doesn't want to involve Jack. I think about the collective shame of everyone at the care facility, the urge to salvage a last bit of pride. I think I understand.

"I want it back," Mr. Carlotta says, the declaration sudden, his voice firm. "Can you help me?"

"Your Purple Heart?" I ask.

"No. My ghost."

OUR TINY CONFERENCE room brims with caffeine. In addition to the coffee I've brewed in the percolator, Malcolm's tea scents the air with its exotic blend of saffron and spices.

"It's different today," I say to him, blinking my eyes against the steam.

He holds his index finger and thumb together. "Just a pinch of cardamom."

Nigel sits at the end of the conference table, which is really nothing more than someone's discarded dining room set. On either side of his laptop sits a cup—one of tea and one of coffee. He takes a sip from each, alternating precisely, never playing favorites.

"I've traced the patterns of the thefts," Nigel says after a sip of tea. "About three days after Katy went on a call, alone, without you"—he points to Malcolm—"something went missing."

"Which is why they didn't arrest me, I'm guessing." Malcolm leans over Nigel's shoulder, gaze on the laptop's screen.

"So it looks like I was staking out places to rob," I say, "after living all my life in Springside?" I roll my eyes.

I haven't been in everybody's house, it's true. Some people like their ghosts, especially the sprites, who are usually harmless. Some people refuse to believe, like Chief Ramsey. Still, this is a rather clumsy attempt, I think, to make me look guilty.

"Bad blood, Katy. Blame your grandmother."

The voice startles me. I shoot to my feet, my chair careening backward into the wall. In the conference room doorway, Jack stands, all dark suit and red lawyer tie. He has his hands in his pockets and he leans against the frame. It's a devastating pose, one he perfected against the lockers at Springside High School.

I grope for my chair and plant myself in it. "Who said anything about blood?"

"It's an expression," Malcolm says, his voice grumpy.

Well, yes, I know that. I cast him a quick glance and fight the urge to roll my eyes again.

"And I don't think that assessment is fair to Katy or her grand-mother," he adds. This last is directed at Jack.

"You're new here, aren't you?" Jack says. He is frozen now, an ice sculpture of a man.

"I live here now." In the echo of Malcolm's reply, I catch: *and you don't.*

My gaze flickers between the two men, then lands on Nigel. He gives me a shrug, but I notice his lips twitch, as if he's trying not to laugh.

"Anyway," Jack says, turning his attention to me, a smile melting some of the ice. "The charges are dropped, but you shouldn't leave town."

"Funny," Malcolm says. "That doesn't sound like the charges have been dropped at all."

"Please, it's not like I ever leave town except to release ghosts," I say. "The last time I went anywhere was the school trip to the state capital."

This confession brings silence. I wonder if something of Mistress Armand lingers in the air of Springside, for certainly I've managed to blurt out several things that can kill a conversation. Again, that sense that I'm odd weighs on me. I don't feel deprived for not traveling. Sometimes I think the world comes to me, or at least, history does. I've trapped enough old ghosts that sometimes I feel old myself.

"When this is all over," Jack says, lawyer-striding into the room, "I'm making sure you leave this town—at least for a weekend."

"Is that a promise or a threat?" With Jack, it could go either way.

He laughs. "Katy, you know me better than that."

He's right. I do. And my question stands, at least in my own mind.

"What's missing?" I ask in an attempt to change the subject.

Jack pulls a cell phone from his suit coat pocket. "A couple of flat-screen televisions, some high-end video equipment, a brand new MacBook."

"And what would I do with those things?"

"Pawn them, I guess."

"Where? In Springside? Don't you think someone might catch on?"

"Up in the Twin Cities—"

"But I never leave town," I interrupt. "Remember? Has Chief Ramsey really thought this through, or am I just convenient?"

Jack folds his arms over his chest. "I think you're stubborn. His theory is you could also use the equipment in your business."

"To do what? Make ghost pornos?"

Once again I have silenced the room. After a moment, Nigel snorts. Malcolm glances away; I think he might be laughing. An angry pink blazes across Jack's cheekbones.

"You know it doesn't work that way," I say, more contrite now.

"You can't film ghosts. Not really. I don't need all the stuff he says I do."

"Unless your business is failing." Jack pauses. "Is your business failing, Katy?"

His words sucker punch the air from my lungs. I open my mouth to contradict him, but I can't draw a full breath. Words lodge in my throat. I can't look at anyone, not Nigel, and especially not Malcolm. I don't understand, either, why Jack is acting this way. So I do what any wounded thing does when desperate. I attack.

"So I stole all these things *and* your grandfather's Purple Heart? How much sense does that make?"

Jack heaves a sigh. "He probably just misplaced it." His voice is patronizing. Does he speak to Mr. Carlotta this way? Has he always spoken this way? My mind searches the past, trying to dredge up old images of Jack. I don't remember him being quite so abrasive. I don't like it. I'm starting to not like him.

I turn to not Jack or Malcolm, but Nigel, who still has his hands poised over the laptop's keyboard. "Let's say someone came to town and did steal all those things. What would be the next steps?"

"Pawn them." Nigel's fingers fly over the keys. "Probably up in Minneapolis or one of the suburbs."

"Even the medal?"

His fingers stutter, then start up again. He squints at the screen. "Oh, well, this is interesting. Apparently there's a market for medals, Purple Hearts in particular. Collectors' items. Does Mr. Carlotta's medal still have the original box?"

"It does." This is Jack, his voice devoid of arrogance now. "And the citation."

"Could be worth something to the right collector," Nigel says. "And ... there's a Military Relic Show going on this weekend at the State Fairgrounds."

"That can't be a coincidence," I say.

Nigel shakes his head. "Doesn't look that way."

"When this weekend?" I ask.

"Tomorrow, eight to six and Sunday, nine to three."

"I think—"

I never get to say what I think. In that moment, both Malcolm and Jack burst out with something, something I can't understand. They talk over each other, talk about me, but neither considers that maybe they should talk *to* me. I'm about to climb up onto the table, maybe stomp my feet, just to silence them, when Nigel catches my eye.

"Oh, Katy!" Nigel stands, a feat considering Malcolm has an iron grip on the back of his chair. "I almost forgot. Sadie's sprites are getting out of hand. I don't suppose you could—" He nods toward the door. His lips twitch again.

I take the offer for what it is: a chance to escape. "Of course. I have supplies at my house."

Sadie Lancaster is my next-door neighbor. She believes herself plagued by ghosts, although in reality, it's only two mischievous sprites. I've caught them dozens of times. They always return. They have nothing but affection for her, but sprites being sprites, they're also annoying.

We escape, leaving Malcolm and Jack glaring at each other. I wonder if they'll still be like that when we return.

Since I don't need my truck, we decide to walk.

"I thought Sadie was going to embrace her sprites," I say.

"She was. She's trying. Thing is, they're troublemakers."

"Sprites usually are."

"And ... I'm coming over for dinner tonight."

Oh. Interesting. Something's been brewing there, between them. My mind goes to last night, how Nigel gathered Sadie's groceries, the comforting hands on her shoulders. Still, the two of them make such an unusual couple that I've dismissed the idea. Clearly, I shouldn't have.

"The steam from the food," Nigel continues. "You know how they like the steam. Well, if food goes in my mouth, and there's a sprite in the steam..." He trails off because I can fill in the rest.

Nigel used to swallow ghosts, was addicted to them, the way you might be to alcohol or heroin. He's only been ghost-free for a little more than a month, and I'm not sure that's long enough for any addict. Accidently swallowing a sprite along with the green beans? That could cause a relapse.

We turn off of Main Street. The wind whips up funnels of leaves. We're closer to winter than summer now. Soon it will be Halloween. Business should be good—there's something about the winter holidays that brings out the ghosts. Of course if everyone thinks I'm a thief, we won't get any business at all.

"Thank you," I say.

"Thank *you*," he echoes. "As excuses go, this one is real."

"I just don't—" I shake my head and try to shake off the image of the strange showdown in our conference room. "I have no idea what's going on."

"Don't you?" Nigel laughs, then pauses at the gate in front of Sadie's Victorian. "The thing about Malcolm is he's never had to work to get a girlfriend. You've seen how women fall all over him."

Yes. I have. It's disgusting.

"I don't know this Jack guy." Nigel plants his hand on the gate and drums his fingers against the slats as if he's thinking. "But I'm guessing it's the same for him, especially now that he's a fancy lawyer with a fancy car."

"He has a fancy car?" I ask. "I didn't notice."

Nigel throws his head back and laughs. In that instance, he is very much like Malcolm, especially along the jawline and with the humor lighting his eyes. But although he's only a few years older, that gap could easily be two decades. His hair is pure white where Malcolm's is inky black. The lines around his mouth and eyes speak of things he probably doesn't want to think about, never mind discuss.

"That's your charm, Katy," he says. "You didn't notice the fancy car."

"I was supposed to?"

"It was right out front."

"It was?"

"Yes, and you were supposed to be suitably impressed as well." He laughs again, softer this time, and more to himself. He unlatches the gate and holds it open for me. "And now? Well, now they're both gunning for the same girl, and the best part? Neither one may win."

"Do you mean me?" I step through the gate and start up the sidewalk.

Nigel doesn't answer. Instead, he hums to himself. I decide to put Malcolm and Jack, fancy cars, and all the rest from my mind.

I have some ghosts to catch.

I DO a quick check of Sadie's to confirm that yes, the sprites are in residence and they're in a particularly naughty mood. Grit beneath the soles of my sneakers tells me they've knocked over the planter with the fern—again. Certainly they would upset dinner plans.

"I think I told you," I say to the air. "That if you aren't good, you're out of here."

Something whirls by my face. Something else ruffles my hair.

"Kona blend."

I also say this to the air. Nigel is—wisely—waiting outside. Sadie is upstairs, I think. She will be where the sprites are not. I'm alone with the sprites, and speaking as if they can understand me. This last, I'm not sure of. I used to think I knew everything there was to know about ghosts. Lately? I'm not so sure I know anything at all.

In five minutes' time, I return with my supplies—the percola-tor, cups, sugar, and half and half. And of course, the Kona blend, not that these two deserve it. Still, it makes them easy to catch. I won't even need to pour twelve full cups, like I would during a normal eradication job.

The third cup does the trick, one with extra sugar and cream. They swirl in the steam, and the air sparkles with their presence. I trap them both in a Tupperware container. They thump the sides, more put out that I've spoiled their fun than in anger.

"You two," I say, "are causing problems."

Thump.

I snap the lid on tight before calling up the staircase.

"I've got them. You can come down now." I peek out the front door and wave Nigel inside.

I'm concentrating so hard on the sprites in the Tupperware that I don't notice Sadie at first. Then, all at once, she blooms before me. Her hair, which normally is a mix of salt and pepper, now glows with hot pink highlights. I step back, not certain about this new transformation. A moment later, I'm plucking a strand of my own hair and considering highlights for myself. Green? Or maybe a neon blue.

She shakes her head, the short curls bouncing. "Too much?" she asks.

"No, it's great. I was just thinking." I tug at my hair again. "Maybe blue?"

"The girl at the salon said even women my age are doing it now, so I figured why not? It's not like Harold's around to criticize."

And a certain ghostly-haired Nigel will understand. I remember, years ago, my grandmother and Mrs. Greeley talking. They kept calling Sadie a young bride. Looking at her now, I see that was true. She isn't even close to fifty, but she's always seemed old to me. I think that comes from having been married to Harold and then having him die in another woman's bed.

Nigel raps on the doorframe. "All clear?"

I hold up the Tupperware. The sprites whirl about. Often, when trapped, ghosts will manifest grotesque—or obscene—images. These two are all sugar and light, just like their preferred coffee.

"Would you like to stay for lunch?" Sadie directs this at both of us, but I suspect she only wants Nigel to stay.

"I'd better get back." I tap the container with my charges. "And do something about this."

Nigel opens his mouth. I think he might refuse, so I rush a few more words.

"Nigel, you should stay."

"But—"

"Stay, unless you really want to run interference between Malcolm and Jack all afternoon."

"You shouldn't have to alone."

I tap the container's lid. "Who says I'm going back to the office?"

His grin is filled with relief and gratitude. Sadie is already chattering by the time I'm at the front door. So I slip from the house, leaving them to their lunch. The ghost eater and the woman terrified of ghosts. It occurs to me, now, that this coupling is not as odd as it first seems.

I'M ONLY a block away from Sadie's when a cherry red convertible pulls up alongside me. Have I noticed his fancy car before? Honestly, it's hard not to notice Malcolm's car. But I'm not sure I've given it the proper consideration.

"Hey," he says, killing the engine. The street is quiet except for a crow and the light thump of two naughty sprites. "Catch of the day?" he adds.

I examine the Tupperware. "You could say that."

"I'm sorry," he says, "about earlier. I was a ... jerk to your friend."

"You mean Jack?"

Malcolm makes a sour-apple sort of face. Yes. That's exactly who he means.

"We went to school together," I say. "I've known him since kindergarten. But I'm not sure I'd call him my friend."

"He thinks you're friends."

"Jack thinks a lot of things that aren't always true."

Malcolm nods toward the Tupperware in my hands. "You want to get rid of them?"

"Yes, otherwise they'll ruin the romance."

His gaze goes from me to Sadie's Victorian. His eyes cloud. His mouth goes slack. "No. You're kidding me. Nigel and Sadie?"

I nod and then shrug. "Nigel and Sadie. It's kind of a ... not May-December, but I don't know. July-October sort of thing."

I choose this moment to launch myself into the front seat of his convertible. It's much too cold to have the top down, but Malcolm drives it this way every chance he gets.

"Older woman, younger man?" I say. "It's very twenty-first century."

"How far out do you want to drive?" he asks. "Should we lose these two permanently?"

At the suggestion, the sprites sink to the bottom of the container, as if weighed down by sorrow. I study them, considering their persistent haunting. They are so playful, like puppies or children. Oh. *Children.* Ghosts search out emotion, either fueled by their own or that of a living person. In this case, I think these two are filling an emotional hole.

I shake my head. "No, let's take them to the usual spot. They won't make it back before dinner, but they won't be missed for long either."

Malcolm has just put the car in gear when I cover his hand with mine. His skin is so warm in the autumn air. For a moment, we sit like that. I've held his hand before. He's taken mine while we're out on a call.

Something about this time is different.

"I want to find Mr. Carlotta's Purple Heart," I say. "If we leave early tomorrow morning, do you think we could be the first in the doors at the Military Relic Show?"

"Katy, you're not supposed to leave town."

"I don't care. Besides, if I find his Purple Heart, won't that clear me?"

"Maybe. Maybe not. Besides, you don't even know it will be there. Those exhibition halls at the State Fairgrounds are huge. Even if it's there, you might not find it. You could leave town, get in trouble, and it would all be for nothing."

"Where would you sell a stolen Purple Heart?" I counter. "Where would you sell a haunted one?"

Malcolm turns in his seat to face me full on. "Mr. Carlotta's ghost?"

"It's attached itself to the medal. Whoever has it will want to unload it, and fast. I think the show is the best option. It won't matter how huge the hall is. I know that ghost. I'll find it."

Malcolm drums his fingers on the steering wheel. He gazes through the windshield, then turns back to me. "How fast can you pack a bag?"

"What?"

Instead of answering, Malcolm puts the car in reverse and backs up until we're even with my house.

"How fast can you pack a bag?" he asks again.

"Five, ten minutes? Why?"

"Let's go now. I'll show you around the Cities, the U of M campus. We can park at my old frat house and jump on the Green Line."

"Green Line?"

"Light rail. We can ... go out to dinner?"

Out. To. Dinner. Is Malcolm asking me out? Should I say yes?

Should I really date my business partner? But is one dinner really dating?

"There's this Persian place. It's where I get all the spices for my tea. I'd love to take you there." The words stream from him as if he's convinced the more of them he uses, the better the chances are that I might say yes.

His chances were already pretty good. "Is it fancy? Because all I really have to wear is my skater skirt."

His eyes light up in a way I can't decipher. He nods. "Pack the skater skirt."

So, I'm not supposed to leave town. I shouldn't go on a date—or an overnight—with my business partner.

I hand Malcolm the Tupperware container.

"Five minutes," I say. "Ten at the most." I leap from the car.

I make it back in seven.

I TRY NOT TO GAWK. But when Malcolm drives us through downtown Minneapolis, convertible top open to the autumn air, I crane my neck as far back as it will go and stare at the blue, glimmering buildings on either side of us.

He parks the car at his old frat house and we wander the campus until we reach the Mississippi River. Students stream here and there, some with backpacks, others with soccer balls tucked beneath an arm. I inhale as if that alone will let me breathe in the entirety of this place. When I exhale, it comes out as a sigh—a sad one.

"Didn't you go to college?" Malcolm asks, his fingers brushing my wrist.

"No. I ... we didn't have the money for that, and I didn't have the grades for scholarships. Besides, I was doing most of the chasing and catching by then." I turn from the view of the Mississippi and the paddleboat that's chugging its way up the river. "I couldn't leave her."

Her. My grandmother. I wonder where she's gone. I haven't sensed her for days, and that secondhand report from Mr. Carlotta wasn't reassuring, either. Every time I feel her presence, part of me is convinced it will be the last.

"You could still go," Malcolm says.

I nod, unconvinced. I like my work. I like catching ghosts. But as I take in the golden leaves, the green grass, the campus with all its buildings and that undeniable buzz in the air, a yearning tugs at me. There is so much more in this world than Springside Township —and I've been working very hard trying to tell myself there isn't.

My contemplation turns toward Malcolm. He had all this—the campus, the glimmering downtown. Does he miss it?

"Hungry?" he says.

"Maybe."

"Come on. You're going to love the restaurant. Actually, you're going to love the frat house."

"There's no way I'm going to love your frat house."

Granted, I've never been inside a fraternity house, but I've done my share of ghost eradications in the boys' locker room at the high school. I can't imagine it's all that much different.

"Want to bet?" Malcolm grins at me. Those fingertips at my wrist slip until our palms meet and our fingers lace together.

On our way back, I catch glimpses of dorm rooms. I find one I like and pretend it's mine. I pretend Malcolm and I are students here and we're on a study date. For the ten-minute walk, I don't think of ghosts, or Purple Hearts, or my grandmother. For those ten minutes, I simply dream.

THE SECOND WE step into the old Victorian that houses his

fraternity, I know Malcolm is right. The rush is immediate, icy against my cheeks. Something tugs my hair.

"It's haunted!" I say.

"It is." Malcolm glances around as if tasting the air. "A few new ones since I was last here."

"Are they always this rowdy?"

"Only when there's a pretty girl around."

Since no one else is around, my cheeks blaze at this, more heat for the ghosts to absorb. But it makes me wonder where all the humans are.

"Is it always this quiet?" I ask. It is a frat house, after all. Granted, my only experience with them is what I've seen in the movies. Still. I was expecting more than ghosts.

"Everyone is either at class or getting supplies for tonight."

"Tonight?"

"It's Friday."

"So?"

Malcolm gives one of the ghosts a sidelong glance. "I know. She doesn't get it. Someone is out getting a keg as we speak."

"For a party?"

"Yes."

"What kind?"

"Friday. It's a Friday party."

As if to send the point home, two of the sprites go whipping around my head. I laugh and reach out a hand as if to capture them. "They're almost tame," I say. They're almost like pets.

He holds out his hand as if he, too, might like to hold or pet one. "I used to catch the nasty ones," he says, "and keep them in my samovar."

"At least now you can catch and release."

"At least now I can," he echoes, his voice oddly nostalgic.

Again, I wonder if he misses his college days, his life here. I think he must. It's in the set of his shoulders. They're not slumped in defeat, nothing like that, but determined, as if now that he's chosen a path, he won't alter his course.

But then he turns a grin on me. "Let's change and go out. Trust me, you don't want to be here when they tap the keg."

"Do ghost drink beer? Do they get drunk?"

I always thought they loved the coffee for both its heat and the flavor. But beer? Could you catch a ghost with that?

"They like the foam," he says. "And yes, they do get drunk."

The rowdiest ghost, the one that has been tugging strands of my hair, whips about in a frenzy of ghostly anticipation.

"Plus," Malcolm says. He has both our bags and is urging me up the stairs. "I don't want to introduce you to any of my fraternity brothers."

I climb the first steps. "Aren't they nice?"

"They're fine."

"Then—"

"I don't want the competition." With that, he dashes up the remaining stairs.

When I'm locked alone in the bathroom (yes, it really is just like the boys' locker room), I try to sort out what he means by that. I try to sort out how I feel about that—and him. Before I can, there's a thump against the door, jarring me from these thoughts.

"If you peek," I say to the apparition on the other side, "I will return with a Tupperware container that has your name on it. Don't think I can't catch you."

The door rattles a second time, but nothing more.

Before I can step into the hallway, my cell phone buzzes. The display reads Springside Long-term Care. My insides ice, and I'm so cold, I think there must be a ghost in here with me.

"Hello?" I keep my voice low, quiet. I glance around as if someone is listening in.

"Katy-Girl! Where are you?" Mr. Carlotta's voice is equally low and muffled, as if he's speaking from beneath a blanket or inside a closet.

"I'm getting your Purple Heart back," I say. "And your ghost." I hope both these statements are true.

"Jack was just here. He's looking for you. Chief Ramsey is looking for you. He wants you to check in."

"That's going to be hard to do."

"Come home now. I don't need my Purple Heart. I don't even need my ghost. I don't want you in trouble. Jack says it could mean jail."

"I was already there," I say. "Besides, Chief Ramsey let me go. He said I shouldn't leave town, not that I couldn't. I'm not under arrest. If they come around, tell them I'm doing a big release out at the state park."

"I have to warn you. Jack has your phone number."

"And he got that how, exactly?"

"Not me, Katy-Girl. I pretended I couldn't remember."

Of course he did.

"Works every time," Mr. Carlotta adds. "He asked the manager, and she gave it to him." His voice is now thick with disgust, at himself, it sounds like, as if he could have somehow prevented it.

"It's okay," I say. "I'm at the state park, remember? I'm probably out of cell phone range as well."

"Ah, that's my girl. Be careful and come home soon, ghost or no. An old man and an old ghost aren't worth it."

Before I can contradict him, he hangs up. Immediately, the screen flashes with another number, one I don't recognize. My guess? Jack is calling. My response?

I refuse the call and then turn off my phone.

～

FOR THE ENTIRE RIDE, I clutch my ticket for the light rail. It's an idiotic thing to do. It won't get lost in my bag. But it feels like a talisman, and I feel like a gaping tourist again.

"It's okay to have fun," Malcolm says, as if he's reading my thoughts.

We're sitting side by side. Even with the blast of air that comes with the doors opening and closing, I catch his scent—nutmeg and Ivory soap. His hair gleams. I can't decide if he adds product or if it's naturally shiny. Once upon a time, I might have reached out to test a strand in my fingers to see. That was before. Before what? This, I don't know. All I know is I can't bring myself to tease him about it the way I might have. I'm not sure I like this either.

It's only a few stops and a few blocks to The Taste of Persia. Inside, the entire space smells like the tea Malcolm brews—warm and rich, the scent has a life of its own, almost like its own ghostly presence. I cast my gaze about, breathing in the air, tasting it.

The space is split in two. On one side is a market filled with exotic fruits, spices, and mountains of rice straining their burlap sacks. On the other is a cozy restaurant with deep red carpets lining the walls and floors, and tiny tables lit with candles.

"Malcolm!" A man emerges from behind the deli counter and embraces Malcolm. "It's been too long!"

"I've moved out of the Cities," Malcolm says.

"Then you must need a resupply." His gaze darts to me. A graying eyebrow arches.

"Hamid." Malcolm's hand hovers over the small of my back. "This is my business partner, Katy Lindstrom. Katy, this is Hamid Kassem."

Hamid shakes my hand, inclining slightly, almost in a regal bow.

"And I do need that resupply," Malcolm adds. "Can I pick it up tomorrow? Tonight—" He nods at me and then the tiny tables to our right. "We're hungry."

"Of course!" He grips Malcolm by the shoulder, a gesture that's both familiar and affectionate. "Mariam will seat you."

I have never eaten in such a place. Springside has a pancake house and the Jade Dragon, and of course, all the fast food you could ever want. There's the country club, but I've never been there, either. Here, it's like I've stepped into the Arabian Nights. Fortunately, I don't need to be Scheherazade, because I'm speechless for a good ten minutes into our meal.

"Do you like it?" Malcolm says at last.

"I love it," I say. "I don't even have words for how much."

"I'm glad."

He offers up a bit of his kebab, but I shake my head. I'm not so overcome that I forget I'm (mostly) a vegetarian. Besides, my baked eggplant is incredible. The tea, served in dainty glasses, is far more elegant than wine or champagne.

"Let's split a dish of ice cream," he says as the waitress clears our plates. "It's amazing."

The waitress returns with a scoop of rosewater pistachio in a silver bowl and two spoons.

"Try it," Malcolm urges.

So I do. With my first bite, I nearly drop my spoon. "It's soft!"

He laughs.

"It's like eating lotion," I say, "only lotion that's sweet and tastes good."

"It's the rosewater. They use that to make a lot of beauty products, so you're right. It's like eating lotion."

We scrape the bowl clean.

Outside, the street glows with yellow lamplight. My mouth is still cold from the ice cream, and I can feel the bite of October in the air. A shiver runs through me. Malcolm steps closer, eases an arm around my waist. The heat of his body sinks into mine. For a moment, we just stand there, although there isn't much to see. The station for the Green Line. Cars zipping past. A few stars strong enough to penetrate the city lights.

"Do you like music?" he says.

"Sure. Everyone likes music."

"Not everyone. But there's this great little club. I don't know who's playing, and sometimes there's dancing, but I think you might like it."

"In the same way I liked your fraternity house?"

"Maybe."

"Then how can I say no?"

What happens then—exactly—is hard to say. Malcolm turns one way. I turn the other. We're face to face, my hand planted on his chest. I tip my head back. He leans down. And then my business partner, Malcolm Armand, kisses me.

It's a soft, intimate thing because his lips are laced with rosewater. I clutch at his coat, wondering if this is a bad idea, while knowing at the same time that it is. I also know I won't stop this kiss. Not yet. I want more of his warm, soapy smell. I want to taste the nutmeg that's so elusive. I don't want this to end because I'm afraid of what might happen when it does.

Of course it ends. All kisses do. But he smiles at me, eyes bright in the dark.

"Has anyone mentioned you know how to kiss?" he says.

"Not recently."

"I thought you said you've never been on a date."

"That doesn't mean I've never kissed before."

With that, I break away and make a dash for the light rail station. I'm halfway there when he catches me by the waist and swings me around. We run the rest of the way hand in hand.

IF THE INSIDE of the restaurant was heavy with spice, the air inside the club is weighted down with beer. I could get drunk just from inhaling. The sprites that swirl around my head already are. They make clumsy passes at my cheeks, as if trying for a ghostly kiss. I wonder, just briefly, if we should switch from coffee to beer. It might make them easier to catch.

Bass thrums in my ears, vibrates through the soles of my Mary

Janes. Malcolm's hand is snug in the small of my back, and we inch our way toward the bar.

"Something to drink?" His mouth brushes my ear, the only way I'll hear him with the unrelenting thump, thump, thump from the stage.

"Just water."

He goes fancy, getting me something bottled along with a beer for himself. It's too loud to talk, the music too jarring to dance to, although some couples are attempting it. We settle against the bar, me in the crook of Malcolm's arm, and it feels as though I've always meant to be here. With the thought, my heart races, its beat counterpoint to the one on stage.

I'm halfway through the water when something feels off kilter, beyond my erratic pulse, our earlier kiss, and the way his fingertips are playing with the fabric of my sleeve. The air is different, not lighter, but not as beer-drenched as before. I touch my cheek, then look for the telltale glimmer the sprites leave behind whenever they dance through someone's drink.

Nothing. In fact, I don't sense them at all.

"The sprites," I say, not that Malcolm can hear me.

Something flutters in my peripheral vision, something that makes me think of bed sheets and bridal veils, something that grips my throat so tight I can't swallow.

No. Not here. That ... thing can't be here. But bit by bit, the club drains of sound, of scent, of life itself. No wonder the sprites have fled. If I had any common sense, I would too. A screech tears through the speakers. People cry out, slam hands over ears. Several knock over chairs on their way out of the club. The lights flicker.

Malcolm and I exchange a single glance. Our hands lock together. We turn to leave, but the main door slams shut. The club goes dark except for a single spotlight that shines on the center of the dance floor. A low, metallic laugh fills the space.

"Ah, ghost hunter, you look lovely this evening. May I have this dance?" The voice clicks and grates, but it's stronger than I remember.

The last time I met this ... thing, whatever it is, I was outside. Perhaps the enclosed space makes it sound stronger than before. Perhaps this is my wishful thinking. I take a step toward the dance floor and the spotlight, but Malcolm's grip on my hand keeps me in place.

"It can't hurt me." I tug on my hand. "It's not strong enough."

"Is that what you think, ghost hunter?"

"It's what I know. You play tricks, just like any other ghost, but you're not any different."

The speakers erupt with a burst of static and smoke. Overhead, lights spark and pop. Behind us, bottle after bottle explodes, spraying shards of glass and streams of alcohol along the surface of the bar. We duck, but liquid soaks my jacket. The back of my neck breaks out in pinpricks. I swipe my free hand across the skin. It comes away red.

"Parlor tricks." Admittedly, I say this once I've caught my breath and wiped the blood from my fingers. Still, random and petty destruction is standard for an angry ghost.

Malcolm's grip on my other hand tightens. "Wrong thing to say," he mutters.

But the entity is silent. A bit of hope sparks that it has worn itself out. The air is still too stale, too lifeless. That fluttering again. This time, I swear I see an actual bridal veil.

"Why don't you step into the light, Katy dear," the entity says, its voice metallic-y sweet. "She looks so pretty tonight. Don't you agree, Necromancer?"

Necromancer? Next to me, Malcolm is statue-like. Despite the dim light, I can tell his skin has an ashen cast to it.

"Don't do this." Malcolm's voice cracks. In it I hear doubt and fear, and something that goes beyond both, something desperate.

"Do what?" The thing is gleeful in response. "You mean to say you haven't told her what you really are? And here I thought things were getting so cozy between you two. My mistake."

"Necromancer?" I try out the word. "What ... I don't understand."

"I'll explain," Malcolm says, "but not here."

I'm not certain I want an explanation at all, but he's right about one thing: here is a poor choice. I ease my hand from Malcolm's grip. He's in shock, I think. His normally warm skin feels chilled. I press my fingers against my throat and then my forehead. My skin is burning. Maybe I'm abnormally hot. Or the club is. It's hard to distinguish where the air stops and my skin starts.

"No, my dear, it's not hot in here, it's simply you."

This is one obnoxious entity. I step onto the dance floor. The soles of my Mary Janes are soft, so I don't make a sound on my way to the spotlight. I enter it. This, of course, is exactly what this entity wants me to do. With this thing, there is no around or away or under. I must barrel through, do what it wants me to do—for now—and look for a way out on the other side.

A dark, inky mass descends from the club's ceiling. How easily it hid itself in all the exposed pipes and vents. It's larger now, larger than when we encountered it outside the mausoleum, but then, my grandmother had just defeated it then.

The entity expands and contracts, contracts and expands, and each time an outline shimmers before collapsing. The thought strikes me that it's trying to take on the form of a man.

"I'm afraid we won't be able to dance tonight, my dear," the thing says. "I'm currently in no shape for it." It cackles, the laughter booming through the space. "But I can do this."

Before I can even think to move, one inky tendril surges forward and touches my cheek. I cry out, jump back, and Malcolm sprints forward, intent not on me, but that thing.

His hands reach for it, but despite its sluggish appearance, the entity shoots up toward the lights.

"Oh, no, you don't, Necromancer. I won't be captured so easily. Besides, I've marked my choice. See for yourself."

Malcolm turns slowly, almost reluctantly. "No, no. You can't do this to her. She has no idea—"

"All the more fun for me, then. Thank you, Necromancer. You've played your part brilliantly in all this. And, Katy?"

I crane my neck. One vent appears darker than the rest, more sinister. Once again, something flutters. Bed sheets. Bridal veils. The taste of metal against my tongue.

"I'll be seeing you soon."

With the entity's final words, the speakers burst back to life, music blaring. Colored lights flash. The disco ball above our heads throws out a million fake stars. The club doors open and people rush the stage, footsteps and bass thumping the floor. I can feel the crunch of broken glass in my jaw. Only now do fumes from the alcohol fill the air, mixed with the odor of a hundred bodies.

I don't search for Malcolm. I don't know what I'd say to him. I don't know what to think about him. Or this. Or anything. I push against people forcing their way onto the dance floor, grabbing elbows and shoulders to leverage myself out of this space. If I can leave this space, I can figure things out. If I can leave this space, it will all start to make sense.

When the cold air of outside strikes my face, I'm no closer to understanding anything but this: I must get away.

I run. Footfalls sound behind me. I think I hear my name. I don't look back. I don't slacken my pace. There's a train at the light rail station. I don't care what line or where it's going. I slip through the doors just as they're closing.

I'm without a ticket, without my partner, without a plan. I press a hand against the glass of the door and peer out in time to see Malcolm stumble to a halt, brace his hands against his knees. He looks up, mouths my name.

And then he's gone.

~

EVENTUALLY, I stagger to a seat. I dig through my bag and pull out my ticket. I clutch my talisman, although I doubt it's much of one. My ride time has expired. I scan the aisle, hoping there's no conductor on this train. A few people occupy seats in front of mine. A group of college-age kids lounge behind me, in the very back of the train.

I don't relax so much as pull in a full breath—at last. I'm on the Green Line, headed toward St. Paul. St. Paul. Where the State Fairgrounds are. I pull out my phone.

A flurry of missed calls and text messages assault me the moment I switch on the power. That number I assume is Jack's. Malcolm's number and a series of text messages, all frantic and popping up much faster than I can read them.

Katy, please...
I can explain...
It's not what you think...

That last text is a lie. I have no idea what to think, not about tonight or about him. I ignore all this and open up the map. The State Fairgrounds are on Snelling Avenue, about two miles from the Snelling Avenue station, which is two stations up ahead. Plan in mind, I tuck the phone back into my bag. That slight movement kicks up scents from the club, the aroma heavy with beer. I reek. This might explain why no one has sat near me.

Then I catch my reflection in the window. There's something on my cheek, right where the entity touched me. I press my fingertips against the spot, and they come away chilled. I rub, but the spot remains. I can't tell what it is, but I can tell this:

Other people notice it.

At the Snelling Avenue station, I step off the train. I study the traffic, the pedestrians, but I see no sign of Malcolm. Will he follow on the next train? Double back to get his car and follow that way? My destination is a fairly obvious one. I check my phone. After that initial flurry, his messages have stopped. My first—irrational—thought is: I hope he's okay.

I give myself a shake and brace for the long trek to the fairgrounds.

I'm HALFWAY THERE when the idea of a taxi makes more and more sense. Of course, now that I'm halfway there, a taxi is no longer an option. I tuck my hands under my arms to ward off the chill as best I can. My over-the-knee stockings keep slipping, reminding my legs that it is very much October and I very much live in Minnesota. My Mary Janes are more sensible than sexy, but they're not made for hiking.

I am alone, after dark, in a strange city.

I am certifiably an idiot.

Someone approaches me, an older man, stocky, but I tense. That could be muscle, not fat. He might not be fast, but he could be strong. Something predatory flickers in his eyes, but the moment his gaze lands on my cheek, it vanishes. Despite the traffic, the man steps into the gutter when he passes me. Horns blare. Even so, he gives me a wide berth.

I stop and stare after him, fingertips on the spot on my cheek. I need a mirror, I think. I need to get to the State Fairgrounds. I need ... a bodyguard?

Two sprites swirl around me. When, exactly, I picked them up, I can't say. Have they been following me since the station? The club?

"Hello, you two," I whisper into the night.

Yes, they plan to travel with me. In fact, they insist I start my trek again with a bit of nudging against my shoulder blades. So I do. With the sprites urging me on, I make it to the fairgrounds in time to slip through the gates before closing.

I'M HOLDING what might be the worst cup of coffee ever brewed. But since it's the warmest thing I've encountered in the last ten hours, I'm grateful. The sprites dip and dive in the steam rising from the coffee's surface. They shudder, and the steam breaks apart. The heat of it doesn't reach my face, but then, neither does the aroma. This makes it easier to drink.

"If you're ever in Springside," I tell the sprites, "I'll brew you some Kona blend."

They whirl around my head before shooting off into the crowd that's gathering by the exhibition hall doors. They will cause trouble today, I'm certain. But with them gone, I'm free to sip the coffee, warm my bones, and scan the area for Malcolm.

And if I see him?

I take another sip of coffee and burn my tongue.

Even though I spent the night hidden in the skeletal shadows of amusement park rides, I am not the first in line for the Military Relic Show. People glance my way before averting their gaze. I don't know if it's because I look like I've spent the night outside or if the spot on my cheek remains. I still haven't had a chance to inspect it or my face. My first stop once inside the doors will be the restroom.

When at last I confront my image in the mirror, I'm not sure what to make of it. Something blue and iridescent swirls beneath the surface of my skin. Its pattern is like that of a hurricane seen from above. The clouds of blue shift and grow thicker before thinning out. It's a slow movement. I must concentrate in order to track it. If there's a message in the pattern, I can't decipher it, although I spend several minutes with my nose grazing the mirror trying to do so.

When someone enters the restroom, I jerk back, heart thudding. Since I can't make the thing on my cheek go away, I must make do, and I must find Mr. Carlotta's Purple Heart. With caution, I ease open the door to the lobby area and scan the crowd for that gleaming ebony hair. Malcolm is tall. He should be easy to spot.

I don't see him and swallow back equal doses of relief and disappointment.

The woman who sells me a ticket for the show darts looks at my cheek. The line is growing behind me, and she counts out change one bill at a time, her gaze always lighting on my cheek. The question fills the space between us.

"It's a tattoo," I say when the silence—and the line—goes on for too long.

"Oh ... wow." She gives it an appraising once-over. "Wicked."

Yes, I think, it really is.

I walk into the exhibition hall, the enormity of it striking me all at once. Malcolm was right. It will be nearly impossible to find Mr. Carlotta's Purple Heart, but not because hundreds of vendors crowd the room. Finding a single ghost, even in a space this large, wouldn't be too difficult, especially one with such a distinctive personality.

No, it's the number of ghosts attached to all the items in this particular space. Old items with old ghosts. The air is thick with that telltale glimmer. Some people might mistake the closeness in the room for poor ventilation. I know better. Other than the time the ghosts of Springside gathered in my house, I've never felt so many spirits in one place.

Some are sullen, heavy things. Others careen frantically around their displays. Some are attached to the person working the booth. Some scare away potential customers, their presence making the air so unpleasant that people skirt the displays filled with medals and other memorabilia.

Except for me. I snag a few business cards. Maybe instead of waiting for the haunted to come to us, we should go to them. We. I freeze, the cards chafing my palm. Me and Malcolm. Is there a *we* anymore? Are we still partners? I glance over my shoulder but still see no sign of him.

I travel the aisles, all manner of apparitions surging forward as if to greet me. There is only one ghost I want. Even if I find it, I'm not sure what the next step is. I catch and release. I've never captured and returned before.

Then something familiar swirls around my face. This is a ghost I know. This ghost is not so old—at least in ghost terms—and not melancholy.

"How...?" I begin, but clamp my mouth shut. I'm already the girl with the freaky tattoo. I don't need to add *girl who talks to herself* to the list.

My grandmother swirls and nudges, swirls and nudges, leading me to Mr. Carlotta's medal. We arrive at a vendor who specializes in World War Two memorabilia, a woman who calls herself G.I. Joan. I'm pretty sure this is not her real name.

Her face lights up when I approach her booth. More than one ghost haunts her or her items—it's hard to tell with so many of them whirling in this space. But it's Mr. Carlotta's ghost that's scaring away customers. It thickens the air around the booth. Each breath is a chore. It's as if the glow from the overhead lights must fight to illuminate the items on the tables.

"How's business today?" I ask.

Joan gives me a wan smile. "You're my first. Is there something I can help you find?"

"My grandfather collects World War Two stuff," I say, "and his birthday is coming up. Do you have anything from World War Two?"

I've parked myself in front of a Pearl Harbor commemorative plate, so clearly she does. It's such a stupid thing to ask, but considering I'm in last night's skater skirt and have a swirling tattoo on my cheek, I figure I look less than erudite. Also? My credit card has a limit, one I'm dangerously close to. I can't act like I want the one item I so desperately need.

Joan pulls out several things to entice me: canteens and lighters, an equipment belt, a hat.

"What about medals?" I ask. "He likes medals."

Joan holds several in her cupped palms. None of them the Purple Heart. I want to confess that I can see all the ghosts. I want to tell her that if she sells me the Purple Heart, business will pick up. The other ghosts here are mild or apathetic—or both.

My grandmother whips around, nudging me toward the Purple Heart as if I can't see it. At last, I give in.

"What about this?" I point to Mr. Carlotta's Purple Heart. "That looks awesome."

"It's really more for the serious collector. I was hoping—"

And I don't have time. "How much?"

She rattles off a price, and my mind blanks. I keep my mouth shut, so neither *yes* nor *no* will pop out. I try to visualize my balance. Can I afford this? If G.I. Joan runs my card through her reader, will it come back declined?

Before I can respond, she says, "Well, I guess I can knock fifty off of that."

I shut my eyes, resigned to the whole exercise all over again. My mind is foggy from lack of sleep, and I've grown lazy with Malcolm as my partner. I never calculate anything in my head anymore, not with him around.

"Okay." Joan sighs as if she's about to make a great concession. "How about seventy-five off the asking price? I can't go any lower than that."

That should work. Or at least, it's worth the risk. From my bag, I pull my credit card and hand it over to her. My throat tightens, and my lungs feel as if they're taking in molasses. This last, though, is the fault of Mr. Carlotta's ghost. It has oozed its way over to me. It fills the space around my head and shoulders. Miffed, my grandmother's ghost bats against it. This thing? It doesn't care.

"Just sign here," Joan says.

I startle at her voice, not sure what she wants. Pen. Receipt. I release a sigh of my own and sign my name.

"Be careful with this," she says to me while wrapping my purchase. "It's not just a collector's item, but a significant part of someone's life. See that?" She points to a pin attached to the award. "That's an oak leaf cluster. That means he was wounded more than once."

I sway a bit, but manage a nod. "I didn't know."

"Most people don't, unless they know something about the military."

That isn't what I meant, but I don't correct her. I thank G.I. Joan, and I'm only a few feet from her booth when three customers converge, exclaiming over her display. The Purple Heart, in its case, feels heavy in my palms.

"You stay with me," I say to the air in front of me. "Both of you. We're going home."

Outside, I jostle the phone from my bag. I scroll until I find what must be Jack's number.

"It's Katy," I say when he answers.

"Good God, where the hell have you been? I've been running interference with Chief Ramsey, but he knows you haven't been home all night. He knows Malcolm hasn't been home either, and he's thinking of—"

"I have your grandfather's Purple Heart," I say.

This can't be the first time someone has silenced Jack Carlotta, but from the tense, edgy quiet that fills the line, my guess is that it doesn't happen very often.

"What?" he says at last.

"I have your grandfather's Purple Heart. I'll be standing outside the gates to the State Fairgrounds if you want to pick me up."

With that, I hang up. I'm pretty sure Jack will make the trip.

Sixty minutes later, a black BMW pulls through the gates. I am suitably impressed—that he broke the speed limit to get here. I don't say a word when I ease into the passenger seat. I only hold up a finger before he can put the car in gear, checking for my charges. Mr. Carlotta's ghost settles sullenly in the backseat. My grandmother caresses my cheek and then knocks Jack's sunglasses askew.

"Okay," I say. "Let's go home."

WE SIT in the Springside Long-term Care Facility parking lot. Both ghosts made the trip, and Mr. Carlotta's has inched its way from the backseat until it infiltrated the box that holds the Purple Heart. As heavy and melancholy as that feels, something clicks into place. For whatever reason, this ghost has claimed this item, and the medal wouldn't be complete without it.

"You want to come inside?" I ask.

"I was thinking about it, but you know what?" Jack shakes his head. "I don't want to steal your thunder."

I can't help it. I laugh.

He raises a hand from the steering wheel as if he's trying to silence my laughter. His grin says he isn't. "I'm serious. Besides, when I was there yesterday, I noticed my grandfather's chess set was missing a few pieces. I was going to pick up a new one, come back this afternoon and play a game with him."

This is a new side to Jack Carlotta. I kind of like it.

"Thank you for picking me up," I say.

"Thank you for finding his medal."

I lean in to kiss his cheek, just a friendly, thank-you sort of kiss. My lips have barely grazed his skin when he jerks back.

"Do I smell?" I did spend the night outside, hunkered down in State Fairgrounds debris.

Jack gives himself a shake. "Jesus, no. It's ... it's..." He reaches a hand forward, but doesn't touch my cheek.

Oh. It's that.

"I want to kiss you," he says. "I've wanted to kiss you from the

145

second I got back into town. But I physically can't, and I can't explain why not, either."

"It's okay. It's been a long, strange sort of day—and night."

"Katy, are you okay?"

I nod. "I am." For now. "Things have been ... different since my grandmother died. Odd things have been happening. Every time I turn around, some new sort of ghost pops up, or someone comes to town. This never happened when she was alive."

"Maybe it's not your grandmother. Maybe it's this Armand guy."

I don't know what to think about that, because yes, it could be Malcolm.

"Be careful," Jack says when I reach for the door handle.

"I will."

"Promise?" He gives me that grin I remember from high school.

"Promise."

I watch him drive off, my fingertips exploring the mark on my cheek. The skin feels exposed, and the urge to pull out some lip balm and smear it across my face nearly overwhelms me. I know it won't help. So I turn and head for the facility's front doors.

I'm halfway up the walk when the manager strides through the double doors, her heels making that staccato click on the concrete. I deflate, my grip on the medal's box loosening. Mr. Carlotta's ghost senses our defeat and seems to gain five pounds. How a ghost can be so heavy, I will never know.

"Katy, Katy," she's saying, her words strung together so I barely recognize my name.

I raise the box. "I just want—"

"Please, let me go first. On behalf of everyone, staff and residents, of Springside Long-term Care, I would like to apologize."

"Apolo—?"

"Everyone was so ashamed. That whole thing with Mistress Armand, but then we heard you'd been arrested, and they insisted

I call Chief Ramsey. He was here all morning, taking statements. You just missed him."

I send up a prayer of thanks.

"We gave him a description of the thieves," she continues, "and explicitly stated it wasn't you who stole from us. Katy, we're so sorry. I understand if you don't want to come back, but will you consider it?"

Stunned, I'm not sure what to say, but the burden in my hands has its own ideas. I lift the box so the manager can see it. "I have Mr. Carlotta's Purple Heart."

She clamps a hand over her mouth. Her eyes grow moist. "How...?"

"It's a very long story. Can I take it to him?"

She nods. "He might be asleep, but yes. Please. Take it to him."

Inside, residents wave to me. They are silently respectful, though, as if they know what I carry with me. When I reach Mr. Carlotta's room, I see the manager was right. He's asleep. Too many late nights of secret telephone calls. I leave the Purple Heart on the nightstand where he's sure to see it when he wakes.

In the corridor, my grandmother's ghost whirls around my head, caresses the cheek without the mark, then she shoots down the hall toward Mrs. Greeley's room.

Unburdened by ghosts, I leave the care facility.

OUTSIDE, the October air clears my head. I will walk home. I will collect all my thoughts along the way. Once there, I will take a hot shower. Then I'll be ready to face this thing on my cheek, and Malcolm, and all the questions I have about last night.

The red convertible at the end of the walk stops this line of thought. Malcolm leans against the door, his normally silky hair rumpled, dress shirt torn and stained. The knees of his trousers are embedded with grime. If he crawled through a sewer he wouldn't look any worse.

"Were you in a fight?" I ask.

"It only feels like it."

"I don't understand." I mean this in every way possible. I don't understand what he said. I don't understand what happened last night. I don't understand him.

"After I couldn't find you," he says, "I decided I'd try to find that ... thing."

"I'm guessing that didn't work."

Malcolm shakes his head, his mouth tight. His gaze locks on my cheek, and I can see the calculation in his eyes, the assessment. He takes a step forward and then another. I hold still, breath shallow in my throat. The skin on my legs puckers with goose bumps, but the cold is something I barely feel anymore.

He stops in front of me, the toes of our shoes almost brushing. He reaches a hand toward my face. My throat tightens, then my stomach. My heart pounds so hard, I'm surprised Malcolm can't hear it. His fingertips graze my cheek, a touch so light I'm not sure it's a touch at all.

Then, suddenly, Malcolm crumples to the sidewalk as if his knees have gone liquid. He clutches one hand with the other. He doesn't cry out, but the pain that etches his expression makes me wish he would. I collapse next to him, go to place a hand on his shoulder, then pull back at the last second. Will that hurt him too? I don't know, and I find I'm shaking my head like an idiot. In fact, I'm shaking all over.

"What is it?" I ask him. "Are you hurt?"

"I know better than to do something like that," Malcolm says, his words low and taut.

"What does it mean?"

"It means that thing has marked you."

Marked me. That sounds ... disturbing. "And what does that mean, exactly?"

"The thing, that entity, can find you again."

Even more disturbing. "Why would it want to find me?"

Malcolm shakes his head. Whether he knows—and won't tell me—or simply doesn't know, isn't clear.

"Why did it call you a necromancer?" I ask.

Malcolm eases from his knees to sitting. My legs are wobbly, and standing isn't something I plan to attempt just yet.

"Because I am one." He sighs. "I haven't told you the whole truth."

I cock my head to the side and give him a hard stare, because that? That is the only thing I do know at this point.

He raises a hand. "Yeah, I know. Pretty obvious, right? I'm a necromancer. I talk to the dead, or as the case may be, with ghosts."

"But ghosts don't really talk."

"Don't they? They communicate with you all the time. Besides, if you invited one inside, you'd hear plenty."

"You mean swallow ghosts, like Nigel used to? Is he a necromancer?"

"Nigel's what happens when a necromancer gets ... careless—or addicted. A true relationship between a necromancer and a ghost is symbiotic. Each partner helps the other."

Something Mistress Armand said to Malcolm echoes in my head. I've always thought he left more than simply his job when he came to Springside.

"The girl you left behind," I say. "That's what Mistress Armand meant. That's your ghost."

"That *was* my ghost," he says, "before Nigel swallowed her."

"Did she escape when we set them free?"

The crinkles around his eyes deepen, his mouth a grim line. "I don't know. Maybe. I didn't sense her, but it was kind of chaotic."

"What was it ... I mean. How...?" My words are nonsensical. How do I ask this question? Were they in a relationship? Can you date a ghost?

"How does it work?" he supplies. "What did we do?"

"Yeah. That."

"She helped me play the market. It's why I was so good. She listened in on phone calls, picked up gossip and pieces of information floating around on the floor, and brought it all back to me. Then I'd make a killing."

"That sounds like cheating."

"Or leveling the playing field. A lot of successful brokers are necromancers."

That sounds insane. I don't say this out loud, but I'm certain it shows in my expression. "What did you do in return?"

"Spent a lot of time in art museums."

"As a ghost, she could go any time she liked."

"According to her, it's not the same, not as enjoyable, not as ... sensual."

Okay, I've heard enough. Malcolm has—or had—an invisible girlfriend. My legs find their strength and I push to stand.

"Where are you going?"

"Home," I say.

"Do you want a ride?"

"No."

"Katy, I know it's strange, but give it some thought—"

"My grandmother never said anything about necromancers, ever."

"Then maybe your grandmother didn't tell you everything. They exist. I'm one. And I'm pretty sure you're one too."

"I'm a ghost hunter." I turn from him and start down the walk.

"Katy—"

"I'll see you Monday. At work."

This time, he lets me walk away without another word.

THE WALK HOME is long and cold. I pick up two sprites along

the way—two that I recognize. They dart and spin about, feeling oh so full of themselves. When I pass Sadie's house, they peel off and zip to the roof and down her chimney.

My own house is dark. Only recently it started feeling like home again, but now, when I unlock the door, emptiness greets me. I think of all the things Malcolm said and all the things that my grandmother never did. I don't feel like Katy Lindstrom, ghost hunter. I'm certainly not Katy Lindstrom, necromancer.

For now, I'll go through the motions. I'll take a shower, brew a pot of Kona blend. I'll drink it slowly and study the walls. I'll pretend I know all the answers. I'll pretend last night never happened.

That will work. For now.

As long as I don't look in the mirror.

MUST LOVE GHOSTS

COFFEE AND GHOSTS: EPISODE 5

A MERE FOUR DAYS AGO, I was behind bars. So meeting Police Chief Ramsey on the front steps of the Springside Township Police Department?

Somewhat awkward.

Chief Ramsey's bulk casts a shadow across the steps. He studies the space behind me, around me, in between us. He coughs, once.

"You're not under arrest," he says. "You know that, right?"

I cock my head and stare. His gaze darts to my face and lingers there—or, more accurately, on my left cheek—before he can compose himself.

I resist the urge to touch my face.

"And you're free to leave town as well." He shrugs, as if the last forty-eight hours were a simple misunderstanding. "Seems there was a theft ring operating here. Pretty clever of them to follow you around. The Minneapolis Police have picked up their trail. We might even get some of the stuff back."

The traffic on Main Street consists of a single VW Bug, sky blue with a convertible top. From the Pancake House comes the scent of bacon wrapped in maple. I want to cross the road, leave Police Chief Ramsey behind, and order a stack of buttermilk pancakes. The fresh-squeezed orange juice is to die for. No coffee, though. They make the worst in town.

Instead, I work a few more degrees of frost into my stare. My grandmother would do this when whatever came from someone's mouth didn't match her expectations. During her lifetime, Chief Ramsey got the ice glare more than once.

"And I really appreciate you finding Mr. Carlotta's Purple Heart." His tone implies that these might be the hardest words he's ever uttered. "That was the one thing that insurance couldn't replace."

It's not much of an apology, but it's close enough.

"So ... you're free to go." He doesn't shoo with his hands, but his fingers twitch as if he wants to.

I would love nothing better than to comply, but I'm here at the police station for a reason. Before either of us can do or say anything further, a van rumbles up Main Street. The vehicle is strange, both in the sense that I've never seen it before—in a town the size of Springside, I've seen most everybody's car—and in the sense that it's ... strange. Bright yellow paint. Black lettering. Antennae sprouting like an untamed garden on the roof.

The van creeps past us, going well below the speed limit. The lettering on the side reads:

Ghost B Gone
Gregory B. Gone, proprietor

Chief Ramsey snorts and shakes his head. He doesn't believe in ghosts, although he should. He has two sprites in the booking area and a more substantial one that haunts his garden shed. We both track the van until it turns off of Main Street.

"What do you know, Katy?" he says. "Looks like you have a little competition there. Gotta love free enterprise."

He steps inside without bothering to hold the door for me. I let it shut, my gaze still on the intersection where the van disappeared. Choices, choices. Do I hop into my truck and follow it? Do I go to the office and confront my business partner, who's been lying to me, and maybe kissed me not so long ago? (Okay, he did kiss me, and I kissed back.) I peer up at the police station's façade. I have business here, too.

I step inside, since of all the things I must do, this is the most clear-cut.

Penny is working in the reception area, her hair frizzed as if she's clutched chunks of it several times in the past hour.

"Not again," she moans. "Third time this morning." Her fingers move across the computer's keyboard in the Ctrl-Alt-Del dance. She flops back in her chair, then jerks forward when her gaze lands on me.

"Katy? You don't ... I mean..." She trails off, her stare more blatant than Chief Ramsey's.

She focuses on the spot on my cheek, her eyes glazing over. I've studied the iridescent blue that mars my skin in the mirror, and I swear it rotates oh so slowly. Penny's current state of hypnosis might be proof of that.

"Penny."

No response.

"Penny."

Still nothing. I slap my hand on the counter. She blinks.

"How can I help you, Katy? Did you leave something here from when ... I mean, last Thursday?"

Yes, when I was incarcerated. "No, I'm good, but I need to know something else."

Penny leans forward.

"What do I need to do to get Belinda Barnes out of jail?" I Googled last night, but I'm still not certain what I might need to do in Springside—or rather, what I might need to do because of Police Chief Ramsey. "Do I pay her bail? How does it work?"

Penny's mouth hangs open. Her computer whirs. It's then I notice the source of her technical difficulties. The two sprites that haunt this place are at work—or, more accurately, play. Sprites love to annoy, startle, pull pranks. You find them in twos and threes because they also love an audience.

"Belinda?" I prompt. "Is she still here?"

Penny clamps her mouth shut and nods.

"Then what do I do? Penny, help me. Do I sign her out? Give you money? Talk to Chief Ramsey?" This last is something I'd rather not do, but I'll try anything.

She shoves from her desk. "Let me go talk to Chief."

Her chair spins as she passes by, then keeps spinning long after she's left the room.

"Nice trick," I say to the sprites. "Don't get out of hand, or I'll come back with Kona blend and some Tupperware."

The chair continues to spin. I continue to wait. All the while, I keep my palms glued to the countertop. I will not touch my cheek.

For a full five minutes, my resolve actually holds.

TEN MINUTES LATER, Penny ushers me into Chief Ramsey's office. He's a big man, and he has a big chair and desk to match. But the space we're forced to share is tiny. Morning sunlight filters through a window that's more of a vent. Dust motes dance in the sunbeam, but it's devoid of sprites. This is just as well. I'm not certain we could cram another being in here, ethereal or otherwise.

"Belinda Barnes is free to go," Chief tells me.

"Does she know that?" From what I gathered during my stay on Thursday, I'm not so sure.

He raises his hand and then tips it this way and that. Maybe yes? Maybe no? Then he uses that hand to rub the back of his neck.

"I'll be honest, I bring her in sometimes when I think she can use a shower and a decent meal, somewhere dry to sleep."

"So she really isn't under arrest."

"Drunk and disorderly. That's the charge, if anyone cares to check." Chief shakes his head. "Shame, bright girl like that, drinking her life away."

"But she *is* free to go," I say. "Right? She can come with me."

"To do what?"

"I have a job for her and a place for her to stay."

"A job." Chief shifts into full-on skeptic mode. Two words never held so much doubt.

Because what can the crazy girl offer the drunk one? I go with the truth, or at least, the piece of it Chief Ramsey might believe.

"It's been lonely since my grandmother died. My house has lots of bedrooms. I thought Belinda could stay in one." I give what I hope looks like an innocent little shrug. "Room and board in exchange for a few chores. That takes care of food and showers and a dry place to sleep."

Chief strokes his chin as if my request takes great consideration.

"And the only thing I have to drink in the house is coffee."

This gets a laugh, although he steels himself almost immediately. With a sigh, Chief Ramsey heaves himself to his feet.

"Go wait in the reception area. We'll start the paperwork and bring her out to you."

I don't release my own sigh until I've passed the front desk and landed in one of the hard, molded plastic chairs. Penny leaves her desk, and the sprites sag. Other than myself, Belinda is the only other person currently in the station who is aware of them, and I'm stealing their audience.

"Be glad I'm not driving you out to the nature preserve," I tell them.

"Oh, I don't know. That sounds nice."

Belinda's voice startles me. She's standing in the doorway to the booking and holding cell area, Chief Ramsey glowering behind her.

"I was just talking—" I begin.

"To yourself?" She nods toward the sprites. "Careful, or Chief Ramsey will start locking you up on a regular basis, too."

"Now, Belinda, I promised your father—"

"Oh, don't worry about Daddy. He's not around to haunt you. Trust me. I'd know." With that, she breezes out of the police station.

"Reckless girl," Chief mutters.

I dash out the door without a goodbye—or a thank you. No matter. Chief wouldn't hear me. No time, either. Belinda is halfway down the block before I catch up to her. At first, she won't adjust her stride. I'm not short, but Belinda is six feet tall, and most of that is leg.

"Thanks, Katy," she says, boot heels clacking on the sidewalk. "But I don't need your pity."

"Would you just stop, or at least slow down? You have no idea what you're talking about." I'm close to begging, but I'm not sure that will work with Belinda. Again, I try the truth. "I need your help."

She halts so suddenly that I shoot past her. I whirl around, afraid this is a ruse. But she's standing there, arms crossed over her chest.

"My help," she says, her tone nearly as skeptical as Chief's was. "What on earth could I ... what the hell is on your cheek?"

I deflate. I tried makeup this morning, but clearly it isn't working. "I wish I knew what it was. It ... happened on Friday night."

Belinda steps closer. "This doesn't look like the result of too much tequila and a trip to the tattoo parlor."

"It isn't."

She leans in. Since Thursday—when we shared the holding cell together—she's had a shower. Someone must have taken the overcoat she wears to the drycleaner. The khaki material hangs in smooth lines, the stains gone, or at least faded so you might not notice.

"Don't touch it," I say.

"Not going to. It's sending out a serious keep-back message."

"The last person who did got hurt," I add.

"Who was the last person to touch you, Katy?" Her provocative lilt implies volumes more than her mere words.

My heart beats volumes more than I think it should.

"That would be Malcolm." My throat is tight. I try to swallow, but it doesn't do any good. Malcolm, my business partner, the man I kissed not too long ago. Malcolm, who calls himself a necromancer. Malcolm, who is expecting me in the office about ten minutes ago.

"It's too bad no one was taking bets on that," Belinda says. "I would've made a killing."

"I don't want to talk about Malcolm," I say, hoping to steer the conversation in another direction. Except Malcolm's involved in all of it, and in ways I'm not sure I understand. "I want to hire you," I blurt out, certain this will do the trick.

"What?"

"I want to hire you."

"To do what? I have no skills beyond scooping ice cream."

"All I can do is make coffee."

Belinda snorts a laugh. "You can do a lot more. You didn't see Chief Ramsey go after Mr. Carlotta's Purple Heart, did you?"

"You heard about that?" I only arrived back on Saturday afternoon. But Springside Township is small, and word gets around.

"Penny." Belinda holds up her hand as if it's a talking puppet. "And the sprites. You'd be surprised how much I hear."

"Actually, I wouldn't. Not anymore. It's one of the reasons I need your help." I nod toward the Pancake House. "I barely ate yesterday, and I'm starving. Can we talk over breakfast?"

Maybe it's the maple syrup drenching the air, but she wavers. Hardly anyone turns down breakfast at Springside Pancake House.

Belinda doesn't nod. She doesn't say a word. Instead, she strikes out across Main Street, cutting in front of the No Jaywalking sign.

I run to catch up.

～

ONCE UPON A TIME, I thought I knew everything there was to know about ghost hunting. You don't need high-tech gadgets or sensors or a (usually faked) connection to the other side. You don't need to wait for dark. What you need is a really good cup of coffee.

It might sound immodest, but I make a great cup of coffee. This, however, is the only thing I can do. As recession-proof skills go, it's a mediocre one. When she died, my grandmother left behind the family business. She left me her house. What I'm finding out now is that she left a lot of unanswered questions as well.

I think Belinda can answer some of those.

I wait until we've plowed through a first round of silver-dollar-size buttermilk pancakes. They cook them all day long and will bring you as many as you can eat.

"This beats the burnt toast Penny made me this morning." Belinda raises her glass of orange juice to mine. "Thank you," she adds. "That should've been my answer before. Thank you."

"I do need your help, but I don't know if you want to talk about it." When she doesn't respond, I say, "Ghosts. I know they've always harassed you."

Belinda sets down her glass. She's always been so golden—well-to-do, adoring parents, hair both naturally wavy and blonde. Add in academic success in high school, all the extracurriculars, and all the awards—prom queen, homecoming queen, most likely to succeed. It could make you crazy with jealousy, if you let it. Or if you could see what I do—and did see all through our school years.

Something about her attracts the nastiest ghosts around. Sprites are playful. The ghost that haunts Mr. Carlotta's Purple

Heart is melancholy to the point of thickening the air. The ghosts that find Belinda are cruel, twisted things that resent not so much their afterlife but the life they missed out on. So they like to make hers as miserable as possible.

They can be difficult to catch, too. I've scalded myself more than once going after them. In high school, before big tests, I'd pack a thermos of coffee. During the four years at Springside High, I managed to splatter Kona blend over the tile of every single girls' bathroom in the building. The last of Belinda's ghosts I captured, in the rehab center, I drove out a good sixty miles before setting it free.

"You might not want to answer this," I say now, picking my way through the right words. "But can you hear them ... talk?"

Before my grandmother died, I would've said, with full conviction, that ghosts don't talk. They don't send messages from beyond the grave. They're not looking to unburden themselves so they can cross over into the light. Now? At least the talking part?

"I ask because I'm starting to think there's a lot I don't know." I cut a pancake into quarters, dip it in syrup, but don't bring it to my mouth. "And I'm starting to think I can hear ... suggestions?" It's more of a question than a statement.

Belinda nods. "It's like that. But when one of them latches on, it's like having your worst enemy in your head, criticizing everything you do. Only without words. Feelings, maybe? The meaning is there, even if the actual words aren't." She shakes her head as if to clear it of ghosts and words. "It's hard to explain."

"I think I know what you mean."

"And if you drink? You can blot them out for a while." She presses her fingertips against her temples. "At least until the alcohol wears off."

"Then it's worse."

She nods, once.

"Only now," I say, "I'm starting to hear them. I don't understand why."

"Oh, well, that's simple. Because your grandmother never wanted you to hear them."

Never ... what? I gape, and I must look hungry, because the waitress plops down another plate of pancakes in front of me. By rote, I spread butter, all the while searching for words.

"How do you know?" I ask finally.

Belinda shrugs. "She told me once, when she was trying to teach me, I don't know, self-defense. The whole coffee trick you do. Even when she made the coffee, I still couldn't trap them. She told me that a lot of it was up here." Belinda taps her head. "If she told you that you couldn't hear the ghosts, then you simply wouldn't. It would make you a better ghost hunter in the long run. More focused. Less distracted by their chatter." She pushes her hair away from her face. "God, they love to chatter."

I consider this. My grandmother taught me everything I know about ghost hunting. But lately, I believe she didn't teach me everything she knew. Each day, the gap grows a little wider. Each day, I worry I may miss something crucial, something I should know.

"I'd like to hire you," I say.

"Katy, I can't take your money—"

"Place to stay? Room and board? I live in a really big house with a lot of bedrooms. No ghosts. I almost wish there were. It would liven up the place."

Belinda laughs, and I decide not to mention the time when nearly all of Springside's ghosts invaded the old Victorian. It was harmless. Mostly.

"I'm lonely," I admit.

Belinda gives me a wan smile. "Me too."

"So? What do you have to lose? If we end up hating each other, you can move out. Deal?" I extend my hand across the table.

My fingertips are sticky with syrup. So are hers.

"On one condition," she says, scooting from the booth. "We stop at the drugstore first."

AS A SAFETY MEASURE, I brew a pot of my very best coffee, a blend I make from a select group of beans. The aroma fills the kitchen, the steam of it warming every part of my face with one exception—the spot on my cheek.

Belinda waves a makeup brush in front of her eyes. "If I stare at it too long, it's like I forget where I am." She takes a breath and anchors me to a chair, her palm on my head so she can tip my face upward.

"I don't think you should touch it," I say.

"Why do you think we went to the drugstore?" She points the makeup brush at some cream foundation and a makeup sponge. "Tools of my trade. I don't actually need to touch your skin."

"Just be careful."

Belinda brushes and dabs, bottom lip caught between her teeth. The spot on my left cheek feels unreal and waxy. I hope it's not spreading. I don't want a blue face. I don't want to be unreal and waxy. At last she sits back as if the whole process has exhausted her.

"It's better. Here." She opens a compact and turns the mirror toward me. "Take a look."

Better. Not gone.

"I can still see it swirl," I say.

"Yeah. That's freaky."

"It's like a tropical storm has invaded my face."

"How did you get it, anyway? Thursday you were looking fine and had two hot guys fighting over you."

"First, no one is fighting over me."

Belinda snorts.

"Second, it's a long story. It wasn't a ghost, but it's a ghost-like ... thing. An entity, maybe? I think I walked into a trap." Or was led there. That the entity was lurking at the very club Malcolm and I ended up at seems less coincidental than I'd like to admit.

"I'm sorry," she says.

"It's not your fault."

"No." She shakes her head, and then her whole body shakes, like she's fighting a chill. "It's just when one of those ... things finds you, they have a hard time letting go. So, I understand, and I'm sorry it happened to you."

"That's why I'm brewing up some coffee." I try for bright and cheery. I pour the fresh brew into a thermal carafe. "This will keep it hot all day long. If you get an uninvited visitor, just uncap it and then run next door and call from Sadie's. She has sprites, but they won't bother you."

Belinda wafts some of the aroma toward her face. Her eyes close, and she sighs. "If I don't end up drinking it all first."

I divide the remaining coffee between a second carafe and a half a dozen thermoses. "That's what this is for. Plus, I need some for work."

She raises an eyebrow. How she makes that single gesture imply volumes, I'll never know.

"Malcolm is my business partner," I say. "Nothing more."

"Yeah, well, if he were my business partner, I'd work overtime."

I decide that doesn't need a response. I tighten the lid on my thermos and leave the house.

FOR A LONG TIME, I merely stand in front of our office, my eyes tracing the gold leaf lettering on the front window.

K&M Ghost Eradication Specialists

I was so thrilled when Malcolm unveiled that finishing touch. When my grandmother was alive, we always worked out of the house. But then, I'd been working since I was five. Something about that gold leaf makes all of this feel real.

Inside, everything is how I left it on Thursday, like nothing has changed. We have a reception desk but not enough money to pay a receptionist. We work mostly in the conference room. That's where Malcolm's brother, Nigel, keeps his computer. He's building us a ghost database, making a website, and can probably do other computer-related things I haven't even thought of yet.

The conference room is where I find both brothers. Something sparks in Malcolm's gaze when I enter the room. Relief? Hope? Or something I can't read?

"Is it..." Malcolm squints. "Is it fading?"

"Makeup. It was too distracting. It kept hypnotizing people."

He swears.

Nigel glances up from the computer screen. "Oh, Jesus, Katy, I'm sorry. Something like that shouldn't happen to you."

The spot on my cheek is not Nigel's fault. It might, however, be his brother's fault. But Nigel knows ghosts; he used to be addicted to swallowing them. And for a few minutes, he even had the entity in question inside him. He might be able to help, or at least have some information I can work with.

"Then did it mark you in a way, when it was inside you?" I ask.

"I didn't think so, not at first. But there are memories that are just out of my reach, and every once in a while, an inappropriate impulse." Nigel pulls his fingers through the shock of white hair on his head. "That's why I had you clear Sadie's house before dinner. It kept suggesting that a sprite side dish would be totally harmless."

So we're both marked. Through all this, Malcolm sits to one side, arms braced on his thighs, hands clasped. His gaze never leaves the floor. I won't condemn him, not yet. Besides, we may have other problems.

"Have either of you heard of Ghost B Gone or Gregory B. Gone?"

"Oh, sure," Nigel says. "He has a web show. I watch it all the time."

Really? A web show? "What does he do?"

"Ghost evictions, as he calls them. Streams them live over the net."

I pull a thermos of coffee from my bag. "So I don't need to bribe you with this to do a little research for us?"

Nigel grins. "You can always bribe me with coffee. What do you want to know?"

"What he's up to. He pulled into town this morning. I saw his van on Main Street."

"Seriously?" Nigel rubs his hands together and pulls his chair closer to his computer.

Within moments, we land on Ghost B Gone's YouTube page. He scrolls through videos and comments, and both seem to go on forever. One video starts to play, and the tinny, squeaking music makes me wince.

"Theme song," Nigel says.

"And you watch this?" Malcolm asks, stealing my question.

"Well, yeah. It's unintentionally hilarious. He doesn't actually catch anything. He just thinks he does because the sprites making mischief get bored."

"You can't see the sprites, can you?" I ask. Ghosts don't show up in photographs, digital or otherwise—or so I've always believed.

"No, you can't, but if you know the telltale signs, it's pretty obvious." Nigel leans forward now. "Oh, look at this."

On the screen is an announcement for the next episode.

Springside Township's Haunted Shame.
One family's dream became their nightmare.
On Halloween, Gregory and the Ghost B Gone team
will rid this dream home of its uninvited and malicious visitors.
Live streaming! 8 p.m. CST/9 p.m. EST

The image of a house replaces the fading words. The Victorian is new construction. I recognize the forest green paint and white trim.

Malcolm turns toward me and gives his head a shake. "This isn't one of our clients."

"That's because it isn't really haunted," I say. "Well, it is, but that's not why it's empty. The builders went bankrupt, the buyers backed out of the deal, and now I think the bank owns it. It just sits there. Kids sneak inside, and it's attracted a trio of sprites who like to scare them. Halloween is their busy season."

"So no one's dream has been denied?" Nigel says.

I roll my eyes. "Hardly."

Malcolm looks at me. Despite everything that's happened, something zings inside me. A connection, the thought we both have at the same time. Like he's still my partner.

"Want to investigate?" he says.

"You read my mind."

~

"KATY, WE SHOULD TALK."

Well, yes, we should, but it would only be one of those messy, emotional talks no one likes to have. I'm overflowing with feelings and hollow at the same time. But I can walk and think and investigate. I don't want to spoil any of that. Because that? That feels right.

Having Malcolm at my side still feels right. He's all Ivory soap and nutmeg, with a hint of the saffron that he uses in his tea. It should be a crime for a man to smell this good.

"We should take my truck," I say, "in case we need supplies."

I keep an emergency stash in my truck—coffee, sugar, percolator, a little camp stove for brewing. The only thing I don't have is half and half. Some ghosts insist on it; trust me, you don't want to see what they do when they're presented with the powdered stuff. Catching a ghost that tough requires a more deliberate approach.

"Can we talk about what happened?" Malcolm follows me to the alley behind our building, where I park my truck.

The thing is old and unsightly, and the mayor has asked that I not park it on Main Street. Malcolm's cherry red convertible? That gets its own designated parking spot between our storefront and the deli.

I climb into the driver's side, put the key into the ignition, but don't turn it. I wait until Malcolm's seatbelt clicks.

"Are we still partners?" I stare straight ahead, as if I'm speaking to the windshield.

"Of course we are."

I shift slightly in my seat. He does the same.

"Then can you tell me the truth, from the start? Because I don't think I can be your partner if I don't know that."

So maybe I do want the messy, emotional chat. I'm certain I won't like what I hear. I also know I can't physically turn the key and drive to investigate Ghost B Gone with all these doubts in my head.

"I owe you that." His voice is quiet, contemplative. "I owe you a lot of things. And it's not so much that I lied. Well, not exactly. I just didn't tell you the whole truth."

"And what is the whole truth?"

"First? You saved me. I really did lose my job. Part of it was Nigel, but no one minded that, not when I was the top broker quarter after quarter. They threw bonuses at me, trips to Cancun. As long as Selena—"

"Wait. Is Selena your ghost?"

He nods.

Of course. Malcolm's ghostly girlfriend would have a glamorous name. I shake my head and try to shake off the irrational jealousy.

"As long as she was around," he continues, "things were fine. But when Nigel swallowed her, there went my streak." He shrugs, palms skyward. "I was still a good broker, but I wasn't spectacular

—and people noticed. And they noticed enough that when things got tight and Nigel got out of hand, they fired me."

I'm torn between telling him I'm sorry and berating him for cheating at investing in the first place. But then, is it insider trading if your source isn't alive?

"I didn't come to Springside with a plan, but I did come here on purpose."

This gets my attention. I scoot against the slippery vinyl seat as if moving a few inches closer guarantees I won't miss a word.

"Your grandmother has—had—a reputation beyond Springside. I knew she didn't practice necromancy, but she was powerful. She could've been one of the best." He sighs. "I was hoping for some advice."

"But you found me instead."

The grin he gives me is a slow, seductive thing. "I'm not disappointed by that."

For three full seconds, my head buzzes. I blow out a breath and steel myself.

"I was at a crossroads. Catching ghosts with you was more fun than working at the brokerage, even if it didn't pay nearly as well. And you..." He breaks off, rubs the palm of one hand with the thumb of the other. "I'd never met a necromancer as strong as you are."

"I'm not a necromancer," I say.

"But you could be. Don't you see it, Katy? Part of the reason Springside is so haunted is you. Ghosts like you. You have an affinity for them. My grandfather would've called you a natural—"

"Or maybe a supernatural?"

Malcolm pauses, then throws his head back and laughs. Part of me melts, just a little. Part of me is thrilled I can still make him laugh like that.

"Yes," he says, still chuckling. "That. I've never seen anything like you, and I can't understand why you've never even heard of necromancy before now."

Well, I've heard of it, but that's not what Malcolm means. But ever since he zoomed into town in his cherry red convertible, I've discovered there are many things about ghosts and ghost hunting I never knew.

"I don't understand why your grandmother never told you, at least."

The sad thing is, I don't either.

"Wait." He sits up straight and strains against the seatbelt. "What about your parents?"

"They died not long after I was born. I don't remember them."

"How did they die?"

I bite my lip. "Car accident."

"Huh. That's a leading cause of death for necromancers."

"It is?" I shake my head because this? This is starting to get weird.

"When there's an imbalance, or when things go wrong—like with Nigel's addiction—accidents happen. If we hadn't intervened, at some point the ghosts would have decided to free themselves. Or sometimes, if a necromancer takes on a ghost that's too strong ..." He trails off. "Car accidents are good for that."

"So the ... host." Is that what you call it? I'm not sure, but since Malcolm doesn't contradict me, I continue. "Has to die in those cases?"

"I'm afraid so." His expression turns tender. He reaches out to touch my cheek—the right one. "One more reason I'm grateful to you."

I shiver, although the air inside the cab is warm. Our conversation has fogged the glass. If anyone walks by, they'll think we're doing something other than talking in here. For a moment, I ponder the possibility of my parents being necromancers. I don't remember them at all. Photographs of them evoke no memories, not even manufactured ones. My few questions always made my grandmother so sad that I eventually stopped asking.

"What about Friday, at the club?" I say now. This notion has been eating at me for the past two days. Did we walk into a trap or did Malcolm lead me there?

"I didn't know that thing, that entity, whatever it is, would be there. It was a coincidence."

"It's an awfully big coincidence."

"Maybe, but you know, ghosts gossip just as much as people do. Plus, I took you to a haunted dance club, a spot where a lot of necromancers hang out. If anything, it happened because I'm really predictable."

"You are?" If anything, Malcolm leaves me off balance.

"Sure. A trip to my alma mater? I was showing you around. Frat house, favorite restaurant, favorite club. That's Psych 101."

"Then why did that thing thank you for playing a part?"

"Because the part I was playing was simply a guy trying to impress a girl."

This should not please me as much as it does. Malcolm has lied. For all I know, Malcolm may still be lying. I will be cautious. I will clamp my lips together so no hint of a smile shows.

"If I'd been thinking—really thinking—I would've seen the theft of Mr. Carlotta's Purple Heart for what it was: bait for a trap." He sighs again, adding to the fog on the windshield. "Do you really care about anyone's flat screen TV?"

"I don't even own a TV."

"There you go. But you care about Mr. Carlotta. So this entity manipulates a couple of weak-minded individuals to steal a few things, including the Purple Heart, and I unwittingly do the rest. And I'm sorry, Katy, really, really sorry." He rubs his jaw as if it aches. "And I'm scared of what this means." He points to the spot on my left cheek.

"You said it meant that thing can find me."

"It does."

"Does it..." I begin, then pause. I'm so tired of calling it *thing* or *entity*. "Does it even have a name?"

"I'm sure it does. I was trying to find out more yesterday.

Called in a few favors, talked to a few old friends, that sort of thing. Made me wish my grandfather were still alive. He would know what to do."

"So you don't know its name."

"You don't *want* to know its name. To speak the name out loud is to invoke the entity."

"You mean, poof? There it is in front of you?"

"That's exactly what I mean, and only a well-prepared necromancer would ever do that."

"So even if someone knows what it's called, they won't tell you."

"Exactly."

"Could you write it down?" I venture.

Malcolm laughs, not a full-throated one, but the sound of it fills the cab with warmth.

"You never give up, do you?" he says.

I shake my head.

"Katy, I don't want you trying anything. I'm worried what this might mean for you. Remember at the mausoleum, when I kept getting that vendetta vibe?"

I nod.

"I think it means you."

"But ... I haven't done anything to this entity."

"What about your grandmother?"

A week ago, I would've declared *of course not*. Now? Now I have to consider that I may have never fully known the woman who raised me and taught me all about ghosts.

"This thing is ancient," Malcolm says. "Time means little to it. So, if it feels like it, it might take its revenge on you. Or wait and take it on your granddaughter. But I think it finds you ... intriguing."

"So you're thinking sooner rather than later, but sooner for it could be when I'm sixty. Or it could be tomorrow."

He raises a hand and lets it drop onto his lap, defeated.

"Well, then," I say, and turn the key in the ignition. "We'd better get going and investigate Ghost B Gone while we still have time."

~

THE DOORS to the green and white Victorian are flung wide open. A tech crew is tramping up and down the porch stairs, lugging in all sorts of electronic equipment. Two people are wrestling a generator toward the side of the house. Out front, a card table holds sodas and sandwiches. Static buzzes in the air, and the tiny hairs on the back of my neck prick up, but it's not from fear or even the sensation of someone watching us.

No, just the cool kiss of a sprite before it veers off through the open doorway.

"See?" Malcolm whispers. "You brought them another ghost. They should put you on the payroll."

"Hardly. This?" I gesture toward all the activity. "Is like setting a cake in front of toddlers and asking them not to touch it. I'm sure the sprites are overjoyed. All this attention? On Halloween? The most they usually get is a few screeching kids."

Together, we take a few steps up the walk. When no one stops us, we take a few more. At last we cross the threshold without anyone noticing. Inside, we pick our way through cables and electrical cords. The buzz of static is more insistent here. Someone is feeding lines from the generator through an open window, and the breeze that sneaks in makes the space feel more abandoned, despite the crowd.

"Welcome!" someone booms out. "Welcome, friends!"

A man approaches, hand extended. His face, behind round lens glasses, beams. At sixty, he'll make a jolly mall Santa Claus. Now, at about thirty, he's wiry and bearded and quite possibly the true source of all this buzzing static.

He pumps Malcolm's hand and then mine. "Good to meet you! Good to meet you! I'm Gregory B. Gone, and this is my show."

"I'm Katy Lindstrom—"

"The ghost catcher! Of course." He turns toward Malcolm. "And you must be Malcolm Armand. So good to have the local talent on hand."

Local talent?

"Really lends an air of authenticity to the show. My viewers love that. Did you hear? I just broke one million."

I glance at Malcolm. Because really? I have no idea how to respond to such a statement.

"Any luck with sponsors yet?" Malcolm asks.

Gregory lights up. Yes, leave it to Malcolm to know what to say.

"Not yet, but I have a line on a couple. But then, you know how tough that is."

Gregory tugs Malcolm away in a move so slick I barely notice. That's fine with me. I head off on my own to peer beneath tables, thump on walls, and trace cables. I can't quite tell if this is nothing more than elaborate stagecraft or if Gregory B. Gone truly believes in all of this.

At my side, the thermoses of coffee I made this morning slosh in the canvas bag we use as a field kit. I push open a swinging door and land in the kitchen. The space is empty. No chairs. No table. I ease onto the island, a bare and icy marble slab, the rack above it like a black skeleton. It's just a little bit creepy sitting beneath it, like the metal arms will reach out and grab me.

I decide I need company, so I open a thermos, pour a small cup, and then hold it out like an offering.

"Yeah, I know it came from a thermos," I say to the air, "but I just brewed it this morning and it's some of my best."

The metal cup warms my fingers. The aroma flows throughout the kitchen as if this space has been longing for the scent of food. I study the steam rising from the coffee's surface. Within a minute, a glimmer appears. That didn't take long.

"Thirsty?" I ask.

The steam wavers, and the sprite basks in the heat and flavor, clearly enjoying itself.

"I'm not sure I know you."

Some ghosts feel familiar. My neighbor Sadie's sprites are like playful children or puppies. Mr. Carlotta's ghost is heavy and sad, and of all the ghosts I've encountered in Springside, it must be the oldest. My grandmother, whom I now realize I haven't sensed in the past two days, is vibrant, feisty, and very much like she was in her life.

This one, here in the steam? I think it's new. Or maybe we simply haven't crossed paths before.

I've just topped off the cup when the swinging door flies open. Gregory B. Gone fills the space with his booming words.

"So here's where you're hiding."

"I'm not hiding." I hold the cup so the steam—along with the ghost—is in his line of sight.

He eyes the coffee. "Doing a little reconnaissance? I think it's going to take more than that to draw these entities from their hiding places, and I'm not sure you should attempt it on your own. They have an evil reputation. But then, living here, you would know that."

I open my mouth to contradict him, but Malcolm stands at the threshold, a finger pressed to his lips. So I bite down on my words.

"Would you like some coffee?" I say instead. "For you and your crew? It's perfect drinking temperature, so I won't be able to use it to catch anything. Hate to see it go to waste."

I'm certain my offer doesn't carry past the kitchen door, but it's like I've broadcast it through the entire space. The kitchen fills with people. Someone brings in the sandwiches. Someone else passes around Styrofoam cups. I pour out every last drop that I have in the thermoses. People tap cups, make toasts, and drink.

The sprite leaves in a huff, smacking Malcolm on the back of the head on its way out.

"Like it's my fault," he whispers when he reaches my side.

"Let me introduce you to a few of our regulars," Gregory says. "Nick, our tech support. Rajeev keeps us electrified. And of course, we couldn't make contact at all without our medium, Terese."

The two men nod, more interested in coffee than ghosts. Terese, ethereal, with flowing white hair and dusky skin, kisses first Malcolm and then me on both cheeks.

"And while you won't see much of his face, we have Tim, who runs the cameras," Gregory says.

I whirl around and confront the lens of a video camera, its eye trained on me.

"Are you filming this now?" I ask.

Gregory bursts out laughing. "Of course we are. And we'll be streaming live tonight for Halloween, when we'll finally rid this place of its ghosts. We'd love to have your help."

"Halloween is our busy night," I say.

"Trust me, all the action will be here. So, what do you say?" Gregory urges both Malcolm and me closer, placing a hand on each of our shoulders. "Can I count on K&M Ghost Eradication Specialists?"

I'm paralyzed by the lens trained on my face, but Malcolm's voice comes sure and smooth.

"Of course. We'll be here tonight."

Gregory does something—I can't say what, exactly—but Tim relaxes his hand and the camera sags in his grip.

"Perfect," Gregory says. "Splice together a promo. Be sure to include Katy saying 'Are you filming this now?' It's adorable. And plenty of Malcolm for the female demographic. In fact, fire up some of our sock puppets and have them start talking about the haunted hottie. That'll up the views."

He squeezes our shoulders before letting go and then claps his hands together. "Tonight's the night, people. Tonight's the night Ghost B Gone makes a true name for itself. No more scraps. No more begging. Everyone will come to us from now on."

He shoos them from the kitchen and, as quickly as they arrived, they vanish, leaving behind stains on the marble countertop, a scattering of Styrofoam cups, and the scent of stale coffee and sweat.

"Is he going to put me on the internet?" I ask, although I'm pretty sure I know the answer.

Malcolm frowns. "I think he already has."

"I don't like this," I say. "I don't like that I can't figure out whether it's stagecraft or if he believes in what he's doing."

"Or if it's a little bit of both."

"And what did you two talk about that I wasn't privileged enough to hear?"

Malcolm snorts. "He talked. Tim trailed us with his camera. I'm beginning to think I'm along just as eye candy."

"The haunted hottie?"

His lip curls as if I've handed him a cold cup of coffee. He looks as appalled as I feel.

"Well, you do dress nicely," I say. Malcolm does, in crisp oxford shirts and pressed trousers, all leftovers from his days as a broker for an investment firm in Minneapolis. "And you are handsome. You're probably photogenic, too."

"What did you call me?"

A flush invades my cheeks. Or more accurately, my right one. The spot on my left is stubborn and cold and waxy. Something about that pings in the back of my mind, but with Malcolm staring at me, one eyebrow slightly raised, I can't grasp what that might be.

"Photogenic," I say.

"No. The other."

"Handsome." My voice is maybe more breathy than it should be.

"Do you think that?"

"Maybe," I say, giving my shoulders a shrug. "Or maybe it's just a simple fact."

His lip doesn't curl at this, at least. For a long moment, he simply scrutinizes me. Then he laughs.

"So, partner," Malcolm says, the humor still in his voice. "What do you think we should do tonight?"

I survey the kitchen. True, the electricity is out, and I doubt Gregory B. Gone will spare any from his generator. Still, there's plenty of room for the camp stove. Through the window, I notice cloud cover has rolled in. The dark, menacing sky might just cancel Halloween.

"We could set up in here," I say. "Halloween is one of the few nights Sadie's sprites don't bother her. We might even find them here."

"So you don't think there's anything here but sprites?"

"I just saw the one. You?"

Malcolm shakes his head. "This place doesn't even feel haunted, just empty."

"Like it should have a family in it, some life," I add.

He opens his mouth to speak, but no words come out. He takes a slow turn around the kitchen. "Does this place feel *too* empty to you?"

"Too empty, like what?"

"The mausoleum?"

Before I can inhale a deep breath, gauge whether the air here feels like that of the mausoleum with all its stale, lifeless stillness, thunder rumbles the house with so much force, the windows rattle. The rack above our heads creaks and sways. A fine sprinkling of plaster from the ceiling coats the marble slab. Malcolm grabs my hand and jerks us both away.

"Why don't we go get ready for tonight?" he says.

"Are you sure?" I say. "This place could fall down around everybody's ears."

"If we're here, with supplies, we can stop things. If the sprites get out of hand, we'll just fire up the camp stove."

I nod. That makes the most sense. Once the ghostly word gets out that something is happening here, it will draw the sprites. So many in one spot can be a problem. They aren't the awful, evil things of movies and books, but so many together results in chaos.

"All right," I say. "Let's go get ready."

We race through the rain to my truck. By the time I fling myself into the cab, my hair is slicked to my scalp. Drops slither down my spine. Malcolm's shirt is so soaked, it's gone from light blue to dark.

"You might want to change before tonight," I say.

He squeezes water from a sleeve. "I think you might be right."

I drop him at his apartment, and we agree to meet back at the Victorian half an hour before Ghost B Gone starts streaming their show. But as I turn the truck around and drive back the way I came —a way that takes me by the house again—I wonder if I'm missing something about tonight.

I let the engine idle, truck blocking the road, but this is a residential street that never sees much traffic. I blink, certain what I see is my imagination—or possibly part of Gregory's stagecraft. The clouds hang lower over the place, the rain pelts harder, the air is darker, somehow.

Terese emerges from the house, hair whipping in the wind, and the strands look alive, like snakes or tentacles. I think that this, too, must be part of Gregory's stagecraft. Her gaze lingers on me before she offers a smile.

I blink again. In that moment, I lose sight of her. She is no longer on the front porch, hair taking on a life of its own. She is not in the yard. I did not see her step back inside. She is not here.

She is nowhere.

I LEAVE Belinda with a second pot of coffee and some sandwiches from the deli.

"I'm a terrible hostess," I tell her. "Leaving you like this."

"Are you kidding?" She already has the sandwiches cut into quarters, a cup of coffee poured, and my laptop fired up on the kitchen table. "This." She points a sandwich quarter at the screen. "Is going to be awesome."

On the screen is Ghost B Gone's YouTube channel. And on their channel, right now? The promo for tonight's show. Belinda has paused the video so I'm frozen in time, my mouth open to say: *Are you filming this now?*

I sigh. She laughs, then sobers.

"Be careful, tonight, Katy," she says. "I'm not sure I'd trust this Gregory guy."

"He's a lot of hot air and words."

"Yeah, and if he manages to say the wrong ones? Who knows what he'll conjure up?"

"It's just sprites," I say. "Malcolm and I checked out the place this morning. Low level, mischievous sort of haunting."

Belinda is silent.

"You don't think there could be anything more, do you?" I ask.

She shakes her head. "It's just that your grandmother always told me not to go around looking for ghosts, or even asking if any were around. It draws them out."

This is true. When we called out the meaner ones, we always did so with a cup of coffee and some Tupperware at the ready.

"They crave attention," I say.

"Then again, this guy is so obnoxious, he's lucky it's Halloween. Otherwise, he might not even get any sprite action."

"I was thinking of sneaking through the house and catching them all beforehand."

"Oh, wouldn't that ruin his day."

She clicks play on the video. I leave before I can hear myself utter those inane words one more time.

~

THE VICTORIAN IS ablaze with light when I pull up in my truck. Other vehicles crowd both sides of the street, so I have to park two blocks down and dodge raindrops on my way to the house. Someone on the porch is handing out candy to children and flyers to the adults. Someone calls my name, but when I turn around, I can't see who it might be.

I stand in the rain for a heartbeat, considering whether I really did hear my name or not. Too many children squeal and cry out, too many adults scold. I can barely hear my thoughts. Pink cotton candy dresses and sparkly tiaras compete with black capes and white fluttering sheets. My heart stops at this last.

A child's idea of a ghost.

Oh, there are so many tonight. All children, I tell myself. Just costumes, from the store. No bed sheets. No bridal veils.

No entity. Not here in Springside, and not here in this modern replica of a Victorian mansion. The rain splatters harder and chases me inside.

Gregory's tech crew crowds the front part of the house. I push past the flow of people and duck into the kitchen. There, I find Malcolm. I exhale. I didn't realize I'd swallowed a good dose of anxiety along with dinner.

"Hey," he says. "You okay?"

I nod. "It's just crazy out there."

"Yeah, I'm not sure the sprites wanted that much attention. I can't seem to tempt any of them out."

His samovar is throwing aromatic steam into the air. I catch the hint of saffron and other exotic spices. That alone should be enough to lure a sprite. It certainly works on me.

"Is there enough that I can have a cup?" I ask.

"For you? Anything."

He pours. I sip. The warmth spreads through me, melting away the last bit of my unease. Then I start in on my own brew.

"I'm beginning to think that if there's going to be a show at all," he says, "it'll be up to us to bring the sprites. I mean, really. Do you sense anything? You're better at that than I am."

Maybe, but not by much. After I measure the coffee and set the percolator to brew, I take a slow walk around the kitchen.

"I called out that sprite earlier today, but I'm not really getting anything. You'd think with all of that—" I wave toward the front of the house. "They'd be ecstatic. Kids, grownups, everyone shrieking at their antics."

The kitchen door flies open, and Gregory sticks his head in.

"Hey, you two, the show's out here," he says. "Don't want to start without you."

"We're just getting some supplies ready," Malcolm says.

"What did I tell you? Coffee won't catch this thing."

"It's for the crew," I pipe up. "In case it's a late night."

"How sweet." He trains a dazzling grin on me. "Come on. The viewers will be disappointed if you're not there when we start streaming. The haunted hottie already has a fan club."

Malcolm waits until Gregory vanishes. Then he lets out a groan. I can't help it. I giggle.

"Come on, partner." I hold out my hand. "We wouldn't want to disappoint your fan club."

He contemplates my hand, but the expression on his face is odd, like he's uncertain, but not about me. More like, he's uncertain about himself. But he takes my hand, his skin warm like always, and we push through the kitchen door and into the main part of the house.

IN A MATTER OF HOURS, the Ghost B Gone crew has transformed the living room from airy and modern to cramped and closed. The space feels as though it has aged. Heavy drapes hide the big bay windows. The fireplace mantelpiece is loaded with ornately framed photographs of unsmiling ancestors. The red in the rolled-out Persian carpet looks like blood. The muted lighting gives the space a dank feel.

It looks like a child's idea of a haunted house.

"Do you think he supplies his own ghosts, too?" I whisper to Malcolm.

He nods toward Terese, whom Gregory is leading center stage—for lack of a better term.

"Ladies and gentlemen!" he booms. "Welcome! Tonight Ghost B Gone will confront its toughest foe yet, but confront it we will. And we will drive this malicious spirit from this space and reclaim it for the family dream home it should be."

Terese stands beneath the lights. They cast a blue tint on her hair. The strands flow and undulate, and I glance around for a wind machine or even a fan, but I don't see any. Stagecraft, I think. He's nothing but stagecraft. Still, that doesn't explain why the floorboards rumble beneath our feet.

"Ah," Gregory says, his stage whisper echoing through the space. "As everyone knows, Mistress Terese does not speak until she's made contact. She saves her strength in order to communicate with those beyond our realm."

Terese shoots her arms into the air, a look of ecstasy on her face.

"Touchdown?" Malcolm whispers in my ear.

I stifle a laugh and nudge him. He squeezes my hand.

The chandelier above Terese's head rattles, the crystals clinking against each other. Plaster clouds the air and coats Terese's skin and hair, the red robe she's wearing fading beneath the dust.

"Terese," Gregory says, voice low and urgent. "Have you made contact?"

She looks as if she's about to speak, and her expression is that of an actress uttering well-rehearsed lines. So this is a play, I think, with some well-managed stagecraft, and we've all been fooled.

But Terese's words never come. Instead, her eyes grow wide

with shock. She stares straight at the camera. Then she collapses to the floor, robes billowing around her.

"Terese!" Gregory throws himself at her. He kneels at her side, patting her hand, checking her pulse. "Get our EMT," he calls out.

Behind us, the crew chatters. A woman pushes through the crowd and shoves Gregory out of her way.

"She's unconscious," the woman says.

Gregory gives her a *no kidding* sort of look, then schools his face for the camera. "Ladies and gentlemen, it appears this entity is stronger than we first imagined. In fact—"

A howl echoes through the house. It's exactly the sort of sound you expect to hear on Halloween, low and almost mechanical. I've heard this sort of noise a hundred times while walking through the costume aisle at the store. And yet, something about it makes me grip Malcolm's hand even tighter.

"Perhaps our ghostly friend would like to make contact," Gregory says.

Behind him, the EMT continues to care for Terese, although I suspect the only thing to do is get her out of this place and take her to the emergency room. No one suggests this. I'm about to when something flutters in my peripheral vision. I whirl, but whatever it was has vanished.

"Malcolm," I say, keeping my voice even and quiet. "I think we should leave."

I turn to do just that, Malcolm's grip still firm, and watch as the front door slams shut. The fluttering comes again. Bed sheets on a clothesline. A bridal veil. The metallic undertones in that howl.

The lack of sprites. The empty feel of the kitchen. I shake my head, but denial isn't going to keep this entity away. My fingertips itch as if they long to touch that spot on my cheek. It's colder now, waxier, as if it really isn't a part of me.

"That's because it isn't, my dear. It's a part of me."

The voice trumps all other sounds in this space. The crew's

chatter dies. Gregory stands, slack-mouthed, eyes darting, searching for the source.

"Have ... have we made contact with the other side?" he manages at last.

"That would be a first," one of the crew mutters.

Something inky peels itself from Terese's inert form. A blob at first, the thing solidifies into shape, more or less. It still lacks substance. It is still ethereal. But it looks like a man now, tall, with angular features. If you saw this silhouette and nothing more, you might think him handsome.

"Ah, yes, my dear. I thought you might like this incarnation. Tall. Dark. Handsome. Of course, I don't have my own fan club, but then I'm not as needy as some of the people in your life."

Gregory storms toward the entity. "Who are you? What do you want? Who are you talking to?"

He is either stupid or naive or completely clueless about this thing. Can't he feel its menace? How stale the air is? The taste of cold metal against his tongue? I break free from Malcolm and lurch forward. My fingers skim Gregory's back just as he reaches the entity.

"Don't touch it!" I cry out.

Too late. Gregory is there, ready to shove a hand through the thing's murky chest. His fist goes straight through. Gregory pulls back, studies his hand in awe.

"What the—" he begins.

Something flutters. Gregory soars through the air and crashes against the fireplace. The photographs teeter and rain down on him. Glass shatters, shards scattering across the hardwood floor and embedding themselves into the carpet. Drops of blood speckle the tile surrounding the fireplace.

Someone screams. Someone else barks orders. In between, voices rise again, the undertone frantic, panic filling the air.

"Silence!" The entity's voice shakes the entire house.

The shouts and urgent voices die, the only sound the hitched breathing of someone who might be crying.

"Much better," it says. "Now, could someone come sweep up this buffoon?" Again, a fluttering, a flick of a bed sheet. Rajeev from the tech crew rushes out and heaves Gregory to his feet.

The entity turns toward me. Or should I say, it oozes. It is not corporeal. This, I can tell. What it truly is?

I have no idea.

"Now, Katy, my dear. Didn't I warn you? You can't run. Not then, and certainly not now."

He is right about that. I will have to puzzle this out, figure a way to fight this thing. I can do this, I think, even if the enormity of the task overwhelms me. Despair—that this thing is too big to fight—fills me. I pull in a breath and widen my stance.

Malcolm slips in behind me, one hand at my waist, the other on my shoulder. He is warm and solid. Even in the stale air that surrounds us, I catch a hint of nutmeg and Ivory soap. I exhale.

I won't have to do this alone.

"Katy's not prepared," Malcolm says. "She doesn't even know what you are." He gives my shoulder a squeeze and then steps around and in front of me. "On the other hand," he continues, "we've been doing this dance for some months now."

The entity shifts, loses its new form for a moment, then solidifies its shape. "Necromancer, are you still here? How amusing."

"She isn't willing," Malcolm says, his voice preternaturally calm. "You can't take her if she isn't willing."

"I can be most persuasive when I wish to be. Once she understands what will happen to Springside Township should she refuse me, I believe she'll see things my way. I almost persuaded her grandmother, after all, and Katy isn't half the ghost hunter she was."

Something that starts as a cry clogs my throat. I move my mouth, but can't make actual words emerge. The thoughts that cloud my head I can't process. Malcolm? My grandmother? This entity? Why am I the only person here—other than Gregory B. Gone—who doesn't understand what's going on?

The entity oozes toward Malcolm. When they're a mere foot apart, it takes on more of his features. "I will give you this, Necromancer. There was a window of time when you were my equal. You and me?" The entity sighs, a strange sound of longing and regret. "It would've been good."

"It still can be," Malcolm says.

"Oh, but now your desire isn't pure enough. Your attention has been ... fractured. And who can blame you? I find myself unusually distracted by her as well. But you couldn't hold me. I'd burn through you in a matter of months. Look what I did to your brother in a meager five minutes. Love makes you weak, Necromancer. Remember that."

I take tiny, staccato breaths, as if some invisible hand is squeezing the air from my lungs.

"This isn't fair," Malcolm says. "It isn't fair to Katy."

"Fair? *Fair?*" The entity's scorn fills the room. Another dusting of plaster drifts from the ceiling. "Was what her grandmother did to me fair?"

Malcolm casts a glance my way and lunges. Before he can reach me, something white and fluttering snaps between us. Less bed sheet and more bridal veil, it cuts Malcolm from me. When I reach for him, my fingers become ensnared in what looks like an intricate pattern of lace and feels like a spider web. I jerk my hands back and cradle them against my chest.

"Are you enjoying the weather, my dear?" The entity shifts again, its attention on me now.

As if on cue, lightning flashes, illuminating the heavy drapes. The thunder in response shakes the house, knocking the last framed pictures from the mantelpiece.

The entity swipes the air. There, in the middle of the room, is a portal to the outside. It's like a viewfinder, and the scene shifts from one part of town to the next. The little creek where we release ghosts overflows its banks. In the Springside Long-term Care Facility, the staff races to place bowls and buckets beneath relentless leaks in the ceiling. Shingles fly from the roof of Sadie's house. She stands in the yard, drenched and miserable, her attention skyward as if she's praying to a cruel god.

"This is only the start," the entity says. "Thanks to your grandparents, I've spent a very long time ... restrained. I'm in the mood for a little havoc—physical, emotional, spiritual."

"The entire town," I say. "You would do that to the entire town simply because you want revenge?" I say these words to buy time. I say these words in hopes this thing will reveal ... something. I never knew my grandfather. He died long before I was born, or so my grandmother always said, but she kept his photograph on her bedside table.

It sits there now. I ponder what that might mean, beyond her love for him.

"My dear," the thing says now. "Revenge, by itself, is a rather petty emotion. I long for some companionship. I've decided yours will be most suitable."

"Katy!" Malcolm's voice is tight with fear. "It can't take you if you're not willing. That's the rule, the pact this thing has made with humanity."

Something flickers in Malcolm's direction, another fluttering bed sheet that sends him soaring into Tim the camera guy. Even as they crash to the floor, Tim keeps the camera elevated, lens trained on the entity and me.

"I must be willing," I echo. "In that case, I need a guarantee that everyone will be safe, that you won't hurt anyone, that..." I trail off, because this is the sort of bargain that cuts more than one way.

"But of course, my dear. I think you'll find me utterly obliging."

I hold up a hand. "I'm not through yet. There can't be any loopholes. When I say I want the town safe, you can't shrink it down and put it in a snow globe. Things like that don't count."

The house quakes. For a moment, I can't tell why or the source. Then the entity itself shivers. It's ... laughing. At me.

"Oh, my dear, you are a delight. I am so going to enjoy our time together. I may consider extending your existence, you delight me so. Would you like that?"

"If I go with you," I say, picking my way through words, through the right phrasing, like picking my way through a barbed wire fence. "I need to know that no one here will be harmed, that my words won't be twisted, that what I say won't be used against me or the people of Springside. No tricks."

"But I'm all about trickery," it says.

"Yeah. I figured that much."

"Ah, you drive a hard bargain. Your grandmother was especially good at bargaining. It must be a family trait."

The entity contracts and grows silent. Is it thinking? Devising some new way to trick me? I need to agree to its terms, eventually. But I won't do so foolishly. I won't throw myself at it in hopes of saving everyone else, not with this cold doubt in the pit of my stomach.

Before the entity speaks again, before I can do something foolish, a force shoves me to one side. Malcolm stands between the entity and me, his breath labored and harsh.

"I will be your willing sacrifice," he declares.

The house rumbles, the floorboards buckling beneath my feet. The entity expands and contracts again as if exhaling an angry breath.

"No interference, Necromancer."

"You can't refuse." Malcolm doesn't waver. "If a willing sacrifice steps forward, you must take it. That's part of the pact." He spreads his arms wide and tips his head back. "I am that willing sacrifice."

The thing expands again, larger this time, as if it means to encompass the entire room. I lurch forward, my arms outstretched to capture Malcolm around the waist, to pull him away from this thing.

One moment, he is there, solid and warm. The next, my arms meet air. I pitch forward, land on the floor. On hands and knees, I stare up at the entity. Its form roils with rage.

"Love makes you weak, Necromancer," it murmurs.

"Malcolm?" I glance around, but he is truly gone, all of him, his warmth, that nutmeg smell, his wonderful laugh.

The entity reforms, again into the shape of a man, more like Malcolm than ever before.

"Well, my dear, it seems we've returned to the status quo."

"Status quo?"

"Where I am.... sated by a willing sacrifice. Do you know who my last willing sacrifice was?"

That cold dread invades my stomach. I don't want to ask. I'm certain I don't want to know. Either way, I can't speak. I shake my head.

"Your grandfather. And do you know why I remained dormant for so long?"

Again, I go with a headshake.

"Your grandmother's tremendous love for him. She never wavered. Unusual. Humans are normally so fickle."

That bed sheet flutters in dismissal, as if this thing could flick away every last one of us.

"Her love alone kept the pact secure for decades, but when she died, so did its hold on me. Null and void, as they say."

And that was when things started to change. I shut my eyes.

"Yes, indeed they did," the entity says. "And now? Do you know what your love for Malcolm is like, Katy?"

I don't know because I haven't even given the feeling that name, not yet.

"It's quite beautiful, like a tender spring sapling. Oh, but so young! So weak! One gust of wind."

The entity expands again, a whoosh of stale, icy air flowing over me. Then the thing oozes forward, touches the spot on my cheek that I know—even now—remains.

"I won't say goodbye, my dear, because I'll be seeing you again very soon. Until then, I'll be anticipating our next meeting."

The entity solidifies into that silhouette of a handsome man. It brings what looks like fingertips to its lips and blows a kiss. The resulting sting flashes across my cheek.

Then, much like Malcolm did, the thing vanishes. I am on the floor, still on my hands and knees, uncertain I have the power to stand.

For several seconds, no one moves. I'm not sure any of us dare to breathe more than quick, quiet breaths. I want to paw the floor where Malcolm stood, but I know it's no use. He's gone. I let that thing take him. I was too slow. And now? What do I do now? How do I explain this to Nigel? That cold dread in the pit of my stomach moves to my heart.

The chime of the doorbell makes us all jump. Rajeev stumbles to the front entrance and flings open the door.

"Trick or treat!"

The air that rushes inside is free of rain but drenched in the aroma of late autumn. Wood smoke and dying leaves. Someone, somewhere, is playing "Monster Mash" loud enough for all of us to hear the words. Children screech. Parents laugh.

It's the status quo.

From behind me, Gregory B. Gone springs up. "Tell me we got that on video!"

He rushes toward Tim, who takes a few faltering steps backward. A trail of blood follows the lines of Gregory's face. The right lens of his glasses is shattered in a star pattern. He grips the cameraman's shirt, a man desperate.

"Tell me, please tell me we got that on video." Gregory glances around, frantic. "Tell me we streamed it. Tell me—"

Rajeev fires up a laptop. "No streaming, at least," he says. "It looks like the feed cut out right when that ... thing appeared."

"Damn." Gregory whirls again on Tim. "Well?"

"I was filming the whole time, but I don't know what I have."

The three of them huddle over the camera. A few members of the crew stand and stare. Some simply wander outside with bags of candy. No one bothers to check on Terese, not even the EMT. I crawl toward her. She is still a plaster-covered lump on the floor, and worry eats at me.

How big of a toll did that thing take on her? Her chest rises and falls, so there is that, at least.

"Terese?" I say, keeping my words soft. "Are you okay?"

She stirs, pushes against the floor, but her arms quake. I catch her hands. Slowly, together, we inch her to sitting. Terese stares at me, her eyes enormous. Her hair is pure white. Not artifice, as I thought before, but fact.

"It wanted you," she says. "I couldn't stop it."

"How did it ... I mean, do you remember what happened?"

She surveys the living area, eyes blinking, gaze confused. It's clear this is the first time she's truly seen it. "A few nights ago, I was conducting a séance."

Oh, those are always a bad idea.

"I often do one before a show," Terese continues. "I made contact with the other side, but this time..."

"It was the entity?"

"Yes. The rest is murky." She reaches out as if to touch my left cheek but is smart enough to pull her hand back before it grazes the iridescent blue spot. "But it wasn't after me. It wanted you."

"I should've known," I say. "You kissed both my cheeks. Were you trying to warn me or did it just slip up?"

She shakes her head, eyes brimming with moisture. Maybe that was an unfair question. I struggle to my feet and offer Terese my hand.

"What do you mean, it's not on video?" Gregory bellows. "We have the show of the century—no, the show of the millennium—and it's not on video? On audio? Did we get anything at all?"

Tim is jabbing a keyboard, mouthing soundless words, and shaking his head. Gregory paces and storms, hands alternately clutching his hair and hapless members of the tech crew. Between the blood on his face and the manic jerking of his limbs, he is fearsome. He whirls. I suspect his next target is me. Before I can dodge his questions or escape the house, a sharp whistle cuts through all the noise.

"This is the Springside Township Police Department! You are all in violation of the law. You have fifteen minutes to vacate the premises."

Police Chief Ramsey is standing in the doorway, bullhorn in one hand and nightstick in the other. While I can believe he'll gladly use the one, I can't imagine him resorting to the other. Officer Millard is standing behind him holding a Taser, so perhaps what I believe doesn't match this new reality.

Gregory charges forward. "I have permission to be here, from the owners. I am ridding this space of malignant spirits so the family may—"

"The Springside Bank owns this house," Chief says. "You're trespassing, and I'm not joking. Fifteen minutes and then I start arresting people."

Around me, the stagecraft disintegrates. Velvet curtains cascade to the floor. Two of the crew roll up the carpet. Near the fireplace, Rajeev clutches a broom, his gaze locked on blood-speckled glass.

From the kitchen, I collect our field kit. I dump the coffee and tea down the sink. It's cold and stale, and the aroma clogs my throat, triggers my gag reflex. For a moment, I clutch the marble countertop. Sweat sprouts along my forehead. I shut my eyes. I yearn for Malcolm's reassuring hand on my shoulder. If I try hard enough, I'll feel it. If I try hard enough, he'll return.

Nothing but the sound of Chief Ramsey's voice—amplified by the bullhorn—greets my efforts.

I pack the percolator into our field kit. There's no room for Malcolm's samovar, so I clutch it to my chest like a life preserver.

Chief grunts at me on my way out. "Funny," he says. "I'm not surprised to see you here."

Without a word, I continue down the steps.

"Where's your partner in crime?" he calls after me.

On the sidewalk, I turn and stare up at him and the house behind him. The green and white Victorian appears benign, like it always has.

"I wish I knew," I say to Chief.

I walk through the clear night to my truck with the knowledge that I am completely alone.

I LET my truck idle in front of my house and contemplate the light that spills from the kitchen windows. When I finally step onto the walk, a hint of spice and molasses fills the night. I stand there, clutching Malcolm's samovar to my chest, the metal a dull cold beneath my fingertips and against my heart, trying to fathom what is going on in my home.

There's one way to find out. I round the house and enter from the back. The moment I open the door, the kitchen wraps me in warmth and spice—nutmeg and clove, and the tang of ginger. Sadie is standing at the oven. She's wearing a pair of mitts I'm certain I don't own. Nigel is slipping cookies from a sheet to a cooling rack. Belinda is pouring a mug of something that she hands to me.

"Don't talk. Don't think. Just sit down and breathe for a bit." She steers me to a kitchen chair and with the slightest pressure on my shoulders, has me sitting.

With caution, I bring the mug to my lips. I brace for coffee or tea, not certain I could stand to drink either. Instead, sweet apple cider fills my mouth. I sigh. The apples are tart, the cinnamon smooth and comforting.

"Sadie's idea," Nigel says.

Sadie waves an oven mitt as if she could wave away his praise. "After the night you had, I didn't think you'd want another cup of coffee."

She's right about that. I survey the three of them, perplexed. "But the streaming cut out," I say.

Belinda wakes up the laptop. Frozen on Ghost B Gone's YouTube channel is the image of Police Chief Ramsey leading Gregory away in handcuffs.

"We don't know what happened, exactly," Belinda says, "but someone started filming again."

She rewinds the video. And yes, there I am, on my hands and knees, my expression shattered. Terese crumpled on the floor. Gregory shouting, arms waving, blood dripping. It's a jerky, chaotic montage of images and sound. Whoever this enterprising videographer is, they track me with their camera as I leave the house.

So there I am, staring up at Chief Ramsey, telling the entire world I don't know where Malcolm is.

I glance at Nigel and something inside me fractures. He already knows, and yet, that doesn't make it any easier. The fact that he— along with Belinda and Sadie—is trying to take care of me makes it hurt that much more. True, I am no longer completely alone. The thought fills a void while easing weight onto my shoulders. I shrug, not used to this new feeling.

"I'm sorry," I say at last.

"What for?" Nigel holds my gaze, his eyes dark and bright.

"For Malcolm. He's ... I don't know. Gone. That thing—"

"Malcolm knew the risks going in." Nigel rubs his hands across his eyes. They're dry and red. They hold sorrow I don't think he dares to speak. "And part of me is petty enough to think he got what he deserved."

I gape, but Sadie smacks Nigel with one of the oven mitts.

"He's your brother," she says, voice indignant. Then she softens. "It's okay to be sad. It's okay to mourn, even if the other person wasn't perfect."

Nigel takes her hand and presses it against his cheek. "Neither one of us is perfect. But yes, my brother—and my rival. It's the way it works in our family. We were both trying to capture this thing. May the best man win and all that."

"Why the hell would either of you want to do that?" Belinda's question echoes my own. She stands, takes my mug, and ladles in more cider.

"Power. Wealth. Lifelong security." Nigel gives Sadie's hand a squeeze and lets go. "A powerful enough necromancer could ... harness that entity. It's an exchange, but one with rules. At the end of the agreed upon time, there's a parting. It's risky, no doubt. But we both thought it would be worth the risk."

"What do you give it in exchange?" I ask.

"That's part of the deal you hammer out once you capture it." Nigel shrugs. "Honestly? It's not like some sort of demonic possession. And it's not like these things are sex-crazed."

Belinda snorts. Sadie's cheeks flush a deep pink, although that might be from the oven's heat.

"Often, all they want is to feel again." Here, even Nigel goes a bit red around the ears. "So, yeah. Sex, maybe. But just moving around, walking, eating. When I had all the ghosts inside me, one of the things they all loved was when I went running." He turns to me now. "It's why they love your coffee, Katy. The steam gives them a bit of substance, and the aroma and flavor make them feel ... almost human."

"So, both of you," I say. "From the start. You came here looking for that thing?"

"And we both knew the rules." Nigel leans forward and grips

my hand. "Remember that, Katy. Malcolm knew, absolutely, what he was doing. We both knew that if we couldn't capture it, our fate wouldn't be pretty."

"So a willing sacrifice isn't the same as capturing this thing?" I say.

"No, not at all."

"Then what happens to a willing sacrifice?" I'm fairly certain I don't want to hear the answer, but I ask anyway.

He shakes his head. "No one has ever come back, so no one really knows."

"Then why did Malcolm—" I begin.

"Honestly, Katy? Don't you know?"

My gaze falls to the mug of cider. The surface is absolutely smooth until a single drop falls from my cheek and sends ripples against the rim.

"You don't suppose it would trade." I say this more to the cider than Nigel. In fact, I nearly hope he won't hear me.

"What?" His face contorts into a scowl. "I'm not sure what you're thinking, but—"

"Nothing, nothing," I say. "But I wonder. That thing was inside you. You wouldn't know its name, would you?"

Nigel slumps in his chair. "Oh, no. No, we're not going there. Look, even if I did know its name, it wouldn't let me tell you. It would be in the part of my memory it erased when it was inside me. Don't go fishing for this thing."

"I don't have a choice." I touch the spot on my left cheek. "It's coming back for me."

Nigel looks away. He must know that's true. He might even know why—that the reason behind its return is tied to my affection for Malcolm. I press a hand over my heart as if it's a tender thing I must protect. As I hold my hand there, something swells inside me. The notion is small, a tiny bit of hope struggling through all my doubt. But it takes root. I feel it grow.

It's a spring sapling of an idea. I barely think on it. I certainly won't speak it out loud. I must protect it from the icy wind. But when I'm at last in bed and shut my eyes, I know this.

It could work.

~

I'M FILLING the fourth thermos with coffee when Belinda wanders into the kitchen the next morning.

"And I thought yesterday's was good." She accepts the cup I hand her.

"Fresh beans from the Coffee Depot," I say. "They finished roasting them this morning."

She slumps against the refrigerator and sighs. "God, I could get used to this. Do you need me to scrub toilets or something? Because you could pay me in cups of coffee to do that."

I almost laugh. The only thing that stops me is the question swirling in my mind, the one I must ask Belinda but dread doing so.

"Actually," I say, "I could use your help."

"Sure."

She pulls up a chair, but before she can sit, I spring my question.

"How do you talk to ghosts?"

Belinda lands hard, chair legs stabbing the kitchen floor. Amazingly, she hasn't spilled a drop of coffee. She takes a long sip, staring down at the liquid in the cup.

"You really want to know?" she says at last.

"I need to know."

"They like small talk. Maybe because they're not fully there?" She shrugs. "When I was younger, I would prattle away, you know, like some little kids do." As she did back at the police station, she holds up her hand as if it's a talking puppet. "My dad was always working. My mother was always organizing this party or that committee or whatever. The ghosts were my friends."

"What happened?"

"What didn't? Middle school, maybe? Somewhere along the line, I graduated from small talk to gossip to rumors. Instead of playful sprites, I started attracting the nastier ghosts. Oh, God, Katy, they say some awful things. Things you know aren't true, but can't help worrying that they might be."

I nod. I remember Belinda in middle and high school. When a particularly mean ghost would attach itself, her hair lost its luster, her skin went ashen.

"When I discovered that drinking made them shut up, I thought I'd solve my problems for good." She shakes her head. "You know the rest."

Yes. I do.

"Small talk." Of all the things I might have to tackle today, this seems like the most formidable.

Small talk is not one of my strengths. My grandmother was good at it. And it was Malcolm who revived the business with sales pitches and marketing and simply talking to people while I chased ghosts around with cups of coffee and Tupperware.

I continue to fill thermoses and pack them in the field kit.

"Can I ask where you're going?"

I set the carafe of Belinda's security coffee on the table. "Nothing should bother you today, but just in case."

She stands and crosses her arms over her chest. "Again, where are you going?"

"On a pilgrimage," I say. "I need to talk to a few ghosts."

MY FIRST STOP is Springside Long-term Care. If my hunch is wrong, then I've wasted a great deal of money brewing a great many pots of coffee. If my hunch is wrong, Malcolm is lost forever. Everything depends on a hunch. The thought makes my stomach jump. My hands, however, are steady. I carry a single thermos with me of some of the best coffee I've ever brewed and head for Mr. Carlotta's room.

"Katy-Girl!" His face brightens when he sees me. "I was just talking to Jack. He's thinking about driving down from Minneapolis this weekend."

"How nice for you." I point to the brand new chess set on a side table. Its carved wooden pieces are glowing in the low lamplight. "Are you going to beat him again?"

"He's not coming down for this old man, Katy-Girl."

I shake my head, going for ignorance. This is not an entanglement I need today.

"You. He wants to see you again." Mr. Carlotta claps his hands together. "Give him a chance. Go out to dinner. He's not the boy you knew in high school."

"The one who set my hair on fire?" I strive for lightness, but it falls flat. I really am bad at small talk.

Mr. Carlotta snorts. "He's grown up. And when you grow up, you see things differently."

I choke back a frustrated sigh. I adore Mr. Carlotta, but he's a product of his times. He won't be happy until he has all his grandchildren married off, or at least his favorite one.

"He'd like to have dinner with you," he says.

"Then he should ask me that himself."

"He plans to. In fact—" The buzz of my cell phone cuts off Mr. Carlotta's words. He cringes and rubs his brow. "I told him not to text you."

I check my phone. Yes, Jack has sent me a text. Yes, he has asked me out to dinner.

"I can't." It's the answer I speak out loud and the one I text to Jack.

The room grows oddly silent. I glance up to find Mr. Carlotta staring at me, pain etched on his features.

"Oh, Katy-Girl, what's happened?"

"I..." I don't know what to say or how to explain what's happened in the past twenty-four hours.

"You look so much like your grandmother right now, that same stoic expression. Every time I asked her to coffee, every time she chased down my ghost. It didn't have to get romantic. I told her that ... how many times?"

He asks this last to the air, or possibly his ghost. Certainly I don't know the answer.

"Don't cut yourself off like she did," Mr. Carlotta says. "No ghost is worth that."

But would a whole town be worth it? I know now what it is my grandmother gave up. The love of this worthy man. A chance for a new life. She kept the vigil, kept herself lonely. That photograph of my grandfather on her bedside table—an image of all she'd lost and all she could never have.

My eyes burn with a quick spate of tears. My stomach ties itself in knots. I struggle to pull in a full breath. Granted, this last might be nothing more than Mr. Carlotta's ghost.

And that ghost is the reason I'm here.

I try to work a smile onto my face. From the one Mr. Carlotta gives me, I know it's a weak effort.

"Mr. Carlotta, would you mind?" I gesture toward the door. "I'd like to speak to your ghost for a few minutes."

He nods. Without another word, he wheels his chair from the room. I shut the door behind him. For a moment, all I can do is press my palm against the wood. Then I reach for my thermos.

"No Tupperware today." I unscrew the cap and pour the coffee into the thermos's cup. "I just want to talk."

Aromatic steam rises into the air. Other than the entity, this ghost is the oldest I've ever encountered. It does not suffer fools gladly and is difficult to draw out, although I know it must be in the vicinity of Mr. Carlotta's Purple Heart. Technically, I suppose it haunts that rather than Mr. Carlotta. In this tiny room, it makes little difference.

By degrees, it oozes its way closer to the coffee. I add a touch more to increase the heat.

"I think it's some of my best," I say. "What do you think?"

In answer, the ghost drops onto the cup. The steam shimmers, creating a lopsided outline that looks as grumpy as this ghost often feels.

"I have a problem." I'm on my knees in front of the side table where the coffee is sitting. Oddly, I don't feel all that self-conscious speaking out loud to what is no more than glimmering air. Maybe it's because I've known ghosts all my life. And maybe it's time I got better acquainted.

"You're old enough that I think you know about this entity. I think you might know what it's called. Can you tell me that? I can't promise that I'll be the one to come back with more coffee, but someone will. You won't be ... alone."

I hold absolutely still, eyes closed, lips slightly parted. The ghost inches closer, the air around my face cooling as it draws ever nearer. Then, it's as if I inhale it. It places its icy caress against my eyelids, my cheeks—making certain to circumvent the spot on my left—and my lips.

A word enters my head, but this isn't Belinda's small talk. Slowly, as if this ghost must pull each syllable from a great depth, I have my answer.

"Thank you," I say, and my voice vibrates the shimmering air around me.

I ask Mr. Carlotta's ghost for one last favor, but I leave before it can respond. I'm working on trust now, and I have many more ghosts to speak to and many more favors to ask.

By two in the afternoon, I've located every ghost, spirit, apparition, and sprite in Springside Township. I raced around the abandoned barn near the edge of town, a thermos above my head as the wild ghosts that live there dipped and dived into the steam. I held a coffee klatch in a gazebo attended by a dozen sprites, leaving behind floorboards far damper and stickier than when I arrived. I even sneaked into Chief Ramsey's garden shed and offered a cup to the ghost that haunts the watering can. I've talked to them all.

Except one.

I'm tempted to return to the care facility and ask Mrs. Greeley if she's sensed my grandmother lately. But perhaps this is something my grandmother can't help me with. Maybe she's known that all along.

My next stop is the green and white Victorian. I expect some sort of barrier to entry. Crime scene tape. A large No Trespassing sign. A closed circuit camera like the one on Main and Fifth. What I don't expect is the bright yellow van with the black lettering and the riot of antennae in a gangly mess up on top. I don't expect Gregory B. Gone to be leaning against his van, arms crossed over his chest, his gaze trained on the house like a despondent lover.

I pull the remaining thermos of coffee from the field kit and grab two Styrofoam cups before I leave my truck.

"I hope you like it with cream," I say, balancing the cups on the hood of his van. "I have sugar, too, if you want it."

He purses his lips and I take that as a no. A butterfly bandage covers a wound on his forehead. The lens of his glasses is still splintered. A strip of silver duct tape keeps the whole thing from tumbling off his face.

"Thank you." He sips and then points the cup toward the house. "You know, that's the first time I've seen a ghost."

"I'm not sure that thing really is a ghost. It's something more." And perhaps, in a way, something less as well.

"Always wanted to," Gregory continues. "Everyone else senses the cold spots, hears the creaking stairs, freaks out and runs away. Me? I don't feel a thing."

I consider the man next to me, the van behind him proclaiming *Ghost B Gone*, and the naughty sprite whirling about his head.

"How do you eradicate ghosts if you can't sense them?" I ask. At this point, I think that's a fair question.

"Terese. She's very ... open to all things supernatural."

Yes. That turned out to be a problem, too.

"She broke up with me," he adds.

Broke up? "I didn't realize you two were a couple."

"Yeah, that might have been part of it. She said I cared more about the show than I did about her."

Well, he did leave her on the floor while he ranted like a madman about what had—and hadn't—been caught on video. But then I let that entity take Malcolm. I maybe shouldn't judge. Instead, I wave my fingers at the sprite, trying to get it to fly away.

"Go on, shoo," I say under my breath.

"Ouch." Gregory slaps his neck. "You'd think it would be too late in the season for mosquitos."

Mission accomplished, the sprite dances off.

"What are you going to do now?" I ask.

He shakes his head. "I wish I knew."

Despite the defeat in his words, his expression shifts. Maybe it's the scent of wood smoke that fills the air. A soft swoosh tickles my ears, the sound of a rake across dried oak leaves. The status quo, in Springside Township, can be an enticing thing.

"This isn't a bad little town," he says. "Maybe I'll stick around. Nice place to raise kids."

I refrain from pointing out that his girlfriend just broke up with him. I strive to keep my face bland, completely noncommittal. But something must bubble to the surface because he gives me a wry grin.

"Yeah ... another one of our problems. Or maybe it was just my problem. Maybe *I'm* the problem." He drains the last of the coffee and then crushes the Styrofoam cup. "Thanks, Katy. You make a damn good cup of coffee."

"Yes," I say. "I know."

∽

I DON'T ENTER the green and white Victorian until the bright yellow of the Ghost B Gone van has disappeared down the road. Once inside, I'm drawn to the living area. Does it matter where I do this? Possibly. Possibly not. In any case, my feet lead me to where I last encountered the entity.

Enough coffee remains in the thermos for two final servings. No Styrofoam for this. I pull out two blood red Japanese cups. I think they're meant for tea, but I'm after elegance, not accuracy.

I fill each cup to the rim and set both on the mantelpiece. When I step back, my heel grinds a shard of glass into the wood floor. Then I stand in the empty space, paralyzed not so much by indecision—I've made up my mind—but by whether I'm being a coward in not saying goodbye to everyone. I'm not sure what will happen when I speak the name I hold in my mind, but I'm fairly certain nothing will be the same. I might not be the same.

I might not be here.

Eyes shut, I inhale deeply, then let it out with a whoosh. No sense in wasting time. The coffee's getting cold.

"Momalcurkan."

I stumble over the word. It feels awkward and unwieldy in my mouth, like it's not a real word at all. Just to be perverse, I add:

"I have some coffee for you."

The floorboards beneath my feet rumble. Plaster dust rains down. This time a spiderweb of cracks appears along the ceiling, marring its smooth surface. The bank will never be able to sell this place.

That inky mass oozes from the fireplace and creeps up the mantel until it reaches the coffee. The blob is nearly solid now, and the cups barely visible. The air grows stale. Around me, things flutter, wilder, more insistent than before. Bridal veils, every last one. White lace teases my peripheral vision until I look at it full on. Then, it vanishes.

The inky mass eases from the mantelpiece. One cup is overturned, but only a tiny stream of coffee flows onto the mantel. The other cup is completely empty. What sounds like an enormous sigh shakes the structure. The jangle of the pot and pan rack comes from the kitchen. The swinging door whooshes.

"Most delicious."

The words echo in my head and all around me. In front of me, the inky blob transforms, once again taking the shape of a handsome man. In this particular case, that handsome man is Malcolm, or a facsimile of him.

"Brava, my dear. Brava. You've managed a trick most necromancers spend years trying to accomplish and never do. Certainly your grandmother never managed it."

"I'm not half the ghost hunter she was," I say.

"Perhaps not. Perhaps you are something more."

"No," I say. "I'm not."

The entity regards me, its scrutiny silent and penetrating.

"It isn't time yet," it says.

My heart thuds, a furious beat in my chest. That proclamation gives me hope, just enough so I can speak my next words.

"I know. I want to make a trade."

"What sort of trade would that be? I see no one here who might entice me. The humans in this place are puny and uninteresting."

"Really?" I say. "No one? Not even me?" I turn in a slow circle like I'm a runway model, despite my hiking boots and coffee-stained jeans.

"Well, that's another matter. What is it you have in mind, my dear?"

"Me for Malcolm, but I have conditions."

"Of course you do."

"He must be alive."

A rumble shakes more plaster from the ceiling, but the sound isn't threatening. Instead, it feels as if the entire house is chuckling and I'm a small child making ridiculous demands.

"Human and in one piece," I add. "And everything he was before you took him as a willing sacrifice."

"Including a liar?"

Three words, perfectly aimed. I press a hand against my stomach as if this thing has struck me there. I pull up everything I know about Malcolm, everything he is to me.

"He's my business partner, and my friend, and I think I've maybe fallen in love with him."

"No maybe about it, my dear. That he still exists means you have."

He still exists. I keep my breathing shallow. I don't want this thing to sense my relief.

"If he still exists, then we can trade. Right? If you return Malcolm, I'll be your willing sacrifice."

"You saw how he did it, what words he spoke?"

I nod.

The entity falls silent again, and everything around us with it. No birds sing outside the window. There's no traffic on the street. The entity in this space has obliterated every last whiff of wood smoke and the sound of crisp leaves. It's stale and cold and I wonder if this is my fate. Bed sheets. Bridal veils. The taste of metal against my tongue.

"Very well," the entity says. "I accept."

As it did with Terese, the entity peels away from the form that is Malcolm. He crumples to the floor, inert. I can only hope he is alive and breathing and everything else he should be. I don't have the luxury to check. Instead, I must hold up my end of the bargain.

I step forward and spread my arms. I tip my head back. "I am your willing sacrifice."

I hold still, mouth wide open, heart kicking up again. The entity oozes toward me, and my limbs lock in place as if I've been cast in bronze. A tendril inches toward my face, reaching for the cheek it marked.

"I've waited a long time for this, my dear."

In that moment, a ghostly stream fills the living area. My mouth is still open, and the first ghost to plunge in is Mr. Carlotta's. Oh, it's fierce, leading the charge like a true warrior. The shock of its memories rattles me. Before I can make sense of any of them, another ghost follows, and then another. The dozen sprites from the gazebo dive in all at once. I can't move, whether from the entity or all the ghosts inside me, I don't know.

Still, they come. The wild ones from the abandoned barn. The grumpy ones who haunt the dark alleyways of town. Sadie's two sprites.

An unearthly cry rends the air. The hold on my limbs loosens and I stumble backward. The ghosts catch me before I tumble to the floor.

"I can still take you, Katy," the entity says.

But Springside Township has a great many ghosts. The thing reaches for me again, but the ghosts don't stop. The entity's hold weakens, but it's still a match. Its power sputters, surges, sputters, surges.

With one last surge, it flows around me. I feel my existence falter, this world receding, and some other one rushing toward me. The light there is bright enough to blind, and yet it contains hidden recesses dark enough to wilt your soul. The house around me fades. I'm still standing in the living room, but I no longer feel the floor beneath my boots. And Malcolm? He's no more than a hazy outline. It's like looking at an old photograph in sepia. It's a world that no longer exists.

But the ghosts won't let me go. They keep me rooted in place until one last ghost dives into my mouth.

This is a ghost I know.

The entity's screech pierces my ears. I'm frozen in place now, my body in a full-on ghost infestation. My sight grows dim, my eyelashes heavy with frost. I feel as if I'm sinking into a dark, icy pool of water. Before I sink all the way, before I lose the last bit of light, I hear my grandmother's voice.

Goodbye, Katy-Girl. I love you.

~

"KATY? KATY, ARE YOU OKAY?"

The familiar voice pokes through the fog clouding my head, the sound of it low and familiar, although it lacks humor. And this is a voice I very much want to hear laugh. My eyelids flutter, my lashes no longer weighed down by ice.

When I open my eyes, the first thing I see is Malcolm. He's here. He's alive. I glance around and find the space warm, a hint of wood smoke in the air. Outside, a bird chirps. I push to sit up, and immediately he's at my side, helping me. I inhale nutmeg and Ivory soap, and I think I might collapse again.

"It's really you," I say.

"It's really me." He gives his head a little shake as if he can't believe he's looking at me. "I don't know what you did. I don't know why, especially since—"

I press a finger against his lips. "That doesn't matter."

He takes my hand, squeezes it. "Actually, it does. Which is why I can't ... I mean, I barely understand what happened. How—I mean, all the ghosts? Did you capture them?"

"No."

"But how did they all—?"

"I just asked for their help."

Malcolm gives me a blank stare as if I've uttered nonsense.

"You kept telling me how much they like me, right?" I say. "I decided to test that theory. I figured none of them wanted this entity around either and they'd be glad to help me get rid of it, one way or another. Also, I bribed them with coffee."

For a moment, that blank stare remains. Then Malcolm throws his head back and laughs.

"You just ... asked them." He shakes his head like I've done something impossible. "I think you've made a breakthrough in necromancy."

"I keep telling you. I'm not a necromancer."

"So you say. This?" He raises his hand, indicating the house and himself. "This proves otherwise." His attention turns to my face—or rather, my left cheek. "Hold on," he says, words softer now.

Brow furrowed, concentration absolute, he raises his hand to my face. He touches the spot on my cheek. I flinch inwardly, certain it will burn him again.

He doesn't wince, doesn't shirk. Instead, he uses a finger to scrape away at my skin. Something dislodges and falls to the floor. Between us, a blue disc shatters into a million tiny crystals. A second later, those million tiny crystals evaporate.

"Am I free?" I ask, my voice barely a whisper. I don't want to hope, but find I'm doing just that.

"I think so."

I sigh, and we're so close that I sigh into his mouth. I inch closer so my lips might brush his, so I might sample that nutmeg. Malcolm pulls me in to him, one arm around my waist, a hand cradling the back of my head. When he kisses me, I taste the nutmeg and the apology and the thrill that we're both here, both alive, both human.

All kisses end, it's true. But this one? This one goes on for a very long time before it finally does.

I POUR coffee into three bone china cups. The porcelain is so fine that the cups are nearly translucent. Wedding china. My grand-mother's. At least, I think it is. I never asked. Now, regret tugs at me that I didn't.

I swallow back the sigh. I'm too full of caffeine to stay sad for long. I'm in Mr. Carlotta's room, the last stop on my pilgrimage to thank all the ghosts of Springside Township. They all helped, but it's this fierce warrior of a ghost who rallied them and led the charge. That deserves something special.

"Ah, Katy-Girl," Mr. Carlotta says. "I think your coffee may even outshine your grandmother's."

"I don't see how it could. She taught me everything I know about brewing coffee."

He sips again. "It tastes different today."

Perhaps it does. Or perhaps it's because today, his room feels lighter. Granted, his ghost is not a presence you can ignore, but the air doesn't feel quite so melancholy, my lungs don't struggle to draw a breath.

Still, I make the offer. "Do you want me to take your ghost when I go?"

Mr. Carlotta strokes his jaw, his eyes on the very spot where his ghost rests. "No, let him stay. He's not thickening the air quite so much, and I get the sense he needs the rest."

"All right," I say, "but there are some things you should know. Your ghost is a warrior."

"I knew it! He has the feel of an old soldier."

"Maybe," I say. "But your ghost is actually a she."

Mr. Carlotta's eyes sparkle with discovery. "A she? Are you certain?"

"Positive."

"An Amazonian, then?"

I shrug. "I don't know. All I know is this ghost is very old."

"Or perhaps Queen Boudica herself!" He nods. "Yes, I think she must be."

The ghost swells at this suggestion. Whether true or not, she certainly seems to like it—and Mr. Carlotta.

"She could use a little R and R," I say. "She fought a big battle the other day."

"I thought you were up to something."

Once we finish, I clear the cups and saucers, tucking each in bubble wrap before placing them into the field kit. I'm at the door, ready to leave, when Mr. Carlotta calls out.

"So, I was talking to Jack last night—"

I shake my head, but I'm smiling. He'll never give up. "I'm seeing someone right now."

He scrutinizes me. "So you are, Katy-Girl. So you are."

I'm halfway down the hall when he wheels his chair into the corridor.

"But you tell him for me that I've got my eye on him!"

WHEN I REACH *K&M Ghost Eradication Specialists*, Malcolm is outside, leaning against the door. The sun glints off the storefront glass and the lettering glows like pure gold. It's one of those rare November days that make you think winter will never invade. The air is warm, but it holds undertones of the cold to come.

"Have fun?" he asks.

I nod, but it's a distracted sort of gesture.

"You didn't find her," he says, "did you?"

I shake my head. "I think she's gone for good this time."

"Remember when you told me that the thing she wanted most was to take care of you?" Malcolm says. "Well, maybe she's done that. Maybe that means she can move on. Maybe … oh!"

Oh? What does he mean by *oh*? "Tell me."

"It just hit me. Maybe she went to find your grandfather."

"Then you don't think that entity destroyed him?"

"Not with the way your grandmother loved him." He pauses and considers the sky. "I suspect his spirit is out there somewhere. It was her love that sustained him." He looks at me now, those brown eyes soft. "That made all the difference. I'm certain of it."

We each wear scars from our own battle with the entity. Silver strands thread their way through Malcolm's ebony hair, a bit a gray settling in around his temples. His eyes have more creases when he smiles. While the spot on my cheek is gone, the skin where it sat has a faint blue cast to it, a stain that no amount of scrubbing can remove.

He shifts and I notice the sign on the door behind him.

Closed for QBR.

"What's QBR?" I ask.

"Quarterly business review. It's been a busy three months."

Yes, it has.

"A lot has happened," he adds.

That, too.

"So, in a QBR you review the business, wins and losses, make plans. Basically, it's an honest look at where the business is at."

"Emphasis on honest?"

He clamps his mouth shut. That only lasts for a second. He bursts out laughing, hands propped on his knees.

"Yes," he says, catching his breath. "Emphasis on honest." He tips his head toward the sky again. "And since it's so nice, I thought we could have a picnic." He gestures toward his convertible.

There, tucked behind the passenger seat, is a wicker basket. Tucked next to it is a red and white checked blanket.

"So this would be what?" I ask. "A date?"

"Only if you want it to be."

I consider this, and Malcolm. I could weigh pros and cons, I suppose. I could walk a careful line between business partner and friend. Or I could trust that we'll figure everything out as we go along.

"Yes," I say. "Let's go on a picnic."

He keeps the top down and cranks the heat. We drive along Main Street until we leave Springside Township behind us. The sky is so blue, Malcolm's fingers laced in mine so warm, and the wind steals our laughter.

We drive so fast that—for once—the ghosts won't be able to follow us.

SNEAK PEEK: GHOSTS OF CHRISTMAS PAST

COFFEE AND GHOSTS SEASON 2: EPISODE 1

IT'S TWO WEEKS before Christmas, and I'm crouched in our storefront display. Morning sunlight shines through the gold lettering on the glass and casts the words *K&M Ghost Eradication Specialists* along my arms. The velvet beneath my shoes makes it tough to gain purchase. My thighs ache. My palms sweat. The scalding cup of coffee I'm holding threatens to spill.

Passersby stop and stare, mouths open. I catch sight of Police Chief Ramsey, but all he gives me is a smirk. He doesn't believe in ghosts, not even when they're right in front of him. If I had any sort of presence of mind, I would've thought to print out a sign, something along the lines of: *Demonstration in progress.*

But that would be a lie. This is no demonstration. The sprite careening around the display window really is agitated. I really need to catch it. I'm really not certain this single cup of coffee will do it. Not this time of year.

There's something about December that brings out the worst in ghosts.

I'm about to admit defeat. The coffee's cooling too rapidly to tempt this one much longer. The sprite shoots back and forth,

215

whipping around the samovar and percolator we keep on display, nestled in the velvet. It slips inside the samovar. The whole thing shakes, then teeters off its perch.

I pitch forward to catch it. My fingertips skim the metal. The coffee in my other hand sloshes, soaks my sleeve, and splatters the window. I'm flat on my stomach in the middle of the display. The sprite does a victory lap around my head and I glance up into the perplexed gaze of my business partner.

He's standing on the other side of the glass. His lips twitch. Malcolm Armand (the M in *K&M Ghost Eradication Specialists*) was once my rival and is now my partner—and sometimes there are benefits with that arrangement. He doesn't move from his spot outside our window. In fact, he looks like he's about to settle in for a show.

"Help?" I mouth.

I can't hear his laugh, but I can see it, head thrown back, the way it lights his eyes. He vanishes from sight and a moment later, the chime over our door rings out.

"Katy, what on earth?"

"We have a sprite," I say.

He sticks his head into the display area. "We have a sprite?" He glances about like he's tasting the air. "Oh ... we have a sprite. Any idea how that happened?"

"None."

The sprite shoots past Malcolm and heads for the conference room.

"Damn," he says. "Is Nigel in yet?"

"Not unless he came in the back way."

Without another word, Malcolm sprints toward the conference room. I crawl from the display as quickly as soggy velvet will allow. Nigel, Malcolm's brother, was once addicted to swallowing ghosts. Granted, there isn't much to a sprite, but it's better if he isn't tempted.

I'm at the threshold to the conference room when Malcolm emerges.

"All clear." He holds up a sealed Tupperware container. "Look what I got you for Christmas."

"Seriously? You caught it that fast?"

He shrugs. "I'm just that good."

He is, actually, but I'm in no mood to admit it. I cross my arms over my chest and stare hard, waiting for the rest of the explanation.

"And I think you wore it out," he adds.

I study the sprite trapped inside the Tupperware. It floats lazily about, giving me a single thump against the side in agreement.

The chime above our door rings for a second time that morning. Nigel strolls in. His shock of white hair always takes me by surprise. Although he's only a few years older than Malcolm, he wears the legacy of his addiction in his hair and in the lines around his eyes and mouth.

Today a grin brightens his face. He looks almost boyish. His steps are quick and light. I think he might break into a song or possibly execute some sort of dance step. Instead, he merely nods at the sprite as he passes by.

"Good work," he says, and heads into the conference room where we keep the computer.

Malcolm and I stare after him. A tune reaches my ears, the melody off key but buoyant.

"Is he whistling?" I ask Malcolm.

"I think so."

"Does he do that often?"

I've only known Nigel for about four months, Malcolm a touch longer. Both brothers still hold a great deal of mystery for me. I couldn't tell you if Malcolm whistles.

"I don't think I've ever heard him whistle before," he says.

Malcolm creeps toward the conference room door and peers inside. Then he whirls, eyes wide, lips pursed as if he's trying to hold in laughter. He crosses to the far side of the reception area, gesturing for me to follow. We bend our heads close together.

"Nigel went over to Sadie's for dinner last night."

I nod. This, I know. Sadie Lancaster is my neighbor. I swept her house for sprites about fifteen minutes before Nigel was due to arrive. It's become an evening ritual.

"Well," Malcolm says now. "He never made it back to the apartment."

"Never made it ..." I trail off, the obvious hitting me with enough force I almost gasp. "You mean they ... that he ... he stayed the night?"

"That's exactly what I mean." Malcolm grins and leans in even closer. "I think it explains his mood, don't you?"

I clamp a hand over my mouth so I won't giggle or do anything else juvenile. Sadie deserves some happiness. So does Nigel, for that matter. Still, Malcolm and I are responding with all the maturity of a couple of twelve-year-olds.

Maybe that's because we haven't taken that step. We're not even close to that step. We are, by my calculation, at least five miles from that step. My gaze drifts from the conference room door to the display window. From here, I can make out the sodden velvet and the way the gold lettering makes it glow.

K&M Ghost Eradication Specialists

My eyes lock with Malcolm's. His are a deep brown, close to black, like an excellent dark roast. We both know why we haven't taken too many steps. What happens to *K&M Ghost Eradication Specialists* if K&M the couple doesn't work out?

"Katy," he begins. His voice is soft, devoid of that earlier glee. He sounds like he might say something quite serious.

Before he can, my phone buzzes in my back pocket. I tug it out, and Malcolm sighs. I can't tell if I hear regret or relief in it, so I focus on the text instead.

Sadie: Katy, can you come over

I hold the phone so Malcolm can read the message. "I just cleared them last night."

"Maybe it's time we took them farther out."

"Maybe."

Sadie's two sprites adore her. They are, I think, like the children she never had. But they're not children; they're sprites. Like the one thumping the Tupperware container Malcolm is holding, they cause trouble. Sprites love to play pranks, get a reaction, soak in attention.

"If Nigel ..." He nods toward the conference room. "I mean, if this is getting ... permanent, they can't hang around."

No, they can't. Nigel's addiction makes that impossible. But something about losing them for good makes my chest ache, just a little.

My phone buzzes again.

Sadie: Katy please

I tuck my phone back into my pocket and hold out my hands for the Tupperware.

"I might as well go. I have coffee at home, and I can lose this one and the other two while I'm at it." I give my soggy sleeve a shake. "And change. I should probably change."

My hands are on the container, so when he pulls it toward him, I come with it. We're close now, with just a sprite and some plastic between us.

"I probably smell like the Coffee Depot," I say, and my voice has gone all breathy.

"I'm not complaining."

Between us, the sprite thumps the sides of the Tupperware, and my heart picks up its beat. If I smell like the brew of the day, then Malcolm spices the air with a strange mix of Ivory Soap and nutmeg—it's warm and exotic all at once. Malcolm's gaze is locked on my face. I couldn't look away even if I wanted to.

And I don't want to.

My phone buzzes a third time.

Malcolm sighs again and then gives me a grin of resignation. We are *K&M Ghost Eradication Specialists* and this is how we pay the bills.

"I'd better." I wave a hand toward the door.

"Yeah. You'd better."

When I'm outside, with my truck rumbling to life beneath me, I can't tell if it's regret or relief that will follow me on this call.

Something green is hanging from my door. The wreath looks festive, like Christmas, but it wasn't there this morning. The front walk bears the slightest imprint of someone's boots, a pair much larger than I ever wear. Instead of heading around back to the kitchen like I normally would, I follow those snowy footsteps up my walk.

A mistletoe wreath is hanging from a hook on my door. It's an old-fashioned arrangement, the perfect complement for the old Victorian house. Berries from a sprig of holly glow blood red against the white of the door. In the center, stuck beneath a plaid bow, is a card.

I strip off my mittens and tug at the card. The entire wreath wobbles, then plunges to the ground. I balance it against one boot while I read the note.

For one speaker to the dead from another:

Did you know that the French once referred to a bough of mistletoe as a specter's wand? They believed that not only could the holder see ghosts, but could induce them to speak as well.

Of course, we don't need those sorts of tricks, do we? Still, what
would the holiday be without such ornaments as this?

The card is unsigned. I turn it over, check the envelope, but
there's no clue to who might have sent the wreath. Malcolm, possibly? Was that why he was a few minutes late this morning? I frown
at the card. It doesn't really sound like him.

"It's bad luck, you know, to let mistletoe touch the ground."

A voice echoes around me, low and masculine. I shove the card
into my coat pocket and whirl to face it.

No one is there. Not on the sidewalk or the street. No one
has crept up behind me on the walkway, although my heart is
thudding like someone has. I scan the area, my back to the door.
Without taking my gaze from the street, I bend down and pick
up the wreath. It takes three clumsy tries before it lands on its
hook once again. Then I decide the best place to be is inside the
house.

Without shrugging off my coat, I brew a quick pot of Kona
blend. If Sadie's sprites are back so soon, I'll need extra enticement
to get them to leave. They've been stubborn lately. Maybe it's the
holiday. Maybe it's because they're lonely.

Maybe I don't blame them. I haven't climbed the stairs to the
attic yet to bring down the decorations. I haven't bought a tree.
Whenever my mind drifts to this first Christmas without my
grandmother, I force myself to think of something else.

Like now. I'll go catch some sprites and breathe in all that is
Sadie's house at Christmastime—sugar cookies and gingerbread
houses, strings of popcorn and cranberries, spiced apple cider.

Although first I take a quick look around outside, but the street
is late-morning quiet with children at school and people at work.

The door to Sadie's house is ajar. Warm, scented air greets me
when I push it open all the way.

"Sadie?" I call out.

I stop at the threshold, pulling in a few deep breaths, tasting the air. Sprites have such a slight presence that sometimes it's hard to tell if they're in residence at all.

Something otherworldly is here. That much I can tell. Normally, when the sprites act up, Sadie will be somewhere they are not. I call out again.

Nothing.

I pull out my phone. On the screen is one final message.

Sadie: he

He? Is there someone—or *something*—else in the house? Or is it the start of a word—a word like *help*? I don't think, don't question what I should do next. I dash up the stairs to the second floor, taking the steps two at a time. I call out again, my voice ragged.

"Sadie, are you okay?"

I don't want to barge into her bedroom, but that's the most logical place to search. I push open the door, the sight that greets me freezing me in place.

Sadie, on the floor, clad in a silk robe of deep gold. Her face is far too pale. She is far too still. My thumb is on the phone, ready to dial 911. I step into the room, but before I can cross to Sadie, a force surges into me.

The cold envelops me first. This is no sprite. Its presence fills the bedroom with resentment and dread, the air so stale and sharp it pricks the inside of my nose. A trickle of hot blood runs down my lip and the quicksilver taste fills my mouth.

The thing shoves me against the shuttered doors of the closet. The flimsy wood buckles under my weight. I grip the frame and try to regain my balance, my breath, cursing myself for walking into an ambush.

This ghost is fierce and angry. It moans, the sound like an accusation. Then the room is silent.

In the quiet, I glance around. The thing is still here; that much I know. With my coat sleeve, I wipe away blood. My phone is where?

I can't fight this ghost on my own. In fact, I haven't encountered one this aggressive for a while. I need Malcolm. Sadie needs an ambulance. But first, I need to cross the room to where my phone has landed, next to the vanity.

I'm halfway there when the air shifts behind me. It feels like a gathering storm. I launch myself those last few steps. All I need to do is send a text. The ghost slams into me, the force propelling me against the vanity and its mirror, with all its glass.

The room explodes in shards. My head slams against something hard. I crumple to the floor, lungs searching for air, fingers groping for the cell phone. The moment I reach it, an icy blast sends it skittering away.

My vision blurs both with tears and an approaching darkness. I need my phone. I need to tell Malcolm about this ghost.

But it's too dark and too cold and my phone is too far away. I close my eyes. I tell myself it's only for a second so I can catch my breath. But my eyelids are heavy, and the dark washes over me. I taste regret along with the blood in my mouth. What I want is to hear Malcolm's voice. That feels like the most important thing of all.

WHAT THE HECK IS COFFEE & GHOSTS?

COFFEE & GHOSTS is a cozy paranormal mystery/romance that is told over a series of episodes and in seasons, much like a television series. Think *Doctor Who* or *Sherlock*.

Ghost in the Coffee Machine, which I think of as the pilot episode, began life as a short story that first appeared in *Coffee: 14 Caffeinated Tales of the Fantastic*.

Once, a very long time ago, I wrote a murder mystery that involved a ghost. During the research phase, I came across a tidbit about catching ghosts using coffee and glass jars. The novel never went anywhere, but years later, when I saw the call for submissions for Coffee, something clicked. Katy, her grandmother, and their business of catching ghosts with coffee and Tupperware (a far more practical and, frankly, safer option) were born.

Not too long later I realized that I wasn't done with coffee and ghosts—or rather, they weren't done with me. They demanded their own type of storytelling as well.

Serial fiction is exciting and fun to write. It's different from a novel in that each episode has its own story arc but also supports a larger one for the season.

I've recently consolidated the episodes into three season bundles. This makes both finding the episodes and binge-reading them much easier.

I can't tell you how much fun it was to write COFFEE & GHOSTS, and I want to thank you for reading and coming along on this journey with me.

ABOUT THE AUTHOR

CHARITY TAHMASEB has slung corn on the cob for Green Giant and jumped out of airplanes (but not at the same time). She spent twelve years as a Girl Scout and six in the Army; that she wore a green uniform for both may not be a coincidence. These days, she writes fiction (long and short) and works as a technical writer for a software company in St. Paul.

Her short speculative fiction has appeared in *Flash Fiction Online, Deep Magic,* and *Cicada.*

ALSO BY CHARITY TAHMASEB

YOUNG ADULT FICTION (WITH DARCY VANCE)

The Geek Girl's Guide to Cheerleading

Dating on the Dork Side

YOUNG ADULT FICTION

The Fine Art of Keeping Quiet

The Fine Art of Holding Your Breath

Now and Later: Eight Young Adult Short Stories

PARANORMAL

Coffee and Ghosts, Season 1: Must Love Ghosts

Coffee and Ghosts, Season 2: The Ghost That Got Away

Coffee and Ghosts, Season 3: Nothing but the Ghosts

Coffee and Ghosts, Season 4: The Ghosts You Left Behind

FANTASY AND FAIRY TALES

Straying from the Path, Stories from the Sour Magic Series of Fairy Tales

www.ingramcontent.com/pod-product-compliance
Lightning Source LLC
Chambersburg PA
CBHW031238120726
47905CB00002B/646